Letting the
Body Lead

ALSO BY JENN CROWELL

Necessary Madness

G. P. PUTNAM'S SONS

NEW YORK

Letting the Body Lead

Jenn Crowell

G. P. Putnam's Sons
Publishers Since 1838
a member of
Penguin Putnam Inc.
375 Hudson Street
New York, NY 10014

Library of Congress Cataloging-in-Publication Data

Crowell, Jenn, date.
Letting the body lead / Jenn Crowell.
p.   cm.
ISBN 0-399-14859-0
1. Americans—Iceland—Fiction.   2. Women graduate students—Fiction.   3. Young women—Fiction.   4. Iceland—Fiction.
I. Title.
PS3553.R5928 L48   2002   2001048247
813'.54—dc21

Printed in the United States of America
1   3   5   7   9   10   8   6   4   2

This book is printed on acid-free paper. ♾

Book design by Meighan Cavanaugh

For Sigga,

who kept me brave enough

to tell the heart of it

Acknowledgments

I would be remiss if I did not begin by thanking all those whom I met on my four journeys to Iceland while doing research for this book. Though far too many to mention individually, you have my utmost appreciation for your gracious hospitality and willingness to extend your time and friendship to a young American novelist, and for that, I extend in return a heartfelt *Takk fyrir mig.*

Special thanks to my North Atlantic soul sister Sigríður Pétursdóttir for proofreading my Icelandic, and to dear Þórunn Valdimarsdóttir, my tireless literary ambassador in Reykjavík.

On the homefront, many thanks to my agent, Jane Gelfman, and my mentor, Madison Smartt Bell, neither of whom lost confidence in me even when I was at my most angst-ridden. Thanks also to my former and current editors, Liza Dawson and Christine Pepe, for their helpful insights, and to Putnam for their patience, as well as K Edgington at Towson University, for her keenly intelligent reading of the manuscript.

Lastly, much love and thanks go to my friends and family, especially to Stephanie Simon-Dack, who cheered me (and Isobel) along from the beginning, and to my husband, Scott Lindsey-Stevens, for reasons far too voluminous for these pages to hold. My gratitude to all of you renders me wordless.

*Letting the
Body Lead*

Chapter One

Reykjavik

*I*sobel Sivulka flew to Iceland on the night she should have received her doctorate, with the last seat on the plane, courtesy of a loan from her parents. Her head churned with frantic dreams of epiphany and escape as she watched the blue lights on the runway at Kennedy slide by, but she left with no agenda, no neat list of milestones to accomplish. She took only a guidebook she would never read, fragments of stories she'd heard, and the starved, supplicant gaze of an exhausted woman with rings of darkness beneath her eyes, a woman with fingernails bitten down to bloody half-moons, a woman seduced by the promise of flight.

Isobel slept on the second half of the journey, a blanket clutched around her shoulders, her head slumped against the window and intermittently rattled by the roar of the northbound plane. Several times the attendants woke her with their polite choruses of "Coffee or tea? Extra pillows? Something to eat?" as they pushed trolleys bearing cold sandwiches, cups of orange juice, headsets for movies she could have seen months ago in New York had she not been drowning. Their fourth trip down the aisle, the hospitality they proffered was alcoholic. Isobel's hand curled around the ten-dollar bill stashed in the pocket of the fuzzy blue pullover her mother had given her for the trip. It reminded Isobel of her mother herself: warm, brightly colored, pragmatic.

"Beverage, sir?" a female flight attendant asked the man seated beside her. Still drowsy, Isobel glanced at him as he requested a glass of wine. He wore pressed khakis and a navy blazer, not quite stylish and businesslike enough for Saga business class but meticulous just the same, his dark hair painfully parted and combed perfectly straight, as if he knew someone he loved was waiting for him, setting a vase of fresh flowers in the center of a polished table in a Reykjavík apartment, walking across a thick burgundy Oriental carpet in her stocking feet to open the curtains and gaze up into the sky, down onto the harbor. Isobel wanted to ask him but saw that the juggernaut of delights was about to roll away and raised her arm.

"Excuse me," she called out.

Tall, perkily dressed, hair glistening, the woman turned. "Yes?" she said.

"I'd like a drink, please," Isobel said.

Her brow furrowed. "Could I see some ID?"

Isobel pulled out her passport and handed it over. She watched wide-eyed surprise spread over the woman's face as she took in the usual details—name, nationality—and then noticed Isobel's date of birth.

"I'm sorry," she said. "You just didn't look twenty-five."

Isobel smiled, burning inside. "It's okay," she said.

Later, as she sipped her champagne, decadent and shivery with anticipation the man in the navy blazer asked, "Are you really that old?"

"Really," she said. She suddenly realized she was sitting there with the scratchy wool blanket still draped around her, her thin fingers gripping the plastic cup so tightly it might implode, the guilty, indulgent grin of a child allowed to stay up late with the grown-ups stretched wide across her mouth.

"Are you a college student?"

His eyes shifted to the faded olive knapsack in her lap, its rugged fabric stuck through with tiny pins reading PRO-CHOICE IS PRO-FAMILY, and, from a rare moment of punchy exasperation, I ONLY LOOK SWEET AND INNOCENT. She knew the picture he'd already concocted in his mind, that of a co-ed adventurer, pedantic in her idealism, delicate yet saucy. Though this assumption angered her, she didn't blame him for it. She would have made it herself had she not known better.

"I'm pursuing a doctorate," she said. The words felt snobbish, hollow. Like a lie.

He took a sip of his wine. "Right now I'm actually going to visit my old college roommate. He was an Icelandic exchange student, and we've always kept in touch."

"Good for you," Isobel murmured. Right now, she thought, my best friend is sitting on a dingy plaid sofa in a tiny house in a small town on a sweltering June evening, stroking the contours of her swollen belly, waiting.

She set the plastic cup of champagne on the tray in front of her. She and the stranger sat in silence, counting the minutes until descent.

༼

Taking the bus to the capital the next morning, Isobel gazed groggily out a huge tinted window and found herself frightened by the sheer magnitude of the sky. Pale gray clouds swallowed the broad shock of flat, verdant moss that caressed the treeless terrain. Light rain misted a shaggy sheep perched on black rock. The occasional car passed by, dwarfed into a toy of the elements on its path along the Reykjanes Peninsula, while a farmhouse stood alone in the starkness like a small white miracle. Watching the same horizon her mentor had viewed a decade earlier, Isobel felt lightheaded, stripped open, as if someone had stuck their fingers inside her flesh and lifted out some trembling, essential part of her.

The bus wound through the suburbs, around squat, primary-colored houses, some with huge satellite dishes anchored to the tops of their tiny roofs. She huddled against the window, still sleepy but impatient for a firm *click* of recognition, anxious for that long, breathless gaze into the face of the city. Even the business hours painted on the sides of buildings in Icelandic that she could intuit—*opið kl. 9–16*—filled her with hope as the bus made one last endless, sweeping turn into the hotel parking lot.

She closed her eyes. The bus hit a rough patch on the gravel road. Her hand jostled against the knapsack in her lap. Above the bus driver's head, a clock flashed *7:15, 7:15* in red neon. She felt broken and grimy.

If this landscape were a body, she thought, it would be mine.

The tourists in front of her filed off the bus, and she slung her knapsack over both shoulders and stepped down after them. She took her place in a cluster of bewildered fellow Americans ready to be ushered to their respective transfer minivans. "I need to get to Hótel Saga," a middle-aged woman said loudly as she struggled with her mammoth wheeled suitcase. "This isn't Hótel Saga, is it?"

"No," Isobel said, pointing to the sign that clearly stated the building's name. "It's Loftleiðir."

Letting the Body Lead

The rest of the group turned to look at her, a tall, shivering young woman bent by her bulging pack. The driver motioned in her direction. She dug a scrap of paper out of her coat pocket and handed it to him. He glanced at the address of her destination. "Near Hótel Borg?" he asked.

"I . . . I guess so," she said.

Other drivers called back and forth in Icelandic. She followed hers to a van and climbed inside along with a group of clean-cut men in their thirties who were going to a convention at Hótel Holt. "No college pals traveling with you?" one of them asked as he sat next to her.

"I'm a graduate student, actually," she said.

"No kidding. Where are you studying?"

"NYU."

"Nice. What for?"

"Psychology."

The van pulled out of the lot, and she turned her head away. Gazed toward the silver dome of Perlan.

The man beside her was still pressing her with queries. "How did you get to grad school so young?"

Isobel shoved her bangs off her face. She was tired of this question. "I skipped a year of high school and crammed a B.A. into three years," she said.

"So are you in Iceland for research, or a grant?"

As they turned the corner onto Bergstaðastræti, she glimpsed a child's plastic slide in the backyard of a royal blue concrete house. The sight cut into her with a fierce tenderness.

"No," she said softly. "Just me."

⚜

Her first few nights in Reykjavík, in her borrowed flat near the harbor, Isobel couldn't sleep. She would get out of bed and wander through rooms, turning on lights even though she didn't need them, inspecting the daily minutiae of a couple she'd never met—a book of British pop songs propped on the upright piano, the Hollywood action-movie posters taped to their teenage son's wall. Her head swam with a terse catalogue of guilty losses, a litany of everyone she'd left behind: Gavin; her mother and Nick; her roommate, Elika; Colette and her unborn child. Finally exhausted, Isobel would crawl onto the deep sill of her bedroom window in her nightgown, both calmed and disturbed by the fact that darkness had not fallen.

At three A.M. on a hilltop dotted with wildflowers, overlooking the stillness of the same northern city, a woman with a bruised lip had stood hugging herself, waiting for the contusion to heal, for the strength to fling her arms wide, for the sky to open up.

And outside, a chorus of youthful shouts. The clear, painful beauty of cathedral chimes in the distance.

ॐ

Isobel was staying on the second floor of a squat gray concrete building in the western section of town. The area was quiet and calm, soothing to stroll home toward, but five minutes away from countless other, louder possibilities.

She could walk to the harbor, where the air smelled sharply of fish; she could go east onto Hafnarstræti, where the facades turned freshly painted and the sweater-clad tourists meandered, or she could continue downtown to window-shop for long, slim skirts and trendy shoes. The city was full of safe diversions, afternoon pastimes to keep her occupied. She would walk around Reykjavík for three or four hours without gloves or a thick enough coat, warmed by her small observations—a glimpse of lace curtains in the window of a basement flat, the side of a house painted in peach-hued half-circles to look like a sunset.

She rarely used a map, even though the streets were a nonsensical maze, both compact and sprawling; once she memorized a few key names, she could wander content with the knowledge that if she found herself in a perplexing side alley, she would loop back eventually to a sign she recognized. Here, at least, she could be continually confused but never completely lost, and this fact gave her solace.

ಞ

Her second week away from home, on a day so saturated with rain that she wanted nothing more than to remain inside, she decided to write a letter to her childhood best friend.

June 12

Dear Colette,

There are so many questions I want to ask you—were finals hell? how was your baby shower?—but I think I owe you an explanation first.

Right now I'm in Reykjavík, staying at the apartment of Einar and Magga, an Icelandic couple who were either crazy or generous enough, I'm not sure which, to offer me their place while they visit relatives in London. All I have to do is tidy up and feed the cat (walking over my page and meowing as I write this), and I can stay for free until August. Thank God for Elika and her father's international connections!

I've been here a little over a week, and I'm overwhelmed already. So many things do that to you when you go abroad for the first time, Colette—alien details, tiny stitches in the fabric of the everyday, like grocery bags and signs posted in shop windows that you can't read, but huge washes of difference, too, the sounds, melodic but incomprehensible, of foreign conversations that swirl past you on the street all morning. Sometimes I have to come home and sit by myself for a while, just for the comfort of stillness and silence.

Usually, though, I take walks. Today the weather is absolute shit (wind and a downpour), so I'm curled up on the living room rug with a cup of tea, half watching American television. I like to read the subtitles, because eventually I want to learn some Icelandic. Of course, since I've seen mainly soap operas so far, I'll only be able to say truly useful stuff like "Oh, my God! You mean she's having an affair with your cousin's wife's estranged brother?"

Seriously, it does humble me to be here, where almost everyone else speaks English plus two other languages, and where I have trouble with such simple actions as unlocking my front door (I've propped it open with the phone book before I've gone out, in my more desperate moments) or figuring out how to turn on the bathtub faucets (there are way too many of them!). I'm trying to be as quiet and unobtrusive as I can, and just take it all in. Reyk-javík is a small city, nothing like New York, so I think I'll get to know it well before I leave. There's something oddly comforting about it—brightly colored roofs, yellow municipal buses that lumber through downtown like slightly sleeker versions of the ones we rode to school back home.

Well, Siggi (that's the cat) has made further musings impossi-ble, so I'd better stop for now. My address and phone number are *at the bottom of this letter, and I want you to know that you're always welcome to write or call, anytime (I'm four hours ahead of you, remember!). I'll send an update later, and I expect lots of godchild news.*

Love,
Isobel

Satisfied, she got up, wrapped the couch's burgundy-hued throw around herself, and took the letter and her now empty cup into the kitchen. The patter of rain on windows coupled with the apartment's warmth made her hungry, so she decided to make herself a sandwich. She hummed as she arranged ham and cheese and flatbread on a plate. Siggi purred, a ball of arched black fluff rubbing against her ankles. She sat and ate while she wrote Colette's address on an envelope, and then her own, careful to place the accent marks correctly. The simple flavors of her late lunch, coupled with her own precision, made her smile. She licked a stamp of a sturdy horse galloping across a lava field and punched it down in the envelope's upper right corner.

The phone rang for the first time since she'd moved in. She pushed her chair back and ran to pick it up. "Hello?" she said, a little breathless.

"Hallo, is this Isobel?" A raspy Icelandic voice, female.

"Yes."

"My name is Ragna. I'm a friend of Magga's."

"I'm sorry, she's not—"

"I know, don't worry. She asked me to give you a call after you got settled in, to make sure you were doing fine."

"Oh. Thank you."

"It was nothing. But you're well? Enjoying the city?"

The woman's speech was kind, yet strangely formal.

"I am," Isobel said. "I'm just a little tired."

"I understand. If you'd ever like company, though, or have any questions, let me know. Reykjavík is a small place, but it might be good to have someone you could call if you needed to. Unless you've met people already?"

"Only a few old women while I was grocery shopping. They were from Brooklyn, near where I live in the States. Here on a stopover, but they couldn't find the checkout line and didn't know the name of their hotel when I asked them where they were staying."

Ragna laughed. "That's brilliant, but they won't be much help, will they?"

"No."

"Are you busy? I could come over today if you want."

Isobel swallowed, disconcerted. "Well, actually—"

"There's no need to be polite. You'd rather be by yourself; it's okay." Her words conveyed neither accusation nor offense, only affirmation. "Have you been to a place here called Café Sólon Íslandus?"

"No, I haven't."

"It's perhaps a bit pretentious, but rather good for a fish lunch and watching people. Shall we go tomorrow?"

"If . . . if you'd like."

"What time shall we meet? One o'clock?"

"That's fine."

"And the café is on Bankastræti, right downtown, near the main shopping street. You have a map, I'm sure."

"I know where that is."

"Good. I look forward to seeing you. You sound like a very brave and interesting girl. But we'll talk better tomorrow."

With that, a crisp goodbye. Isobel hung up the phone and

looked down at Siggi. His huge green eyes stared back. "Brave and interesting," she said aloud, and laughed.

∾ৎ

The next day at one o'clock, Isobel stood in the middle of the airy, brightly lit café in her anorak and jeans, damp from the relentless rain. She noticed a tall, dark-haired woman in a big black coat who stood with a man at the bar. She had a throaty voice and tipped her head back when she laughed. Isobel wondered if she might be Ragna. She moved toward the counter, peering in the woman's direction.

"Excuse me," she said, "are you—"

"Oh, Isobel, hey," Ragna said, much more relaxed in person, and thrust out her hand. She had a firm, warm handshake. "It's good to meet you." She motioned toward the man. "Halli," she said, "this is a girl from America. Magga says you're working on a thesis, am I right?"

"Umm . . . you could say that," Isobel said.

Halli nodded his approval and shook Isobel's hand as well, then turned to go upstairs.

"What's up there?" Isobel asked.

"It's a gallery," Ragna said. "They have showings and concerts."

Ragna folded her arms across her chest. She had on a rose-colored shirt made of crushed velvet, and wide-legged black pants with a pair of large, scuffed black boots. Her long silver earrings dangled. She reminded Isobel of Elika.

"Well," Ragna said, "let's get a coffee."

Ragna led her to a table by one of the windows, slung her coat over the back of a chair, and sat down. Her blouse was short-sleeved despite the cold weather. She sat comfortably, her legs uncrossed. Her pale arms were bony yet muscular. She watched patiently as Isobel struggled out of her cumbersome anorak.

"Are you all right?" she said. "Not getting lost in there?"

"I'm fine," Isobel said, red-faced, as she sat down.

A waiter, dressed in black, swooped by to hand them menus. He brought Ragna a cup of coffee, a glass of water, and a pack of cigarettes without asking. *"Takk,"* she said.

"He knows what you want?" Isobel said.

"I live here," Ragna said, smiling.

"You're an artist?"

"Umm . . . you could say that," she said, her mockery merely playful. "I've got a grant at the moment, but I've worked so many other jobs that it feels like a bit of a luxury to call myself that."

Isobel glanced over the menu. "Is there anything you'd recommend?" she asked.

"Oh, it's all smashing."

"The fish soup? With saffron?"

"Excellent."

"I'll have that, then."

Ragna leaned her elbows on the table. "So," she said, "what do you think of our beautiful, fascinating country?"

"I like it so far," Isobel said, not sure whether the query had been in jest.

Ragna laughed. "Poor girl," she said. "I wasn't playing fair, acting like a member of the tourist board, was I?"

"Maybe not," Isobel said. "But I do like it here."

"I'm sure you do; I was only teasing. A lot of people here would like you to see Iceland as utopian, but it's not. I think you'll find by the end of the summer that it's a very complicated place."

The waiter returned and set an earthenware bowl of soup before Isobel. She swallowed a spoonful.

"Smashing, isn't it?" Ragna said.

"Yes," Isobel said, amused. "It is."

Ragna lit a cigarette. "You mind if I smoke?" she asked, almost as an afterthought.

"Go ahead."

Ragna inhaled deeply, a hard yet ethereal look on her face. She looked good holding a cigarette; she had long, thin fingers, with strong knuckles. Her eyes were so blue they seemed unreal, like marbles, or the colors of a child's painting.

"You're writing a thesis," she said slowly. "I admire that. There are a lot of academics here"—she waved her hand—"like him over there, the one in the brown leather jacket, he's doing research on the Sagas, and her, she's working on social trends in Nordic Europe, see her, in the green dress? I really do admire that, I think it's smashing to be that focused and that . . . cerebral, I suppose?"

"I don't know," Isobel said. "I'd rather be more intuitive."

"Why not be both?"

"That's the question I've been asking myself, but it's a struggle."

"Intuition is a struggle? No, my dear, it's inside you, you know it is." Ragna took a sip of her coffee. "What's your work about, if I may ask?"

Isobel paused. "Young women," she said, "and how they have such a difficult time growing up."

Ragna chewed her lip. "Here," she said, "girls are encouraged to experiment a lot more. There isn't the same kind of stigma as in other places, I think."

She said this as casually as she had told Isobel to try the soup with saffron, but the force of her nonchalance made Isobel wonder.

Ragna dug a pen from her coat pocket and wrote her address and phone number on their lunch receipt in spiky, angular print. "Enough introspection," she said. "Call me. I'll be around."

The waiter slid by again. Ragna handed him her credit card,

even though the lunch had cost barely a thousand krónur, perhaps fifteen dollars at most.

Isobel unzipped her anorak pocket and reached inside for some cash. "Let me at least—"

"*Nei*," Ragna said. "It's no problem. I'm honored. We don't have many twenty-year-old foreign sociologists here, you understand."

Isobel laughed. "I guess not. But thank you."

"Thank *you*," Ragna said. Another one of her friends came downstairs, and she jumped up and ran over to him, talking a steady stream of husky Icelandic punctuated by her trenchant laugh. She kissed him on the cheek and rushed back over to Isobel, girlish in pink velvet. Her face was flushed.

"Smashing boy," she said. "That one owes me mountain climbing."

❧

Isobel had expected Ragna to be swept up by another admirer and part with her outside the café, but she had volunteered to walk her home. "I hope I haven't overwhelmed you," Ragna said with a self-deprecating smile as they went down Austurstræti.

"How do you mean?" Isobel said.

"Well, you know, a crazy Icelandic woman calling you up all of a sudden, inviting you places."

"It doesn't happen every day back home, I'll give you that."

The rain had stopped, but the wind had picked up. Isobel shivered a little.

Ragna put her hand on her shoulder. "You're sure you're all right, my dear? I could give you my coat."

"That's okay. I don't want you to be cold."

Ragna took it off. "I think I'll survive."

They passed a woman pushing a pram, wearing thin slacks and a diaphanous blouse.

"You see?" Ragna said, loud enough for both Isobel and the woman to hear. "We're all like that, in denial. We think that maybe if we walk around in next to nothing, the weather will finally turn warm. I've been trying for twenty years, but it hasn't worked yet." She grinned and tucked her coat around Isobel. "Here you are. You should put a heavy sweater on. Yes, I know, you'll get mistaken for an American shopper and not the observant scholar you are, but you're freezing."

They cut through Ingólfstorg. A teenage girl with purple hair waved to them and ran over in her platform shoes to hug Ragna. Ragna kissed her on both cheeks, and they spoke in hoarse, trilled whispers for a few minutes, without acknowledging Isobel, until the girl gave Ragna another hug and departed. The effect of witnessing but not understanding such intimacy disoriented Isobel, yet endeared Ragna to her as well.

"You know a lot of people," Isobel said.

"That was my niece," Ragna said. "But if you live here long enough, you know everyone."

"Doesn't that get suffocating?"

"It depends. Most of my friends, the ones my age, have moved out of the country. They were bored, they couldn't stand it, they'd been to Europe for university and were ready to move on. This is a smashing place to raise a kid, though. Very safe."

"You have a child?"

"He's eleven. Working on a farm for part of the summer."

"Really?"

Ragna nodded. "We instill that ethic early," she said wryly. "And it gives me a bit of a break from him. Don't misunderstand me, he's a lovely kid, very spirited, but when you're on your own . . ."

"His father—"

She made a sweeping motion with her hand. "Is not worth mentioning, my dear."

They walked on in silence. Isobel wondered if she had pried too much, but when she looked into Ragna's face it was solid with calm.

"It's so quiet and clean here," Isobel said softly, in an attempt to move toward a topic less volatile. "Nothing like Manhattan."

"Just wait," Ragna said. "It's Friday."

"What do you mean?"

"Tonight," she said, "it will be anything but clean and quiet. You haven't been out to the bars or the clubs, I imagine."

"No," Isobel said.

"You might try it," Ragna said with a smile. "I'm sure you'll encounter lots of people for whom intuition is not a problem. Of course, they'll all be drunk, but—"

Isobel laughed. "Where are good places to go?"

"Oh, anywhere on Laugavegur. Some will let you in for free before eleven-thirty, but that's because nothing happens then. The later the better."

They were approaching Isobel's street now, and as she viewed it from a distance, she thought: It looks so forlorn, all damp concrete and empty spattered pavement. She pulled Ragna's coat closer, in search of a smoky comfort she hadn't known she'd wanted. "Maybe I'll do that," she said.

～✺

She finished the afternoon underneath a blanket, watching Australian sitcoms, Siggi at her feet. After her usual flatbread supper, she peered into Einar and Magga's closet, where she kept her few items of clothing that needed to be hung up, and wondered what exactly one was supposed to wear for a night out in the middle of the North Atlantic. Just as her search for the proper out-fit began, the phone rang.

"Hallo, Isobel?" A now familiar husky voice.

"Ragna. Hi."

"I'm not bothering you, am I?"

"No, not at all."

"Listen, my dear, I have a proposition for you. I just spoke with Guðrún, Magga's sister—she's a friend of mine as well—and when I mentioned to her that I had met a quite brilliant girl from the States who was living here for the summer, she asked if perhaps you might like to talk to someone closer to your own age?"

"That would be lovely."

"Guðrún has a daughter, Kristín, and she's a very sweet girl, about twenty years old. She's usually quite busy, you understand, with a small child of her own, but she could meet with you tomor-row sometime if you'd like."

"Of course. That's very generous of you all to arrange."

"It was nothing, my dear. What time do you prefer?"

"Afternoon is better. I'm not sure when I'll be home tonight."

"Ah, so you are going out?"

"I think I'll be brave and try it. Right now I'm figuring out what to wear."

"Oh, don't worry about that," Ragna said. "It usually depends on the place you go to—the exclusive ones are more strict, but some clubs you can get into in jeans. You're young; you'll be all right. It's we old folks who have to be approved by the bouncers." She laughed. "Well, I must get going—I have my own party to get ready for—but shall I call Kristín and tell her we will meet you at your flat around two o'clock?"

"Perfect."

"Have a brilliant time."

Isobel smiled. "I'm sure I will."

After they said goodbye, Isobel went back to the closet and selected the one good dress she'd brought along. A rare impulse purchase bought at the urging of Elika, it was a short, funky sweaterdress interwoven with tiny gold metallic threads. She had yet to wear it or its matching gold heels, but she had tucked the ensemble into her suitcase along with her sensible ribbed leggings, in the hope that—what? She had no idea.

She fingered the shining, nubby texture now, and thought: I want to be one of those girls. The ones Ragna talked about, the ones who—at least on the surface, at least according to a member of the tourist board—are encouraged to experiment, the ones who move with the raw grace of what they know they already know.

She glanced at the clock by the bed. It was half-past six.

༷

Isobel spent the rest of the evening watching more television and attempting to read the day's papers. She preferred *Dagblaðið-Vísir* over *Morgunblaðið*, as *DV* had a children's page, but given her limited Icelandic vocabulary, even that was a challenge. The nightly news came on. Isobel glanced at it and went back to deciphering the classified ads. A few were for phone sex, sandwiched in with the cars and summer houses for sale; she frowned. *"Góða nótt,"* said the female newscaster—tenderly, Isobel thought—as the program ended.

"Góða nótt," Isobel said in return.

She went into the bedroom and took out the dress and heels, then remembered that elegant attire usually involved stockings. She flung the dress on Magga and Einar's bed and searched through her small knapsack, home to various odds and ends that she'd remembered to pack—for no reason—at the last minute. Buried beneath her address book, a pair of too large gloves, and a goofy chenille headband that she used as an earwarmer in cold weather, she found a beige pair.

She took off her jeans, shirt, and socks, and put on the stockings and the gold dress. She wasted no time looking in the full-length mirror; she didn't want to know. Instead she returned to the living room. "We need some music, don't we, *kisa*?" Isobel said, practicing her Icelandic on the cat. She flipped through a box of CDs on top of the stereo and selected the third Sugarcubes album. She turned it up loud enough that she could hear it throughout the flat, and padded into the bathroom.

" 'This wasn't supposed to happen,' " Isobel sang, her words garbled by toothpaste. She spit into the sink, wiped her mouth on a towel. She put on earrings and got out her makeup bag. " 'Accidentally you seduced me,' " she belted out, as if the more cheerfully she sang, the less alone she would feel. She wanted someone else with her—Elika, sprawled on the bed and yelling irreverent style tips, or even Colette, sweetly bustling about to help. Isobel longed to have another woman here, one with whom she could share giddy excitement, swap perfume, burn with invincible twin-schoolgirl flush at the prospect of adventure in a foreign city where darkness never fell. She looked out the window at the pallid sky and thought, I want darkness to fall.

Isobel scrawled on lipstick, tousled her hair in an attempt to transform it from messy to mysteriously wild, and turned off the CD player. "Don't wait up for me!" she called to Siggi.

She wedged a book in the front door for good measure and started down the stairs. Her steps were precarious in the delicate heels, but with her house key in one pocket and some cash in the other, she felt as if nothing could trip her.

Chapter Two

New York City

On an unusually balmy March evening two months earlier, not long before her doctoral defense was scheduled, Isobel had awoken from a restless, prickly sleep to find a young girl standing at the foot of her bed. She gleamed like a waxy angel in the light from the streetlamp behind the drawn blinds, her arms crossed in a slouchy gesture of hurt masked by indifference, too glossy lips coated with a scowl.

Beneath her thin quilt, Isobel drew back, groggy with disbelief and blinking hard, as if to dislodge the image from her grit-filled eyes. She slid farther beneath the covers and tried to comfort herself with the futile mantra always spoken to her by her loved ones in times of distress: *Don't worry about it, it's nothing, you've been working too much.*

As Isobel closed her eyes again, the girl dissolved into a gauzy filament. Against the soundscape of sirens and car horns pouring in through the open window, she was no more than a solemn sigh.

༄

The next morning, Isobel got up and called her mother. Her film-student roommate, Elika, who called her parents once a month at best, scoffed at Isobel's long-distance confessionals. "Next thing you know, you'll be discussing your sex life with her," she chided, while Isobel merely smiled, not wanting to tell Elika that sometimes, after her over-eager boyfriend had left their apartment, she would huddle on the floor, knees drawn to her chest, hurriedly yanked-on jeans still unzipped, all the buttons open on her blouse, and dial the phone, waiting for her mother's voice to tell her about a new skirt she'd bought for work, what she and Isobel's stepfather had made for dinner, anything to soothe the confused pounding that echoed through her body, her eyes closed, her spine bruised as she leaned back against her bed, longing for another touch, hungry for home.

"I've been weird lately," Isobel said to her mother now.

"How so?" her mother said. "I mean, are we talking *really* weird or normal Isobel-weird?"

Isobel laughed. Her mother was the only person from whom she could take a joke without some small shard of offense. She pictured her standing in her blue-wallpapered kitchen back in small-town Staplin, barefoot in her bathrobe, eyebrows furrowed with perplexed amusement at her overworked daughter calling from New York City.

"Really weird," Isobel said. "I'm exhausted, but I can't sleep."

"Honey, it's probably just stress," her mother said, the long vowels of her southern childhood resurfacing. "You know how you get about your studies. Don't look for any deeper meaning. You read into things too much."

Every time she asked her mother for advice, it was so solid that Isobel wondered how her mother could have ever led an irrational life.

"Yes," Isobel said, "but—"

"You should socialize more. Hang out with Elika, or that nice guy you've been seeing—what's his name?"

"Gavin," Isobel said with a sigh. "And I have two words for you, Mom: doctoral defense."

Her mother laughed. "Balance has never been an easy concept for you, has it, Isobel?"

"No," Isobel said.

"I realize you're putting your academic life first, and I admire that, but I worry about you sometimes. You shouldn't let it devour your life."

"That's easier said than done when I've got an assistantship to maintain."

"Sure it is, but think about it. You won't be able to do your best work if you don't give yourself a break."

"I know."

"So give yourself a break, okay? That's an order."

"Yes, ma'am."

"Listen," her mother said, "I'd better run. It's almost eight and I haven't even ironed my dress yet and my one good pair of pantyhose is still in the wash, and, well, you know what it's like around here. Have a good day. And think about what I said."

"I will." Isobel felt her throat tighten. "I love you."

"I love you, too."

She hung up the phone. Sunlight slanted over the windowsill in a dark beautiful curve of shadow. Isobel gnawed her thumbnail. I'm twenty-five years old, she thought, and blinked hard, thinking of her mother thinking of Isobel standing here, watching the wild, moist glow of morning in the terrible city.

Letting the Body Lead

❦

A few minutes later Isobel knocked on Elika's door, still in her nightgown and shaky with the fusion of reassurance and dependent self-loathing she always felt after she talked to her mother. Elika answered in a fuchsia silk kimono, her dark hair gorgeously rumpled. "Come to raid my closet again, dearie?" she asked.

"I can't face what's in mine," Isobel said.

"Let me take you shopping, then," Elika said, taking Isobel's hand and leading her into the bedroom. She kicked floral sheets across the floor, clambered over her bed's purple batik comforter, and in a graceful curve jumped to land in front of her tiny, crammed-full closet. Isobel stood in the doorway, watching Elika's graceful flight, sensing the weight of her own inertia.

"I'm short on money right now," she said, "and besides, I don't have the guts for a full Elika ensemble."

Elika grinned. "Suit yourself, but I still think you need to take more risks."

"Please, nothing lime green."

"I wasn't talking clothes," she said, thumbing through hangers.

Isobel sat on the bed and rubbed her eyes. "I know," she said. "I've just got a meeting with my adviser at one-thirty and I'm really tired."

"Are you getting enough sleep?"

"Hardly. Two hours is a luxury."

Elika held up a long silk skirt printed with abstract green and blue swirls. "What do you think?"

"I like it, but please remember that I'm a good five inches taller than you are."

"Don't worry, it'll be adorable. Now let me see where the shirt that went along with it is."

"You mean you've actually got matching outfits?"

"Isobel, darling, you underestimate me."

Elika had a talent for discordant dress that ranged from endearingly bizarre to enviably stunning. By simply wearing strange clothes, she transformed them into stunning, electric creations that crackled with life: ankle-length velvet skirts in gorgeous William Morris patterns, paired with cropped T-shirts advertising chili cook-offs, metallic blouses, and chunky-heeled black mules. One time she wore a necklace made from paper clips to a bar, and Isobel watched, a thin gold chain of her mother's draped tastefully around her neck, as no fewer than five men wrote down their numbers for Elika. The maddening thing was that it wasn't an act, a conscious stab at the avant-garde; it came to her naturally, just like color-coordinating everything came naturally to Colette.

"Here it is," Elika said, pulling out a blouse in the same green silk.

"Nice, very nice. So anyway, I can barely sleep, and when I do, I—"

"Hey, I think I've got another one you can wear underneath. Let's see, it might be in the back—"

"Elika, are you listening to me?"

Elika peered into her closet, one hand masterfully flipping through a season's worth of impulsive purchases until she found what she'd been looking for. "Yes, and I think you're fucked up," she said.

"Thanks, I love you, too."

Elika leaned over and ruffled Isobel's hair. "I'm only kidding," she said. "Don't worry so much. Don't be so cerebral."

"You're very good at psychobabble, you realize that?"

"Sorry," Elika said, laughing. She placed the skirt on the bed next to her and tucked her third find, a cream-colored chemise, under the green blouse. "Here you go," she said. "Now all we need is a pendant and funky shoes, and you'll be set."

Isobel reached over and ran her fingers across the silk. "So you think I should give myself permission to quit now, or what?"

Elika smiled. "No. I think you should be good to yourself."

"My mother actually said the same thing to me this morning. Not in as many words."

"Oh, no!" Elika wailed in mock histrionics. "I'm turning into a fifty-year-old!"

"I don't think my mother would be caught dead in those red leather pants you've got hanging in your closet, though."

"Don't be so quick to judge her. She's cool enough, she just might go for them."

Isobel's mother had come up around Christmas, and she had taken Isobel and Elika to lunch. Much as Elika laughed at Isobel's compulsion to tell her mother everything, she had loved Jana, who'd entertained them with tales about her own spunky youth smoking pot in Chapel Hill.

"What size shoe do you wear?" Elika asked.

"Ten and a half."

"That's right. I was going to hook you up with the cutest pair of green Doc Martens, but oh well."

Isobel stood, picking up the outfit Elika had selected and draping it carefully over her arm. "Thanks."

"My pleasure," Elika said, and then cried out. "Wait! I forgot!"

She rushed over to her bureau and rifled through her mammoth burgundy velvet jewelry box, digging through Sri Lankan demon necklaces and Mexican silver bracelets until she found a jangly boutique bauble on a black cord. "Here, take this. And don't be too tasteful with the shoes, all right?"

"I won't," Isobel said, even though she knew black dress flats were the best she could manage, and hugged Elika, hard. Then she went back to her room and hung up the borrowed clothes, still not yet ready to trade the pale softness of her nightgown for the skirt's peacock swirls, and curled up on the living room futon with her latest research notes. After a page or two, they blurred into a senseless haze of jargon-filled musings surrounded by a dense cluster of hard data. She yawned, sliding deeper into the cushions and pushing her folder onto the floor to let it resound with a satisfying thud as she slept.

It was rich, deep sleep, the kind that comes only after a rough night and only when sleep can't be afforded. She undulated out of it with slow luxuriance, murmuring in contentment, and sat up and rubbed her eyes. The apartment was still and silent; Elika had already left for her morning class on Japanese cinema. Isobel went into the kitchen, feeling coherent and human and generally pleased with herself, and looked at the clock on the microwave. The vile green glow of the numbers told her that it was one in the afternoon. Her universe cramped and contracted with fresh exhaustion at the thought of making it to her appointment showered, fully prepared, and on time.

"You can't be serious," she said. Her mouth felt sluggish with awakening. *On time* was negotiable, she decided.

Forty-five minutes later, she rushed up the stairs to her adviser's office, hair damp, gathering Elika's skirt in her fingers so she wouldn't trip as she took them two at a time. She was lucky; Natalie still sat chatting with her one o'clock appointment.

"Keep breathing, Isobel," she said in her smoky rasp of a voice, through the open door. "We'll be done in a second."

"Thanks," Isobel said, gasping. She went down the hall to the soda machine, set down her bulging backpack, and searched its front pockets for quarters, stepping on the skirt as she bent down. The necklace clanked in front of her, a noisy impediment. She got a Diet Coke, brought her bag back, and settled on a bench for a review of her notes in earnest this time.

In a few minutes Natalie said goodbye to her last student, an elegantly tall girl with hair swept up in a dramatic topknot, wearing a gauzy floral dress and brown hiking boots. "You can phone me at home if you have any more questions, Christa," Natalie called after her, and ushered Isobel inside.

Isobel adored the office. It had no posters on the walls, no knickknacks on the shelves, no clusters of framed photographs on the desk, just stack after stack of books. She took a seat on a bulky old swivel chair by the door.

"You're all dressed up," Natalie said. "What's the occasion?"

"Well, um . . . none, really." Isobel toyed with Elika's pendant, her face turning red. She felt childish and gaudy next to her adviser, who had on a dark red corduroy shirt, baggy khakis, and a pair of loafers, and looked ready to put her feet up on her desk at any moment.

"Just the fact that it's a gorgeous day in New York, huh?" Natalie said.

"I ran over here so fast I didn't notice."

Natalie laughed. "Seriously? The view from my pathetic little window has been tempting me ever since lunch."

Isobel had forgotten to eat. She swallowed a sip of her Diet Coke, and its sweetness churned in her stomach. Sunlight filtered through the glass in wild patterns. Her head grew woozy.

"So what's the update?" Natalie asked.

"With me or with the program?"

"Either. Both."

"As far as the program goes, we have about six more sessions."

"And as for you?"

"I'm scared out of my mind."

The suddenness and intensity of her own words shocked her.

"Of what? The oral defense?"

Isobel nodded.

"Let me guess," Natalie said. "You've slaved over this, you've handed in the infamous document, and now a multitude of new facets spring to mind and you think, 'I should have done this, I should have incorporated that, why didn't I structure it another way, and now I'm going to be eaten alive'?"

"Yes. How did you know?"

"Been there, done that, bought the T-shirt. Is there anything in particular that's troubling you?"

"Other than my own perfectionism?"

"Other than your own perfectionism."

"Well, there's the issue of quantification. I do a field study, take twenty undergraduate volunteers and pair them up with twenty so-called at-risk eighth-grade girls in Brooklyn for three semesters, and then what? Even if I pass the defense, even if I run screaming with glee through Washington Square at commencement in May, have I really helped the girls? I thought the fact that the mentors were all college-age women would inspire a deeper connection, but . . . I wanted it all to be sisterhood and togetherness and one big slumber party, you know, and I forgot that hey, these are girls who have been screwed over time after time in their lives, and we're just one more futile attempt to break through their bitterness, which angers me. Then I get angry at myself for being angry, because I should either be the objective observer, recording my findings, or the one who's going to revive Ophelia, right? Hell, what am I saying, this is self-indulgent, you don't need to hear what I'm feeling, you just need to get the final—"

"Isobel, Isobel. Slow down."

"I'm sorry. I shouldn't be babbling like this. I just haven't slept much, and I didn't eat at all today, or yesterday, now that I think about it, and—"

"Don't apologize. Go home."

"Are you serious?"

"Yes. Much as I want you to run screaming through the park in May, I want more to see you healthy and sane in March."

Isobel smiled weakly.

"Why don't you talk to the other mentors about what you've just told me, and give me a call after your next session with the girls. You're still swimming the gulf between practice and theory, but you, of all people, can make it to shore, I think."

Isobel felt as if her adviser had summed up her entire existence in the slim metaphor.

"Okay." She stood up. Almost lost her balance.

"Hey, are you all right?" Natalie asked, steadying her.

"I'm fine."

"Take care of yourself this week. Please."

"I will," Isobel said. She waved goodbye, then picked up her bag and made her way down the stairs, head lowered, steps quick. Laughter and fragments of conversation swirled around her. She was the same as she always had been, books clutched to her chest as if to stop a wound that bled and bled, her thoughts racing. Alone.

≈

"You haven't eaten for two days?" Elika said. "Isobel!"

"It was stupid, I know," Isobel said. "But I was so busy planning for the mentoring program yesterday, and today I fell asleep and lost track of time, that's all."

They sat on Isobel's green floral throw rug in the living room, waiting for Gavin. Elika was painting her fingernails metallic blue. She wore a purple velvet T-shirt and black jeans and had her hair gathered off her neck in wild strands. A piece of string was tied around her neck.

"Listen," she said, "don't do that too often. I've been down the starvation road, and it's not a pretty one."

Isobel was about to throw back a joke about how there was no road Elika *hadn't* been down, but she could tell by Elika's dropped voice and rare somber tone that her roommate was being utterly serious.

"How did your meeting with your adviser go?" Elika asked.

"Frustrating as hell."

"Why? Because you were ready to faint?"

"No, because lately I feel there's no use living in an academic fishbowl."

"How do you mean?"

"I'm doing my study on these girls, who are really great once they open up to you, they're not the problem at all, the last thing I want to do is give anyone the impression that—"

"Isobel, I can see where you're heading, and I do not think you are a bitch because your work with them is driving you fucking nuts. Please proceed."

Isobel laughed. "Nothing gets past you, does it? But thanks."

Elika blew on her wet nails. "Go on."

"I read Carol Gilligan's theories," Isobel said, "about the shift in 'voice' girls undergo around the age of twelve, how before that point they're confident, outspoken, but once they hit it, they're tentative, unsure of themselves—"

"And she needed a grant from Harvard to figure that out?" Elika said. "Christ, the alchemy sixth-grade girls go through is beyond theoretical."

"No kidding," Isobel said. "I looked not only at Gilligan's work but also at the studies that had recently been done on girls in the American school system. I put all those things together, and I saw a really disturbing trend—and listen to me, slick as anything, never mind the fact that I went through this, you went through this, my girls over in Bensonhurst are going through this, Isobel's just charting her *trends*."

"I don't think you're being slick," Elika said. "You care about the girls, and you're making an honest attempt to help them. You're already done the research portion, right?"

"Yes, thank God."

"So if you really wanted to, you could just call it quits and never do another session with them," Elika said. "You could just spend your time hyperventilating over your oral defense and forget all their issues, am I right?"

"I could, but I don't care to."

"Well, there you go. You're doing this out of the goodness of your little heart."

"Elika, it's not that simple. I'm not some heroine."

"No, but you're not evil just because you're adopting the trappings of the academy, either."

Isobel sighed. "Think about it," she said. "The main reason why I'm doing this project, when you get down to it, is what? Not to make that twisted labyrinth of being young and female a little easier to get out of, but so I can get an overrated piece of paper."

"You make self-advancement sound criminal."

"I don't think it is, but—"

"It's not a matter of either/or, Isobel. You can be intelligent and emotional at the same time."

Once again, as she had in Natalie's office, Isobel was jarred by the knowledge that someone else had spoken crucial words regarding her. It happened a lot lately and made her feel both more heightened and more passive.

"Maybe after I get the doctorate," she said with a halting laugh. "Enough babble about me. How was your day?"

Elika made a face. "It was spent in an oh-so-exciting tryst with an editing booth."

Elika's current video project revolved around the concept of women and self-image. She constantly begged Isobel to be one of her subjects. "No way, sweetheart," Isobel always said. "You aren't making me curl up on your futon so you can turn a camera on me and watch me struggle to look waiflike."

"I'm sorry," Isobel said now.

"Don't be. It had to be done." Elika collapsed in an exaggerated swoon. "Ah, the sacrifices I make for my art . . ."

"All so you can sit in a smoky loft in SoHo and brag in a languid voice and flip your hair."

Elika looked slightly hurt (or was that an act, too, Isobel wondered), but she laughed. "You see, that's why you'd be so great for my documentary," she said. "You have this . . . this *duplicity* about you."

Isobel scowled. The scowl wasn't so much at Elika and her art-house analysis—she was used to that by now—but at herself, at the adolescent who would have curled up on Elika's futon, ready to spill her secret longings for posterity, for the sad, sick motive of being noticed.

"Duplicity?" Isobel said.

"Yeah. You sit there looking so sweet and timid and cute, but you're really wild and irreverent."

"My dear," Isobel said with throaty dramatics, "you have no idea."

"My point exactly."

"Nice try, but while we're on the subject, how would you like to come in and talk to my mentoring group about your work?"

"Me?"

"Yes, you. You'd be terrific."

"Sure. 'This is Elika, my not-quite-ready-for-PBS friend.'"

"Your credentials won't matter. They'll love you. You're a little older than them but still hip, and you're living on your own in New

York with your own career, despite all you dealt with when you were their age. I think they could relate to you."

"Anyone who does is asking for trouble," Elika said.

"Stop. I guarantee they'll warm up to you."

"If I talk to them, will you at least seriously consider being one of my subjects?"

"Deal."

They heard a knock at the door. "I'll get it," said Elika, scrambling up.

Gavin stood there with a bemused expression on his face. "Elika," he said.

"I hope you intend to take your woman out for dinner," she said. "She's starving."

"I was planning on doing that, actually."

"Good boy. I think you should keep him a little longer, Isobel."

"You hear that?" Isobel said, coming over to kiss him on the cheek. "Hi, hon. Elika thinks I should keep you."

"Well, then, by all means," he said. Sometimes Isobel thought she and Elika in tandem scared him. "Nice fingernails, Elika."

"Why, thank you," she said brightly. "Would you like some?"

Sometimes Isobel thought Elika tried to scare Gavin on purpose.

"No thanks. I went through my metallic phase awhile back." He draped an arm around Isobel, who flinched without realizing it. "Are you ready?"

Isobel nodded. Elika gave her an awkward hug goodbye, punched Gavin lightly on the shoulder, and sauntered down the hall to her room, yelling, "Don't worry, I'm leaving now, you two can start being each other's love slaves!"

Isobel and Gavin looked at each other. *Love slaves?* he mouthed.

"Don't say another word," Isobel said, and got her purse off the table.

꿍

Gavin took her out for Ethiopian food, and afterward they walked through St. Mark's Place holding hands, the sky dark and clear, the lights bright and eerily festive. They didn't say much, which pleased Isobel. She wanted nothing more than silence and fingers to wrap her own around.

Isobel had been seeing Gavin since the previous September, around the same time she began serious work on her dissertation—a nagging confluence that she tried not to contemplate. Elika, who shared a mutual friend with Gavin, had set them up on a blind date. "Trust me," she said. "This guy is painfully decent." And so he had been, meeting Isobel on a humid end-of-summer evening at a quiet bistro, the sleeves of his dress shirt meticulously pressed. He was proud of his recent M.B.A. and his new job at a marketing agency, but over dinner he spoke of other, more mundane pleasures: people-watching on the subway, Rollerblading in the park. As they left the restaurant, he held the door open with one hand and let his other rest in the small of her back, as if to gently steady her. On the street, a light breeze blew her long linen sundress around her ankles. Back in the city after a summer away, ready to work again in earnest, she had surged with elation. She had looked at Gavin and thought: With you, I might pass for normal.

They went into a basement record shop now and meandered through its gritty aisles. "Pick something out," Gavin said. "A belated Valentine's gift."

"Please," Isobel said, "don't remind me."

February fourteenth had been the day her dissertation was due. Enthusiasm dashed by the deadline, she had rushed about her apartment in a proofreading panic, furiously checking and rechecking her sources before she handed over the stack of pages to Natalie. By the time Gavin arrived in the evening, with a single long-stemmed rose in cellophane on his arm, her eyes had blurred with jittery tears, and she'd begged him for a rain check on the whole concept of romance. It was then that Elika began referring to Gavin as Isobel's "insignificant other"—jokingly, but placing a perceptive finger on the moment of their relationship's subtle shift.

"No, really," he said now. "I mean it."

She led him to the shelves of imports in the back and selected what she liked. The industrial album playing in the shop blared way too loudly, and the fluorescent lights assaulted her eyes. She felt tender and exposed, pummeled by her day, and didn't know how to explain to Gavin that she couldn't play the romantic, appreciative girlfriend.

She glanced at the price sticker on the disc as they headed for the cash register. It was a double set and cost forty dollars.

"Shit," she said, "I didn't realize. You don't have to get this for me."

"Relax," he said, taking out his wallet. "No one's keeping a tab."

"Thanks, hon. For dinner, too."

"You're welcome. And seeing as Elika made you out to be a near famine victim tonight—"

"Hence the choice of Ethiopian food. Cute symbolism. Elika embellishes."

"Even still, it's not a good idea to go without eating like that."

His words and tone struck her as gratingly paternal. As they left the shop, she longed to stop him in oblivious midstroll and shout: Can't you see it's not that simple, can't you see how much this dissertation devours me?

Instead, she said, "I want to pay you back for it."

"There's no reason to be rabidly egalitarian. Ten dollars isn't going to break my budget."

"What is *that* supposed to mean?"

"Turn off the women's studies major for a second and stop jumping down my throat. I was trying to be nice, not accusatory."

"Well, you are now. 'Turn off the women's studies major'? There's an enlightened comment for the record books."

"I didn't mean to make a generalization about your work, Isobel. I just think that maybe you're getting too caught up in—"

"Don't go there," she said. "Please don't go there. Not now, when I'm exhausted. Every nerve in me feels like it's on fire."

They walked back to her apartment, silent again. Their bodies bristled. He waited until they were on her front steps to put his arm around her. She looked over at him, his face youthful under the streetlamp. He opened his mouth to speak. She put a finger to his lips.

"Shh," she said. "I know."

He leaned in and kissed her, hard, grappling, too fast for her to feel. She swayed. The plastic bag from the record shop swung madly in her hand.

"I guess you can come in," she said.

༚

In the hushed glow of her room, she sat on the edge of her high brass bed, and he stood above her, short brown hair tousled, eyes wide with childlike delight. She kissed him with absent softness, ready to sink backward into the mattress. He bent down, pulled off her cardigan, and gently lifted her T-shirt over her head, dipping his mouth into her collarbone and neck; his warm fingers pressed into the cold skin of her back as he unhooked her bra. She shivered. "Close the window," she whispered. As he did, her arms came up across her chest in an automatic, ashamed reflex, and she slid onto her stomach on the Irish Chain quilt before he returned to sit beside her. He ducked his head and kissed her shoulder blade. Ran his hands down her spine.

"You're so tense," he said.

She said nothing, her head buried in the pillow.

"Do you want me to rub your back for you?"

She let out a long, muffled murmur.

"I'll take that as a yes," he said, and his hands moved in deep, careful strokes, just enough pain, just enough release. She closed her eyes. All she wanted was that gentleness, that firm touch, his breath and body floating safely above her. Drowsiness settled around her like a silky blanket.

After a few minutes, he sat up. She heard him toss his jacket on the bed, peel out of his shirt. He leaned down and grasped her shoulder in an attempt to turn her over. She stiffened. He smoothed back her hair and put his lips next to her ear. "Hey, you aren't falling asleep on me, are you?" he said.

"Gavin. I haven't had a good night's rest all week."

His sigh seeped into the room. "All right." He moved away, ready to get up. Without looking at him, she reached across and grabbed his hand.

"Don't leave," she said. "It's late."

"I can get back to Midtown all right, Isobel."

She lifted her head. Stared into his face. "No," she said. "I want you to stay."

He squeezed her hand. "Okay."

They both stood. She walked over to her closet, unbuttoned her jeans, and slipped on her nightgown. She turned back and found that he had folded her sweater and shirt and draped them over the foot of the bed. He stood there in his plaid boxers, waiting for her to turn back the covers, to choose which side to crawl into. A little ache stabbed through her.

"Thank you," she said.

She took the left side, her back to him. He curled up next to her, not so close as to be touching, but close enough that she could feel his warmth. They lay there for a while with the lamp on. He reached out a tentative hand, and with his fingers brushed the side of her face, stroking her forehead, her jawline, her lips. She leaned up and turned off the light, and at the exact moment that the room exploded into darkness, he inched nearer to her and moved his hand down to grasp hers, his arm curved around her body. She fell asleep.

❧

When she woke again, the bedside clock read three A.M. The numbers loomed with pale terror. She flailed and flipped over, groped out at Gavin. It took him a minute, but he shook awake. "Isobel, what?" he said. She dug her fingernails into his skin, stuttering with disorientation, and he wrapped his arms around her. "Was it a dream?" He caressed her hair over and over. She shook and clawed at his back. Her limbs quivered with a muddled fusion of fear and passion.

She wrapped one leg around his waist. He slipped his hands under the delicate cotton of her nightgown. Her lips trembled. She gasped at his mouth, sinking her teeth into his lower lip with a desperation that frightened her even more, and he let out a shocked cry. She burrowed her chin into his shoulder as he fucked her, her dilated pupils searching wildly in the dark for some object to set sight upon, to give word and meaning and context to what she was feeling and not feeling. He moved too eagerly, as if grinding against her harder and harder would tranquilize her, but it only hammered her panic deeper inside her body. She screwed her eyes shut. Pictured the thirteen-year-old walking through the doorway, her shaggy hair parted to one side, her frail arms braced across her bare chest. He started to come. She jerked away.

"I have to stop," she said. "Please."

He waited until he was finished before he let her go and moved back. The look of entitlement coupled with confusion on his face made her boil. Couldn't you see what I needed? she thought.

"Jesus, honey," he said, "I only—"

"Don't talk," she said, sitting up. "Go back to sleep."

"Isobel, I'm really sorry."

She didn't say anything.

"Are you angry at me?"

"No," she said. "I'm not angry."

He felt for her hand. "You're still shaking."

"I'm fine."

"Are you sure?"

"Yes."

"Because I'd hate to think that—"

"Go back to bed. Please."

His breathing grew slow and easy, and when she knew he had fallen asleep, she leaned over and kissed his damp forehead, then went down the hall in the dark to the living room. By feel she grabbed a tattered ivory throw off the couch and curled up with it clutched around her in her old bentwood rocker, its creaky rhythm lulling her into a numb trance. She sat there the rest of the night.

Chapter Three

Reykjavík

$\mathcal{T}$wo hours after she had left Einar and Magga's, Isobel sat in a quasi-Irish pub by the harbor, sipping her third Guinness. She had chosen the venue on the basis of its quirky audacity, but its charms had rapidly worn thin. A group of Americans sat at the crowded table next to her, and she half wanted to join them, if only to be a part of some element, even if it meant enduring the same shit of *Oh, why are you here and what is your research about and yes, that's fascinating and I have a friend who's working on a dissertation and—*

Alcohol nuzzled, warm, against her loneliness. It was one A.M.

She stood and walked to the doorway as a flock of fourteen-year-old girls in sheer dresses walked by outside, their lips bright purple, their hair soft and shiny. Boys sauntered past in imported jeans, their barely pubescent faces tender yet tough. The air swarmed with the slur of intoxicated voices and the almost festive honking of horns. The city lay draped in the eerie stillness of streetlamps and dusk's gray glimmer.

Isobel stuffed her hands in her pockets and went outside. She was drunk herself, but not miserable because of it; she felt loose-limbed, as if she could reach her arms up and touch anything, pockets of friendly air billowing into her coat. Behind her a group of boys broke into raucous song, their voices rising and falling in a youthful crescendo, so raw with brittle beauty that Isobel wanted to hold it against her, to wrap her fingers around it as if it were one of the bottles that they alternately swung and gulped from on their midsummer swagger-stroll. In their melody she recognized only a few fragmented words, like shards of colored glass, but for once it didn't matter. Isobel followed the throng as they turned the corner onto Austurstræti, caught in the melding of street into street; for one shivery moment, the rock pumping out of car stereos mingled with the techno pouring out of discos. She tipped her head back, and her hair blew in the night breeze.

At the first club she came to, there was a line outside the door, and she surprised herself by stepping into it. She hadn't planned on dancing, but now she wanted nothing more than to move back into her own body, to warm herself in a feverish whirl. She glanced at the boy next to her. He was tall and slim and narrow-faced, and he held a two-liter bottle of Coke that Isobel knew was spiked even before he nudged her and offered it with a sly smile. She drew back a little in confusion, a half-formed stutter on her lips, but then understood: He thought she was one of the girls, an Icelander. The idea struck her as both mad and delicious.

Isobel took the bottle from him, smiled back. *"Takk,"* she said. He said nothing in response, as if trying to test her. She took an awful, appreciative sip, keeping her eyes on him as she did so. He was about seventeen, she guessed, still at the age when getting smashed as quickly as possible mattered more than anything else, on the cusp of disdain for these Friday nights but not quite there yet. Isobel found him incredibly endearing and, at the same time, envied him his shimmering seventeen-year-old freedom. The Coke slid down her throat, syrupy yet satisfying. She thought: I could get used to this.

The crowd lurched ahead of them, and the next round of patrons spilled into the throbbing cocoon of the disco. They were fifth in line now. From the open door Isobel could see neon light bursting in gaudy splashes like promises before her eyes. She took another sip from the bottle, and some of the drink splattered down her chin in a lukewarm trickle. She and the boy both laughed. He reached over and swiped at her sticky mouth with his thumb. Isobel laughed even harder. She felt as if every broken, self-conscious piece in her were tenderly, firmly being pressed back into place in one supple, giddy wash of second adolescence, forming a new Isobel whom she might not like in six hours but who was perfect for right then. He grabbed the bottle back from her with only half-playful greed, taking one last messy swig before he chucked it onto the sidewalk and slung his slender arm around her. Then he pulled two thousand-krónur notes out of his pocket and handed one to her as they reached the front of the line. Isobel thought about buying him a legitimate drink so they'd be even, but then remembered that, for tonight at least, she wasn't legal. She grabbed him by the hand and led him inside. Between her fingers, his wrist was thin and delicate as a child's.

In the club the music pulsed so loudly it was like a violent lover, battering deep down in her chest and slamming ragged sound into her ringing ears. Isobel swayed dizzily on her feet and watched her boy's face blur into a mere grin and nothing more. A dance track's dislocated beat seeped into her, and she undulated to it with numb, easy slowness, at once entrenched in her own body and floating above the room in a hazy circle of strobe lights and smoke. She was no longer an underage-looking drunk girl in a tight gold sweaterdress, but a bright-colored synergy of heat and motion and light, inhibition spilling like lava from her fingertips in frenetic hues, the red and yellow and purple waves rolling off the movement of her hips and arms and upturned head. She felt as if the room were revolving so softly as to be barely perceptible, segments of the crowd sucked away from her and then swishing back in a tidal gush. Her boy floated out of her field of vision and then reappeared; Isobel didn't rush to him or reach out, simply gave him a disjointed, happy wave of recognition, lost in the sloppy joy of her private dance. She slid toward him, and he took her hands and drew her closer, close enough for her to glimpse the wild glint in his dilated eyes.

With careless glee Isobel slipped her arms around him, loosely, so that she could still lean back to feel the hot glare of the neon and hear the devoid tune as it pounded into her temples. She felt molten, liquid, all flesh, soft but invincible. His hands traveled up and down her body, and she was still herself, she didn't shake, she didn't wonder. He yelled over the din, his breath warm on her throat, *"Hvað heitir þú?"*

"Isobel," she yelled back. She moved nearer to him, drew her palms into the small of his back.

"Isobel," he repeated. Said that way, softer, with an accent on the *I*, her name felt like a transmutation of herself. She thought of asking his name in return but decided not to. She wanted this cloaked, transient. He was whispering against the side of her neck now, hot, choked words, most of which she didn't understand and had no desire to know, his teenager's voice sticky and vague with exaggerated passion. She closed her eyes tight and tried not to laugh. She wanted to block from her mind the ridiculousness of the whole situation that was slowly bleeding in around the edges of her ecstatic game, wanted to relax and melt like the girl she had never been. *"I-so-bel, I-so-bel,"* he said, stretching out the sylla-bles, distorting them until they garbled in the midst of the roaring music. He kissed her throat. She thought: This is lovely, but it doesn't matter. I can just keep dancing.

After a few minutes, he lifted his head with a sudden jerk that told her, *We're leaving.* Isobel took his hand again, and they shoved their way back out onto the street. Her hearing was still swollen with sound. She stepped over another young boy, this one about fourteen, curled up unconscious on the pavement, his bent knuckles pressed to his delicate, full-lipped mouth, his tangled brown hair wet with the drink someone had poured out there. For a moment Isobel wanted to stoop and touch his small shoulder, to stroke back his damp locks and watch his dazed eyes flutter open and ask him why he did this to himself every weekend, but, still ripe with alcohol herself, she walked on and squeezed the hand she held, hard.

It was almost dark now. Up at the corner, a row of taxis shone glossy black under the streetlights, and the sight filled her with a mournful urgency. They stopped at a hot-dog kiosk and joined yet another line. The night air had sharpened. Their laced fin-gers swung.

He ordered them each one with everything, and Isobel paid for her own despite his protests. They ate as they walked, swiping at their mouths with paper napkins, shivering a little. At the corner, he pulled her under the awning of a shop and kissed her. With a strength she didn't know she had, Isobel pressed him up against the glass window, grabbed his head in both her hands, and kissed him back, her tongue running along the inside of his lower lip, seeking the pungent, lingering taste of chopped onion, mayon-naise, youth. His jumpy fingers pushed her jacket down off her arms. *"Nei,"* she said. The foreign word leapt from her, numb.

He mumbled what Isobel assumed to be an apology, then yanked her coat up again and wrapped his arms around her. Her head throbbed. She rested it against his shoulder. I ought to get a taxi home, she thought, and end this.

She took his hand again, and they turned onto Tryggvagata. He sat on the curb. She sat in his lap. He buried his mouth in her neck. She was sobering up.

A taxi approached, and Isobel jumped to her feet and waved, dragging him with her. She leaned down to the window, told the driver her address, and turned around to face the boy. He looked haggard, and terribly young. Isobel took his face in her hands again, gently now, and kissed his forehead.

"Thank you," she said, in English.

Behind them, in the doorway of a bar, a woman quavery with drunken sobs huddled in the arms of her stoop-shouldered lover as he stroked her back, her hair. Isobel closed her eyes. Clutched the boy tight. Thought, Be strong, but be gentle. She felt desperate and dizzy.

"I have to go now," she said.

She pulled away from him with a halting half-wave and ducked into the back of the cab. He stared at her, the contours of his face harsh with desolate anger. She curled up on the seat, as they drove away, her head bowed, her jacket wrapped tight around her. Her temples pounded. She hoped she wouldn't be sick. Outside, under the lights, Isobel could still see them, the gorgeous girls in their purple lipstick and ethereal dresses.

❦

When the driver dropped her off, Isobel handed him the last of her money and hobbled up the porch steps, inside the building, and up the staircase to her flat. She kicked the door open with one foot, sending the book propped there sliding across the vestibule.

In the darkness, she staggered to the bedroom and tossed her jacket next to a slumbering Siggi on the mattress. She took off her pointy metallic heels and padded across the thick carpet in her stockings, hating the childlike sounds of her feet's scuffle. She stood before the bureau mirror and flicked on the lamp. At three A.M. her own visage jumped out at her with frightening force: narrow, hollow, young. Always young. Like a fist clenching and then uncurling, the gates of self-loathing scraped open inside her. You are pathetic, Isobel told herself. Look at you.

She looked.

Her eyeliner had smudged into two brownish streaks. One of her earrings had come out somewhere on Tryggvagata; the other dangled loosely, a precarious gold bauble glinting cheaply at her earlobe. Her lips were cracked, their festive claret color gone, replaced now by rawness. On the shoulder of her dress, near her collarbone, a hybrid splotchy stain glared at her, seemingly irrevocable. She put her hands up to her mouth in a halting gesture of protection, comfort, cold fear, and watched, transfixed, as the face of the girl in the mirror crumpled, shrank back into a senseless pucker of tears, a slobbery wail.

"Shut up," Isobel said to her.

Isobel straightened, wiped her eyes, took her nightgown from her open suitcase, and flipped the light switch outside the bathroom, safe haven of white tile and sink rims to rest weary foreheads against, and went inside. She took deep breaths, clenched her teeth, unzipped her dress, and stepped out of it, all the while looking down to avoid the disheveled truth of the mirror. She hung the dress tenderly over her arm and plucked a tissue from the box on the counter to dab at the stain tentatively, then roughly, her jaw rigid with the effort. The green glow of dribbled mayonnaise and greasy chopped onion mingled with a ringed daub of spilled liquor on the gold threads, stubborn and vile and never coming out, Isobel knew. Her whole body ached. She felt infected. Still, she took the dress carefully and hung it up in the closet, in the back where she wouldn't have to look at it when she got out her windbreaker or a good linen blouse, this pale spangled reminder, throbbing, selfish, sexual.

Isobel went back into the bathroom. Her limbs quivered, but she felt strangely floaty and cut off from this feeling, as if she'd accomplished something important. She blew her nose. She combed her hair. She took off her stockings, gently, precisely, for once with no snags or rips or signs of careless ineptitude. She slipped her nightgown over her head. She removed her lone earring. She wiped off the smudged brown eyeliner. She brushed her teeth, comforted as the taste of processed meat and vodka and her date's warm, searching tongue slid away from her, replaced by the blandness of mint toothpaste and oblivion. I'll crawl into bed and sleep all this out of me, Isobel thought, putting everything neatly back into her makeup bag, and then I'll get up tomorrow and I'll be fine.

She leaned down one last time to splash water on her face. The shock of cold droplets hit her, and nausea welled up in her throat. Her hands gripped the basin. Her eyes clamped shut, so tight she felt as if she were being pushed through a wringer, her body turned inside out so that she was all viscera, vulnerable, reddish.

Isobel waited, crouched there, until the churning in her subsided, and then she went into Einar and Magga's room, crawled under the duvet, and crashed headlong into an instant, murky sleep.

❧

When she awoke again, it was to a scream of sunlight through the drapes, accompanied by the cat's yowls. "All right, all right, I'll feed you," she mumbled, and rolled over to look at the clock. It was one-thirty.

Her hair was still damp from a shower when the doorbell rang half an hour later. Isobel answered it, knowing she looked like a bloodshot-eyed slob in her wheat-colored sweater and jeans, stiff with rain from the day before. She was met by four women who ranged in age from five to forty, and who seemed either oblivious or thoroughly nonchalant regarding her hangover.

Ragna burst inside before the others, eschewing the previous afternoon's handshake in favor of a vibrant hug that told Isobel, *We're not leaving each other's lives anytime soon.* She introduced Isobel first to Guðrún, a stocky yet stylish woman in a teal pantsuit whose hair was an even brasher red than Isobel's, and who apologized for what she called her "pitiful English" while Ragna rolled her eyes as if to say, *She's a linguistic genius, Isobel, don't believe her.* Isobel then met willowy Kristín, who said little but managed to give her a quick smile of muted but genuine interest before little Ásta began querying: "You're from America? Where? How long are you staying at Magga's? Do you have any children I can play with?" Kristín laughed and put a slender hand on her daughter's pale, silky head, admonishing her gently in Icelandic.

"How was your night out?" Ragna asked Isobel.

She blushed. "I'm paying the price today," she said.

"You look fine," Ragna said, and Isobel knew she was being diplomatic. Isobel wondered how her party went but didn't ask; Ragna was ruddy-faced, glowing. "What did you think?"

"People don't do anything halfway here, do they?" Isobel said.

Guðrún laughed. "Those crazy Icelanders," she said, as if she weren't one of them.

"Have you eaten yet, Isobel?" Ragna asked. Isobel shook her head.

Ragna spoke with Guðrún in low, rapid Icelandic for a moment, then turned back to Isobel. "How would you like to walk over to Guðrún's for a late breakfast?"

Isobel's brain felt prickly, imprecise; it didn't like processing words. "That sounds wonderful," she finally said.

Outside, the world was full of sharp, burning color and wind that thrust her senses back into being. She shuffled along in the procession behind Ragna and Guðrún, who talked between themselves, and beside Kristín, who watched, silent, as Ásta skipped ahead of them all, dashing across the street and into an alley, then scampering back without so much as a reprimand.

"She's a lucky girl," Isobel said, "to have that kind of freedom."

"I'm lucky not to have to worry," Kristín said. "We took her to London once, to visit my sister, and I was so scared. She didn't understand that cars wouldn't stop for her."

Kristín's cell phone rang from within her purse. She pulled it out, spoke for a few minutes, her voice and face suddenly more animated, then hung up. Her features went soft and shy again.

"So what clubs did you go to last night?" she asked.

"I honestly can't remember," Isobel said.

"If you want, I can give you a list of good places," Kristín said. "Safe ones, with decent music."

"I'd like that," Isobel said. "Although I'm not really into parties."

"I used to be," Kristín said. "Not anymore."

During their walk, her gaze strayed not once from the bright pink speck of down coat that was her distant daughter.

Guðrún lived near the university, in a first-rate example of what Isobel had discovered to be typical Icelandic architecture: a white concrete block. She led them inside the wrought-iron gate and up the spiral stairs to her landing, where she and the other three women took off their shoes. Puzzled but too fuzzy-headed to ask, Isobel did the same before entering.

Inside, the golden glow of sunlight on waxed hardwood floors delighted her yet made her woozy. Ásta settled on the living room's red jacquard couch to watch American cartoons on satellite television, and the rest of them gravitated toward the kitchen. Ragna read *DV* with her feet up on a chair, smoking a cigarette, and every so often, she would laugh and point out something ridiculous to Kristín. Isobel almost asked them to pass her the children's section but was too ashamed. Instead she watched Guðrún at the stove, who stood pouring a thin batter onto a griddle. Guðrún noticed her, and smiled.

While they waited for brunch, Kristín brought out some family albums, meticulously labeled and organized, and a coffee-table book of panoramic photographs of Iceland to show Isobel. She flipped through them, solemnly pointing out her family's summer house, Ásta's baby pictures, waterfalls and glaciers. "Wait," Isobel said. "Could you go back to that one, please?"

Kristín turned a page in the panorama book, and Isobel glimpsed a familiar sight. In this shot, the sky above was blistering blue, but still she recognized the plain on which Sylvia Johnson and her former fiancé had stood. "This place," Isobel said. "Does it have a name?"

"Oh, yes," Kristín said. "That's very famous. It's Þingvellir, the site of our first parliament, from centuries and centuries ago—"

"Nine hundred A.D.," Ragna said from behind the paper.

"You've heard of it before?" Kristín said.

"I had a friend who visited there once," Isobel said. She didn't know if she could still consider Ms. J. a friend, but it was the simplest thing to call her.

"You can go there, too, if you want," Guðrún said from the stove. "There's a bus that leaves from the city and goes around the Golden Circle—"

Ragna waved her hand. "Don't bother with that, I'll take you."

"Ásta!" Guðrún shouted. *"Pönnukökur!"*

Ásta ran into the kitchen and sat at the table, bouncing up and down in her chair.

"I take it you like pancakes," Isobel said. Ásta bobbed her head, and the rest of them laughed.

Guðrún set a plate of the crêpes in the center of the table, and Ásta plucked the top one from the stack before her grandmother could hand them each a smaller plate. "You can eat these with a little sugar," Guðrún said, "or with cream and jam. We have two kinds, the strawberry or the—" She paused, and turned to Ragna, holding up one jar. *"Hvað er þetta á ensku?"*

Ragna peered at it. "Rhubarb," she said.

Isobel heaped the cream and strawberry jam on a pancake, cut it neatly, and lifted the fork to her lips. Her mouth filled with sugar, light, sweetness, air; her head whirled with the human warmth of the room. In the window hung a piece of stained glass in an ornate pattern she couldn't decipher; it was deep red, the purpled hue you watch emerge from beneath your skin with both fascination and fear when you cut yourself. So this is what living in a body feels like, Isobel thought. Dizzy, stroked by the kindness of strangers, as the sun shimmers through glass the color of blood.

≈

When Isobel left Guðrún's, with her home and mobile-phone numbers and strict orders to call either her or Kristín if she needed anything, Ragna walked with her toward the center of town. "Did you have a good time?" she asked.

Isobel nodded. "I really appreciate all you've done," she said. "I only wish I could have been in better condition to meet Magga's family."

Ragna shrugged. "So you had a wild night," she said. "That's very Icelandic. We even have a name for the weekend pub crawl: *rúntur*." She rolled her *r*'s like no one Isobel had ever heard before.

"It may be Icelandic, but it's very unlike me," she said.

They reached the traffic island at the end of Bankastræti. "You might surprise yourself, my dear," Ragna said, and turned. "I've got to meet a friend at four o'clock, so this is where we part ways, I'm afraid."

She hugged Isobel, and a gust of wind blew the dark tendrils of her hair across Isobel's face. Then she was gone, headed toward the harbor.

Isobel decided to walk up Laugavegur and peek in a bookshop she'd seen earlier in the week. The first floor was crowded with magazines, newspapers, and people in line at the register, so she went up the stairs to the second level. High-ceilinged, minimal-ist, the room and its stacks of books beckoned. She perused a table of works in English and selected an anthology of sociological es-says on Iceland, which cost more than she could afford but which she nonetheless craved. The woman who took her credit card had long, pale hair like Ásta's, and a broad, serene face; behind her funky glasses, her eyes were clear and pleasant. Isobel wondered if the clerk had had a Friday night like hers. Even if it had, she re-mained apple-cheeked, alert, diffident but polite as she in-structed Isobel on how to fill out her tax-exemption form. As she handed Isobel a plastic bag with her pricey tome inside, Isobel wanted to ask her how she did it.

She walked home past the lake. By the time she reached her front steps, Isobel had made a resolution. You will make your time here as productive, as pure, as possible, she told herself. You'll have lunch with Ragna. You'll read books, saturate yourself with history and culture and landscape. You'll eat good things and write in your journal and take long naps and get lots of fresh air, and in August you'll fly home refreshed, enlightened, ready to work again. No more of this impulsive hedonism, this mindless debauchery, this alcohol poured down your throat to loosen your bones, this useless trail of neon and namelessness, do you hear?

Chapter Four

New York City

The day after her rough night with Gavin, Isobel was still reeling. Her body felt distant, unmoored, like a tattered sponge, soaking up while falling apart. Isobel barely sensed Gavin's kiss goodbye when he left for work at six, and she floated through the kitchen barefoot when she arose, oblivious to Elika making breakfast. "Hot night of passion, roommate of mine?" Elika asked.

In answer, Isobel poured herself a glass of water, raised it to her trembling lips, and felt the liquid splash down her neck.

"I'll take that as a no," Elika said.

Later, on the subway ride to her mentoring session, Isobel sat as straight as she could, gripping her knees with her hands, her head tipped back and her eyes straining to stay open. Wake up, she told herself. Think of the girls.

But she couldn't.

Letting the Body Lead

Two hours later, Isobel's detached, shaky mood had yet to sub-
side, and her mentoring session was an absolute disaster. The
girls showed not a shred of interest in the handouts on famous
women in history that Isobel had photocopied—unless she
counted their gleeful insistence on wadding up the pages and
throwing them at one another. After asking them twice to stop,
Isobel finally climbed on top of a desk and yelled, "Okay, do you
want me to go get Mrs. Sullivan or not?"

At the mention of their stern guidance counselor, the girls
scrambled to rescue their paper airplanes and return to their seats.

Isobel smiled weakly. "I didn't think so," she said, and lowered
herself back down into a chair. "Hey, things obviously weren't
working today, and I'd really like to prevent them from getting
this crazy again. Why don't we try this: Everybody take the sheets
of paper they were having such fun pelting each other with,
smooth them out, and write down what you think would improve
these sessions. Be honest, the mentors and I can take it." She
looked at her group of college-student volunteers, who sat in a
state of shock at her dramatic tactics but still nodded vigorously in
agreement. "You can tell me I'm a big dork who dresses funny and
doesn't have a clue what's going on in your life, if that's what you
feel like." Some of the girls giggled. "Or you can just write about
something that bothers you. Get your pencils out, let's go for it."

Most of them sighed and rolled their eyes but did as they were
told. "Do we have to use correct spelling and all that crap?" one
girl called out.

"No, no," Isobel said. "Don't worry about it, that's not the point."

She watched as twenty heads lowered and twenty pens scrib-
bled. One of her volunteers, Kasey, a porcelain-skinned young
woman with a long ponytail, leaned over and touched Isobel's

arm. "Isobel," she said, in her lilting southern accent that re-minded Isobel of her mother, "are you okay?"

"I'm fine," Isobel said, embarrassed. "It's just one of those days when I needed to wing it. Do you . . . do you think what I did was all right?"

"Oh, I'm *sure*," Kasey said, in a soft, soothing tone whose reas-surance veered toward patronizing. "You've heard Mrs. Sullivan say how difficult they can be."

"We're done!" several voices chorused.

"That was quick," Isobel said. "You can fold up your answers and put them on my desk."

"Geez, she sounds like a normal teacher," one girl said with a derisive sneer. Isobel winced.

"Only you guys will read it, right?" another girl asked ner-vously, biting a lime-green fingernail.

"Confidentiality guaranteed," Isobel said. She watched as each girl filed past her and dropped a crinkled slip of paper next to where she sat. Shireen, a shy, stocky girl whom Isobel often worked with individually, leaned over and whispered to her, "I'm glad you bitched everybody out. They were being really stupid."

"Thanks," Isobel said. "How are you doing?"

Shireen gave a jerk of her shoulder. "I'm still here."

After the grumbling girls had been escorted to their next class, and after Isobel had seen off her volunteers, she returned to the empty classroom where the sessions were held and sat there opening each folded sheet as if it were a small poison flower. Most of the answers were terse and unremarkable, along the lines of "This is boring, but better than regular class." One response read, in all capital letters, "THIS PROGRAM IS FINE, ANYONE WHO COMPLAINS ABOUT IT SHOULD GO THE HELL BACK TO STUDY HALL AND SHUT UP." Isobel wondered if that was Shireen's.

The last note, however, really caught her eye. It read, in small, precise print, "Do you really think reading little third-grade articles about famous women who made a difference will help me when my dad's out of the picture, my mom can't think about anything except getting her next fix, and I might be pregnant?"

Isobel sighed and rested her hand against her forehead. When I was her age, she thought, I spent my Saturday afternoons curled up on the windowsill reading. I idolized my teacher and dreamed of foreign countries. My romantic life was nothing more than a few tentative near-misses, cerebral longings from afar. She's absolutely right. I haven't got a clue.

"Isobel?"

She looked up to see Kathleen Sullivan, the girls' guidance counselor and Isobel's liaison at the school, standing in the doorway. "Yes?" Isobel said.

"Your dedication never ceases to amaze me," Kathleen said, "but I think we've got an algebra class ready to start in here."

Isobel jumped. "I'm—I'm sorry," she said, and stood. "I was just—just checking over a project for the girls."

Kathleen leaned against the wall, tucking a rare stray strand of ash-blond hair back into place. "How were they today?"

"Awful," Isobel said, shocked and disappointed at how easily the exasperated, bitter word slid from her mouth. "Unbelievably frustrating."

Kathleen grinned in agreement. "They have their moments, believe me."

"I had to really yell at them," Isobel said. "I hope it was appropriate."

Kathleen waved her hand, let out a dismissive snort. "Don't worry about it," she said. "Some days you do what you have to."

Most days, Isobel thought.

"So when are you bringing in a speaker?" Kathleen said abruptly.

"I'm working on that," Isobel said. "I have someone lined up. My roommate, actually. I just have to convince her."

"Not too much time left," Kathleen said. "You'd better get busy." She turned to leave and, almost as an afterthought, added, "Have a good evening, Isobel."

"You, too," Isobel mumbled. She leaned back against the desk edge for support and shuffled the slips of paper in her hands, as if they were a deck of cards in which she might read some pivotal clue to salvation—for her or for the girls?—before the algebra teacher made his entrance.

❧

When she arrived home, she found Elika studying for an exam, books spread out on the living room floor, and a vase full of roses on the kitchen table. "From your secret inamorato?" Isobel asked.

Elika looked up from her seemingly illegible notes. "No, silly, courtesy of that boy of yours. Read the message."

Isobel reached into the silky red folds and pulled out a tiny card. In Gavin's broad, loping script, it simply read, "I'm sorry." Isobel swallowed.

"When did these come?" she said softly.

"A few minutes ago," Elika said, biting the end of her pencil. "Swanky florist, fuckin' cute delivery guy, the works. Very dramatic. It's a shame you missed it."

"Yeah," Isobel said, her voice tired.

Elika got up and came over to her. "Listen, sweetie," she said, "it's probably none of my business, but I couldn't help noticing what he wrote, and, well, I was wondering . . . if there was anything you needed to talk about, or wanted—"

Isobel shook her head, felt the tears dislodge and spring to the surface. She closed her eyes tightly, fighting them. "No," she said. "Thank you, but no."

Elika put her arm around Isobel, and Isobel rested her head against Elika's shoulder. I don't want a fragrant apology bouquet, she thought. I want a little darkness. I want what I never had, the jagged enigma-boys of my youth.

"Elika, how can I be so stupid?" she said, willing herself not to sob. "How can I be so accomplished in some ways, like it's a reflex, and yet such a relational idiot?"

Elika patted her back. "Isobel," she said, "it's called being human."

Chapter Five

Reykjavík

He happened to Isobel on a Saturday night in late June. She was standing at the bar of one of the clubs on Kristín's list, and then she was lying on the bed in his grungy studio apartment. Or at least that's how it had seemed.

She had ordered a beer, not so much because she had wanted it, but because she wasn't ready to dance yet and she needed something to do with her mouth and her hands. She had been about to reach into her pocket to pay the bartender when she saw a broad, muscular hand slide a thousand-krónur note across the bar.

She turned to find a tall, gangly man in a yellow polo shirt and a pair of khaki pants. At first glance, especially in the semidarkness, he appeared to be the usual Nordic archetype, clear as a passport stamp—tousled blond hair, fine features, blue eyes. The more she stared at him, however, the more ragged around the edges he seemed. He looked insanely beautiful, and deeply wrong.

"Thank you," she said.

"You're Canadian?" he said.

She laughed. "No," she said, "but I'm flattered."

The bartender handed them each a can of beer. Her fingers relished the feel of cold aluminum. She felt brave and dangerous. She wanted to show him. Her throat worked hard, swallowing the contents of the can so quickly she thought she would choke.

"You didn't really want that drink, did you?" he said, with a sly smile.

She shook her head ruefully. "No," she said. "I didn't."

I want to put my arms around you, she thought, just to see how it feels.

"You must forgive my rudeness," he said. His accent was melodious yet impish. "I'm Kjartan."

"I'm Isobel," she said.

"Ah," he said. "Like the South American writer."

"No," she said, impressed. "With an *o*, not an *a*."

"Isobel," he repeated, emphasizing the proper letter. "Woman of isolation. Solitary ice girl. It's a bit loud in here for my tastes. Shall we dispose of our libations and take a walk, my darling?"

He smelled like he had already downed a six-pack. His eyelid drooped; he looked as if he could take her anywhere and do anything to her and feel entitled. Isobel thought: I have absolutely no reason to trust him. I want to follow him out the door into the night air.

"Yes," she said, her voice high-pitched and distorted, as if it weren't sounding from within her own body. "I think we should."

"Have you got a coat?" he asked. She nodded. He put his arm around her, palm on her waist, and led her to the coat check. He took the blue fleece pullover her mother had given her and slipped it over Isobel's head as if she were a small child, pulling her hair gently out of the collar. She let herself go loose. The boundary between where his fingers ended and her neck began felt fluid and supple, like silk. He held her face in his hands and leaned down to kiss her, firmly yet tenderly, on the forehead. The room was acrid with smoke. A white strobe light flashed. On the stereo system, a hip-hop singer crooned, "You're a superstar, that is what you are . . ."

Outside, the street was strangely quiet. Kjartan took her hand in his. She pulled it away, not because she disliked it, but to reassure herself that if she had to leave, she would.

"You're worried," he said. "You needn't worry. We aren't crazy murderers and rapists here."

"Really," she said dryly, not believing him, wanting to believe him.

He yawned. "We're just old men like me who can't handle the club scene."

She laughed. "How old are you?"

"Older than you."

"How old am I?"

"Perhaps twenty-five."

"Yeah," she said, her tongue thick. "How did you know?"

He stopped and drew her close to him for a moment. "You have a young body," he said, "but an absolutely ancient mind, I can tell." He touched her temple, and she felt a ridiculous surge of happiness at the illusion of having been understood.

They walked for a while, not saying much as they passed the glistening lake.

"Here," Kjartan said when they had reached the eastern section of town. He led her into someone's small backyard. "Let me show you something."

He plucked a few small seeds from a fragrant bush, and fed them to her gently, his fingers grazing her lips. A tart taste, sour but lovely.

"It's cumin," he said, and pulled her tight against him. She felt herself spiral and somersault away from her body, then dive back into it as he lifted her chin and slid his tongue deep into her mouth. Her fingernails scraped his back.

"I live just up the street," he said.

She said nothing, just took his arm and kept going. His house was on the corner, and he unlocked the entrance while she waited on the steps below. He held the door open for her and extended his hand so she could step up into the darkness. She stood on the front mat of his apartment while he turned on one dim lamp. Its russet-colored glow coated the lone large room in sepia tones, like an old photograph. She took off her shoes, stood in her stocking feet before a stranger. Touch me, she thought, so I can feel myself. Hold me so I won't fly apart.

Kjartan strode over to her and lifted her pullover roughly off. "I want to see what you look like," he said, kissing her neck, and then her breasts. "I'll bet you're burning beneath the skin, under all these layers."

"*Já,*" she said, because she could think of nothing else. Sweetly, painfully, language failed her, and she knew her real education was about to begin.

�’

Now she stared up at him from the bed, as if she had flown outside herself, while he undressed her like a doll. He had lit candles on the table beside her head, and they sent daggers of shadow flickering across his broad, bare chest.

"What a rare find you are," he muttered, as he unzipped the turquoise silk dress she'd bought the day before on Laugavegur, with money she didn't have. "So ivory-skinned, so fine-boned . . ." His praise disintegrated into a stream of Icelandic that sounded both endearing and dirty. Isobel closed her eyes. Let his hands slide over her, skimming soft as water.

"You look scared," Kjartan said, his voice a wet whisper at her ear. "Are you?"

She shook her head. "No," she said, with a tinny laugh.

He tossed her dress on the linoleum floor. She wanted to tell him not to, wanted to ask him to hang it up or drape it over a chair, but alcohol had left her too languid. She turned her face away from him, stared straight into the flame of a candle. He was calling her his fire-haired girl. *I'm not a girl,* Isobel longed to say. *I'm twenty-five years old, remember? I'm earning a doctorate.*

But she was a set of rose-painted nesting dolls, and all the hollow pieces inside of her, squat crone through scrawny baby, girls fifteen and sixteen and seventeen, shook out into his eager palm.

Kjartan leaned down on his elbows above her, his startling blue eyes strangely tender as he enumerated in a gentle yet discursive voice all the things he wanted to do with her and to her. It felt as if he were speaking to the wall behind her head; surely these scenarios and actions couldn't possibly concern her stunned body, involve such absolute hunger for her pallid, oblivious flesh. I don't know, Isobel kept thinking. You're drunk, I'm drunk, stop talking. She clutched his arm. Her frantic brain stuttered in a dislocated swirl. Brutal sense bobbed, briefly, to the surface.

"You're going to use a condom," she said. "Aren't you?"

Kjartan kissed her ear, her neck. "Don't worry," he said. "I'll take care of you."

"That's not what I asked," she said. Her teeth clenched. She was ready to jolt out of her stupor, sit up, walk out into the empty-armed night if she had to.

Then his mouth moved in a jagged line along the curves of her skin, as if he were drawing a moist, tattered map of her with the tip of his tongue, and there was a shock of sweetness—bright, with a bitter edge—that smacked down her certainty for one crucial moment.

"Okay," Isobel said. "Okay."

~§

Later, after he had fallen asleep, she lay wedged between his back and the wall for hours, her eyes wide. She heard shouts on the street, the ticking of the clock, his snores. She balled her hands into fists and nestled them in the space between his shoulder blades, then lowered her face against her taut knuckles, excited yet stunned. He didn't stir.

Isobel slid across the bed on her knees, so as not to wake him, and crossed the room naked. She grabbed his bathrobe from a hook in the armoire and put it on, tying the belt tight. Barefoot, she went through the kitchen and the hallway into the bathroom he shared with the other tenants in the building. She closed the door and stood before the smudged mirror for a hard appraisal of herself. Her knotted hair spread across the royal-blue velour collar of the robe, more like a stubbed-out cigarette's last ember than a lusty fire. Half-moons of darkness gleamed under her eyes. Her face was stark with triumph and terror.

When Isobel crawled back into bed, she found a tiny, old pink stain on her side of the sheet, like a bland, sad echo of the rich color that shone through Guðrún's window. He rolled over, caressed her groggily, his touch like a reflex. She inched closer, pressed herself against him. She wanted heat, hipbone to hipbone, a circle formed by arms around her back. He moaned in the midst of some dream, shouted out fast, slurred words. She traced a small, faded scar over his eyebrow, kissed the underside of his chin, brushed dark blond hair away from his forehead. It was five in the morning, and she was willing to romanticize anything.

Kjartan yawned and opened his eyes. "You're already awake?" he said.

"I never fell asleep," she told him.

He stretched and, in the process, almost elbowed her in the head. "Isobel the night owl," he said, pronouncing her name as if it began with a long *e*, the same way the young boy with the bottle of spiked soda had. "You don't drink much, do you?"

"Why? Do I look like hell?"

He grinned, reached under the duvet for her. "No," he said. "You look like a beautiful foreigner who should stay here indefinitely."

"Ha," Isobel said. "Only until August."

His large hands settled on either side of her waist. "You're shaking," he said. "Are you cold?" Isobel shook her head. "Nervous?" She gave a quick shrug. "You're quite a strange creature."

She nestled her face in his neck. "So I've been told."

"Don't worry," he said, patting her hair. "I still like you. How could I not, with these marvelous red tresses of yours swirling around me? My fair Celtic girl. Did you know that Icelanders are more Celtic than Scandinavian?"

"No."

"They are. Because the Norwegians brought Irish slaves over."

"Really?" Isobel murmured. "And did you know that Icelanders are very good at inserting miniature history lessons into each and every conversation?"

Kjartan laughed. "It's our national duty."

They fell asleep together like that, her head on his shoulder, his arms around her. At ten they woke for good, and stumbled around the room with the shades drawn, he loosely pulling on the bathrobe Isobel had worn earlier, she searching for her bra. They sat on his couch and drank orange juice and coffee to sober up. Kjartan smoked a cigarette, staring into space, and didn't touch her. Isobel wanted a hand on her knee, a palm against her cheek, some small gesture that would let her know it mattered whether she went home or stayed. Instead he glanced through the day's paper, acknowledging her only when he chose to summarize a choice article or two in English. The phone rang. He answered, and she waited, legs tucked under her, for the end of his twenty-minute chat. As he talked, he absently stroked her thigh.

So this is what you do to chase the illusion of intimacy, Isobel thought. Ramble about fine bones and burnished hair and ivory skin, then smugly sit here.

He hung up, leaned over, and kissed her full on the mouth. He tasted sour, like decay. "Sorry about that," he said, even though she knew he wasn't.

They fell backward on the couch, Isobel on top of him. He started to work down the zipper of her dress. She sat up, put her hand flat on his collarbone.

"No," she said.

His brows furrowed, quizzical. Kjartan had told her last night that he was thirty-five, but below her now he looked like a perplexed little boy, unaccustomed to being refused.

"Why not?" he asked.

"Too sleepy," Isobel said, and kissed the side of his neck. She wanted to snap, *Because I don't want to, that's why,* but didn't.

"Isobel the stubborn," he said. "Maybe later?"

"Maybe."

She had no idea if *later* would exist, or if she would want it to.

༄

By noon they were back in bed again. Her mind still couldn't wrap around the way things just seemed to start; her body panicked at the waves of sensation that pounded through it. Anxiety and pleasure melded into one surreal tremor. Afterward, Kjartan watched her with a naughty half-smile, fingertips brushing against her breasts, and Isobel wondered how someone could touch another person like that, so nonchalantly, as if it were habit.

I need to take a shower, she thought wildly. I need to feed the cat.

She swung over the edge of the bed. He put his hand on her back. "You're going?" he said.

"I have to," she said.

"Write your number there"— he gestured in the direction of an open notebook on the desk beside him—"and I'll call you tomorrow, okay?"

Isobel nodded. Bent down, kissed him gently on the lips. By the time she stood, he had already turned over on his side and fallen asleep. She leaned over the desk and wrote in the book in careful capitals: ISOBEL SIVULKA, 551-4645. She almost turned back a page to see what else was written there, but didn't.

Then she put on her underwear, her dress, and her shoes, picked up her purse, and went outside. The sun soothed her. The air crackled. Isobel felt like she'd been let out of prison. She shielded her eyes and looked for a street sign to lead her home.

᠊ᡈᢓ᠊

When she walked into her flat, Isobel quivered at the quiet neatness of it: the kitchen with its Wedgwood-blue china cupboard, the hall table, the cloak tree. Siggi rushed toward her, meowing. "I know, *kisa*," she said. "I'm sorry."

Isobel fed him and gave him a bowl of milk, then stood in the shower for forty minutes, letting the hot, sulfur-scented water beat down on her in a steamy tattoo of regret and redemption. She emerged red and scrubbed clean, and put on a pair of sweatpants and a T-shirt, soft baggy things. She sat cross-legged in an oversized chair in the living room with a cup of chamomile tea, into which she dropped two perfect lumps of sugar. Let this go, she told herself. Lounge here with a symphony playing on the radio and the cat by your feet.

❦

But she couldn't. As she slept that night, she tossed fitfully, gripped with the memory of tongues and fingers, of Kjartan between her knees. She woke Monday morning, got dressed, and stared severely at herself. So you fucked some edgy drunk, she said to her hungry face. You can't stand the thought of leaving it at that, but leave it.

Her mouth contorted in a scowl at her words, but not merely for their bluntness. She knew she was on the verge of decision, fraught with the dual specters of cautious safety and stubborn longing. How can I choose, aware and awake, Isobel thought, when I'm enticed by a dream of skin on skin, still sleepwalking?

She sat on the sofa and ate passionfruit yogurt from an ivory bowl. She flipped through the television's satellite channels. She tried to read the book of sociology essays she'd bought, but the words spun and blurred. At noon she put on her coat and scarf and went into the city center. She stuffed her hands in her pockets as she walked through an airy tourist shop, full of handblown vases, lava pottery, sweaters in autumnal tones. She tried to pose as a cool, elegant foreign traveler, but she wanted to smash everything there.

Isobel left before the clerk could ask if she needed help, and headed in search of the garden full of cumin. The overcast sky was so huge it threatened to swallow her with one snap of its pallid gray mouth. The wind stung her face raw. She couldn't decide whether the sensation was a caress or a slap. She walked and walked, until her bare hands grew red and numb. She passed a sub shop, the

69

American embassy school, two young boys who looked Vietnamese. She knew his place was near the lake, but she felt like she was going in circles. Her once comforting pilgrimage around the city now felt like a trap. Maybe it never happened, she thought. Maybe I invented him, as the antithesis of Gavin.

Thinking of Gavin made her ache. She glimpsed the tourist boutique again and told herself firmly that she needed to go back to Einar and Magga's. She trudged toward her narrow expatriot street, her concrete-block surrogate home.

She walked faster when she saw the house. Entering the front door, she ran up the stairs to the second-floor landing. She fumbled for her key with swollen hands, shoved it in the lock, turned. No luck. She tried again, and then a third time. Nothing. She slammed her fist against the door, softly, in a passive gesture of defeat.

Isobel sank to the floor of her apartment lobby and began to cry. The tears warmed her frozen cheeks. Get up get up get up, she thought, as she heard the phone begin to ring on the other side of the wall.

Eventually she stood and tried the lock again. This time, mercifully, it worked. She went inside, brushing off Siggi's dervish hellos, and checked the answering machine. No message. She sat on the couch and watched a subtitled BBC production of *Jane Eyre* while miserably nibbling from a plate of cheese and sliced salmon.

As the credits on the film rolled, the phone rang once more. Isobel jumped up and lunged for it, knocking the plate to the floor. "Hello?" she said.

"Is this Isobel?" A male voice, familiar yet new, low and strangely solemn.

"Yes," she said, leaning against the wall, dizzy. "Yes."

"It's Kjartan," he said. "I was just wondering . . . how you survived the weekend."

"I'm fine," she said. It wasn't a lie anymore. "Better than fine."

She pictured him smiling indulgently, and the thought filled her with warmth. "That's good," he said. "I tried to call you earlier, but you weren't in."

"Oh. Right." She flushed with embarrassment. "I was trying to find your place, actually. But I had a bit of trouble."

Kjartan laughed a little; the sound was not unkind. "It was rather dark the last time you were over. Perfectly understandable." He cleared his throat. "You want to see me today?"

"Yes—I mean, if you—"

"I would like that, Isobel."

His voice was rich, desirous, yet somehow offhand.

She took a deep breath. "Okay. When?"

"I'm here right now."

"You'll have to give me directions. Obviously."

He gave them to her, yawned, and said, "I'll see you soon, baby."

She hung up, feeling ashamed of herself yet giddy. She found Siggi happily eating the remains of the salmon off the carpet.

"Oh, all right," she said. "I guess you can celebrate my complete lack of discretion with me."

❧

When Isobel arrived, Kjartan answered the door in his underwear and a polo shirt, hair rumpled from an afternoon nap. Behind him, the television blared. "Our first proper date," he said dryly, and kissed her on the nose. "Welcome to my mess."

He hopped back into bed, and she crawled under the duvet with him. "You were walking for a long time, I can tell," he said. He took her chilled fingers in his mouth, one by one, and warmed them. She felt herself uncoil. He unzipped her jeans, put his hand inside. An involuntary sigh escaped from her; it undulated like a red carpet rolled out, a velvety bridge for her to cross over. "What a lucky guy I am," he said.

They fucked to the drone of the seven o'clock news. Near the end, she raised a hand to her lips, to stuff down the sounds she was on the verge of making. Kjartan grabbed her wrist and held back her cramped knuckles. "No," he said. "Don't hide yourself from me. I want to hear you."

When they were done, she lay on her stomach with her hair covering one eye, feeling floaty and glamorous. Kjartan ran his hand down her back. "Well, Red," he told her, "I think the only sensible thing to do now is to order pizza, what do you think?"

She stretched. "Seeing as the cat ate my dinner, yes."

Kjartan got up to order, and she huddled under the comforter, shame setting in at her loudness, her nakedness. She heard him shout to her from the phone, "What do you want on it?" Ham and pineapple, she thought. She didn't answer. A few minutes later, the doorbell rang, and she slid farther beneath the covers.

He came over, shook her a little. "You can come out of hiding now, my darling," he said, placing the delivery box on the floor. He had put his shirt back on, as well as a pair of sweatpants. He looked long and lithe, slender even in his sloppy garb. "I hope you take pineapple on your pizza."

"How did you know?" she said, sliding into a sitting position, the duvet still wrapped around her.

"I'm rather sensitive."

"What do you mean?"

Kjartan's brow furrowed. "It might be . . . It means . . . Well, perhaps the best word in English would be *psychic*."

She snorted. "Shut up."

"No, I'm very serious." His voice and gaze were both grave. "I am."

"Okay," Isobel said. She watched as he lit the bedside candles. Her eyes had already begun to adjust to the shadings of life with the blinds down. The pizza was burnt, but she ate three pieces anyway.

Kjartan popped open a can of Egils Gull and took a long gulp, head tipped back, the muscles in his throat tight. He handed the beer to her, and she drank a small, polite sip, then grimaced.

"There's a face for a photograph, Isobel *mín*," he said. "You've got rather more refined tastes, I think."

She returned the can to him. "I'm tired of myself," she said, suddenly. "I want to hear about you."

"No, you don't," he said, resting his head in her lap.

She ran her hand through his hair. "Give me the abridged version, then."

"Persistent girl." He grinned. "I've lived here all my life. I came from an upper-class family. My father was a shit. I studied at Menntaskólinn í Reykjavík, the best gymnasium in the city. I went on to university, for philosophy, got good marks for a while, and then . . ."

"What happened?" Isobel said.

"The alcohol, you know, it . . ." He paused. "Let me just say that I possess nowhere near the clarity of mind or strength of character that you do."

"I'm not that strong," she said. "Focused, yes, but that's all."

"How long till you become Dr. Isobel?"

She laughed. "I haven't the faintest idea."

Kjartan looked into her face. His eyes pleaded with false melancholy and real persuasion. In the light, his hair glinted copper.

"Stay here tonight," he said.

❧

The rest of that evening was a kaleidoscope of burnished colors and surging emotion. She put on her clothes. He put on a CD of Cuban jazz. They danced barefoot in a slow, sinewy circle around the coffee table, and he dipped her back with a deep flourish at the song's end. She struggled to gaze up at him, his features framed by spikes of blurry candlelight. She felt drugged. "Don't worry, baby," he said. "I won't let you go."

Drop me, she thought. Let me keep falling, falling, falling into this black hole, into this new mad self, these new wild bones.

Instead Kjartan pulled her to her feet, said, "That's enough for now," and settled on the couch to watch the latest football scores. She joined him, feigning interest in whether Keflavík had won, her legs draped over his lap. On the replay, his team scored a goal. "*Já*," he yelled, and pumped his arm in the air. "That's the best thing that's happened all day. Except for you visiting, of course." He gave her a quick peck on the cheek, then lit a celebratory cigarette.

Her head ached from all the smoke in the room. "I think I need some fresh air," she said.

"You can go out there," Kjartan said, gesturing toward the back door. "It's not much, though, I'm warning you."

She went through his kitchen and onto a small concrete patio. Gulping for breath, she looked up at the setting sun, then back at the row of trash cans, painted with the city seal of Reykjavík, before her. She had lost all sense of time.

"Isobel, my darling!" she heard him call. Dutifully, she rejoined him, and he kissed her over and over. "I've missed you."

She laughed. "I've only been gone a minute."

"I know, but I did." Kjartan yawned. "Perhaps we should go to bed."

He turned off the television, shed his clothes as quickly as he had dashed into them, and got under the duvet. *"Komdu hérna,"* he said.

She pushed herself off the couch with her hands and blew out each of the candles. She wanted true darkness, none of these thrown shadows. She went over to him, and stood beside the bed, hesitant. She could still see the outlines of his face, fragmented by the cracks of light that cut through the blinds in pointy stripes.

"I like the way you move," he said.

A sharp shard of insight twisted inside her, hard, between her ribs, near her heart. He hasn't thought twice about how I move or how I feel, she thought. He knows only how I want to be made to feel.

She worked open the buttons on her blouse. Pulled off her jeans. Held her shoulders square and taut. No moon out yet. Her body still made silver. A little shining fish, mouth open, diving toward him.

This isn't noble, she told herself. But it's enough.

༜

And so her life began to revolve around him. The following Thursday, she went for dinner at the restaurant where Kjartan waited tables every other evening. A woman in silver platform shoes led her to her seat, and in a few moments he came over with a menu. "My favorite customer," he said, and kissed her behind the ear when none of the other servers could see. "You want a good white wine, something to start with?"

She smiled and shook her head.

He pointed out an entrée on the list of specials. "Get this," he said, mischievous, and pointed to an expensive lamb dish in cream sauce.

"But I can't afford—"

"Don't worry," he whispered. "I work here."

Isobel watched as he brought out platters and drinks. Wearing a white dress shirt, hair slicked back, Kjartan moved with grace and assurance, laughing with the other diners, shouting orders to his fellow waiters.

He brought the plate of lamb and sat across the table from her.

"Aren't you supposed to be working?" Isobel said between rich, tender mouthfuls.

"I got off early," he said. "How is your meal? I chose well, didn't I?"

"It's fabulous," she said.

"The lambs here," he said, "they just frolic about on the mountains, grazing on herbs, so they taste much better."

This idyll, Isobel thought, must be tinged with violence.

Despite his urgings to try the chocolate cake, she skipped dessert. The restaurant was near where Einar and Magga lived, so Kjartan offered to walk her home. He didn't touch her while they were on the street, but still Isobel felt buoyant, spinning. The overcast sky sent forth a surprise drizzle as she led him up the front steps and inside.

"Vivaldi weather," he said.

"Excuse me?" Isobel checked the mail that lay in a pile by the door, to see if there was any for the family. She found only a manila envelope festooned with airmail stamps. She tucked it under her arm, without reading the return address, as they reached the second floor.

"Four seasons in one day."

"Cute." She jammed her key in the lock, twisted it to the right, back, and to the right again, all to no avail. "I'm an idiot. Could you get this for me?"

With one deft turn, Kjartan had the door open. "You're not an idiot," he said. "Just not a Viking."

"Very funny." Isobel tossed the package on the table. In the hall, the answering machine beeped. She figured it was Ragna inviting her to lunch and ignored it.

"Nice place," he said. "Mind if I move in?"

Rain accosted the windows. Isobel reached for the pressed folds of his shirt, gripped them in her hands. Kjartan opened the top button on her blouse. An urgent, metallic screech invaded her ears every thirty seconds. He was kissing her fingers now, walking her backward toward the bedroom, whispering in hushed Icelandic.

Isobel thought: I will do anything you tell me.

❦

They fell asleep in Einar and Magga's bed. In the middle of the night, Isobel slid from beneath murky dreams to find the girl standing in front of her. She slouched with her fists balled in the pockets of her cargo pants, hair tangled, eyes narrowed. *You thought you could get rid of me*, the girl said, *but I'm not going away*.

Isobel screamed. Kjartan jolted awake, saw her frightened face.

"Poor darling," he said. "Isobel *mín*. Tell me what it is."

She glanced in the direction of the door, skittish.

"You're seeing things? Been studying too hard? Let me bring you a glass of water, baby." His hasty attempts at sympathy irritated her, and yet she warmed to them, snuggling into the crook of his arm, letting him lift a cup to her lips while he soothed. "There now. Better? It's pure water, from far in the earth."

"You'd make an excellent member of the tourist board," Isobel said, voice light but peevish.

"I'm not quite archetypal enough," he said. "Let's get back to sleep, shall we?"

She lay with her back to him, listening to the rain and the answering machine and Kjartan's easy sighs, waiting for the girl to leave.

❦

In the morning, they got up and had twisted doughnut-like concoctions called *kleinur,* with coffee, as if nothing had happened. "Hold on, let me listen to that damn message," Isobel said.

She went into the hall and played the tape. Over static, Colette Eberly's voice rang out, clear yet tentative. "I hope I have the right number," she said. "I couldn't understand the recording at all, but Isobel, if you're there, I wanted to let you know that you have a goddaughter. I went into labor three days ago, they tried to stop it, but I guess Laura Isobel wanted to arrive a month early. I'm home now, so give me a call when you can. Love ya. Bye."

"Anything important?" Kjartan said, mouth full, when Isobel returned.

"My best friend just had a baby," she said.

He looked away. "I have a daughter and a son," he said. "They live with their mother, up north in Akureyri."

This was news. Isobel leaned forward. "Do you see them often?"

"When I can," he said. "I'm flying there this weekend."

Part of her scoffed, *As well you should,* but another part crumpled, cried, *Stay with me!*

"Don't look so sad," Kjartan said. "I'll be back."

❦

When they finished their breakfast, he stood, gave her a quick kiss, promised to phone on Monday, and left. Isobel sat for a long time with her face in her hands. She breathed in deep, hoping for the fragmented pieces inside her to coalesce, snap back together, validate what she was doing. Do you really want to live like this? she asked herself.

No, she thought, but I want to be wanted.

Then she waited until it was late enough in the States to dial Colette. Colette answered on the third ring, her voice thin and tired.

"Greetings from Reykjavík, home of the weirdest shoes in the western hemisphere," Isobel said.

"Isobel!" she shrieked. "I didn't think you'd call."

"You asked me to, so I did."

"Brian, it's Isobel!" she yelled to her fiancé. "We were just getting ready to go visit Laura."

"How is she?"

"Oh, she's gorgeous. But *tiny*—only four and a half pounds."

"And she's healthy?"

"She has to stay in the hospital a week or two, but she'll be fine."

"How do you feel?"

"Wrung out. Worried."

"You didn't tell me her middle name was going to be mine!"

"I didn't know she would be a girl until I had her, silly. Plus I thought it would be a nice surprise."

Isobel wiped her eyes. "Well, it was. Thank you."

"How's your trip going? You getting some good downtime?"

"Sort of," she said. "I'm having the most bizarre romance. Or antiromance, I should say."

"Good Lord, Isobel," Colette said. "I'm not sure I want to know, but be careful."

"I will."

"Hey, Brian's motioning at me," she said, "and I'm sure this is costing you a fortune. But thanks for calling."

"No problem," Isobel said. "Big love to my little shrimp namesake, okay?"

The last sound she heard before they hung up was Colette's exhausted laughter.

༯

With Kjartan gone, time passed with grave, dispassionate slow-ness. On her daily walks, her body felt heavy and listless. One af-ternoon, she rode the bus for the sheer novelty of motion. Tickled by the air from the open window, she told herself she was doing fine, let the lie caress her as she listened to the kids in the back sing American rap songs. She knew she was fooling herself by the time the bus returned to the terminal at Lækjartorg.

On Saturday, she phoned Kristín. Isobel didn't want to neglect her, and she was bored and restless without Kjartan.

When Kristín answered, Isobel could barely hear her over the din of the television and a vacuum cleaner. "Oh, Isobel," she said. "We were wondering where you'd been."

In the background, Ásta's voice rang out with a question. Her mother answered in Icelandic, mentioning Isobel's name. She heard Ásta shout. "She wants to go feed the ducks by the pond," Kristín said, "and she wants you to come with us."

"How can I refuse?" Isobel said.

"I need to clean up around here, but when I'm done, would it be all right if we came over?"

"Perfect."

They arrived within the hour, and Ásta, wearing an orange child's knapsack, ran over and hugged Isobel. Isobel smiled and touched the top of Ásta's head; it felt like a whisper. Her heart stammered.

"Shall we go?" Kristín said.

They walked through the old city center to Tjörnin, its small lake. Ásta swung between Isobel and Kristín, gripping their hands. The sky was so blue it hurt to look. A warm breeze lifted their hair off the backs of their necks. They passed a trio of young women not much older than they were, in sleeveless dresses, pushing prams.

"All right, *elskan*," Kristín said, stopping. "Have you got the bread?"

Ásta yanked at the straps on her pack, unable to push them from her thin shoulders.

"Here," Isobel said. "I'll get it." She unzipped the front pocket and produced a plastic bag with a few whole-wheat pieces inside.

"Thank you," Ásta said shyly, and ran to the water's edge. Kristín smiled and shook her head, and motioned Isobel over to a bench, where they sat and watched her daughter tear off hunks of bread with stubby fingers and fling them at unsuspecting ducks.

"She's adorable," Isobel said.

"She tries my patience," Kristín said.

Isobel laughed. "I can imagine." She thought of Colette, and of Laura in a few years.

"I have a friend," Isobel said, "who's just had a daughter, and she's very young."

"How old is she?" Kristín asked.

"Twenty-four."

"That's not so young," she said. "Not for here. I had Ásta when I was seventeen."

"And that's . . . not a problem?"

"A problem?" Kristín said. "How do you mean?"

"Well, Colette, my friend, has to get married, and her boyfriend—er, fiancé—is a really sweet guy, I know he'll be good to her, but he's young, too, and she was never sure, I mean, how can you be sure at—"

"She *has* to get married?"

"She doesn't have to, of course not, but she feels like she needs to. That's partly just Colette, but it's hard being a single mother where I'm from. Not that it isn't hard anywhere else, but . . . You get blamed a lot. You don't get supported."

"Here," Kristín said, "it's not like that. My mother and my family help out. I get a grant from the state."

"Ásta's father," Isobel said. "Is he still around?"

Kristín cleared her throat, as if to rid herself of what she really wanted to say. "He does what he can," she said firmly. "He does what he can."

Grinning, Ásta turned and waved to her mother. "Look!" she cried, pointing as a duck paddled toward one of the morsels she'd thrown. Kristín waved back.

"So you're worried about your friend," she said. "Is she not happy?"

"I don't know," Isobel said. "She says she is, and I want to believe her, but . . . I still wonder. She's dropped out of college, and she plans to go back later, but—what if she can't? What if it's too hard for her?"

"I put off my education when Ásta was born," Kristín said, "but this fall I'm going to technical school."

"Do you feel like you wasted those five years?"

"Not at all," she said. "You make choices, and you live with them."

"Isn't it difficult?"

Isobel waited for the response. If she closed her eyes just a little, the lake and the sky fused into one shocking blue.

Kristín sighed. "It isn't easy," she said. "But it's my life."

Chapter Six

New York City

"I'm so glad you could do this," Isobel said to Elika. They sat on the subway, two weeks after her rough night with Gavin, en route to the junior high for a mentoring session.

"It doesn't happen for just anyone," Elika said. She had dressed up for the occasion, in a long red paisley skirt and a silk tank top, with her leather jacket and a pair of genuine army boots. Hair swept on top of her head, fingernails now painted glossy black, she had attracted stares from the tourists before she got through the turnstile.

"What if these girls hate me?" she said now, grabbing Isobel's arm. "What if they laugh me out of the classroom?"

"Trust me. They don't bite. I told them about you, and they're really excited."

Elika relaxed a little. "I'm flattered, but it's still scary. Their age is such a fraught, catty, self-deprecating time. Not one I want to revisit."

"I know what you mean. Every time I walk in and look at them, the old insecurity sucks me in again. And it's hard, because I have to be the authority figure, come down from my safe, self-absorbed ivory tower, when I'm shaking inside."

"Do you ever resent them?"

Isobel stared down at her hands. "Yes," she said softly, so the other mentors chatting beside her couldn't hear. "I do."

"Why? Because you've given them so much of your energy?"

"Sometimes. But it's more like . . . 'Christ, why do you have to make me remember? Why do you have to make me feel that all over again?'"

"Which isn't their fault. It's your own reasonable, stressed-out reaction."

"My own reasonable, stressed-out reaction it may be, but still I can't deal with my own shit."

Elika laughed.

"No, really," Isobel said. "There are days when I feel completely unqualified for this position, the last person in the world who should be counseling adolescent girls."

"Isobel, let it go. People are allowed to have rough days. Even you."

As they rattled closer to their stop, Isobel rested her head on Elika's shoulder for a moment. Elika patted her hair.

"How much longer," Isobel said, "do you think we can keep propping each other up like this before we fall?"

❧

By the time Isobel and her group arrived at the classroom, the girls were already there, lounging on tables and chatting loudly. Kathleen waved to Isobel and Elika as they came in.

"Sorry—sorry we're late," Isobel said.

"That's all right," Kathleen said. "We're glad you brought a speaker at last."

"So am I," Isobel said. "Here she is, Elika Muraski."

"Elika?" Kathleen repeated. "What a distinctive name."

"Thanks," Elika said, extending her hand. "And you are?"

"Kathleen Sullivan, guidance counselor," she said, appraising Elika's black fingernails as she shook her hand warily. "Shall we begin?"

Isobel nodded, and Kathleen called out sternly to her students, "Could I have your attention, please?"

The girls continued to talk. Kathleen clapped her hands and shouted, "Excuse me!"

They all scrambled off the desks into their chairs and grew quiet.

"That's much better," Kathleen said. "Now, Ms. Sivulka has brought a very special guest today, so I'd appreciate it if you would give them both your full attention. Thank you."

Isobel winced. She had repeatedly asked the girls to call her by her first name, but Kathleen always referred to her more formally when speaking to them, no matter how many times Isobel requested otherwise. Formality aside, it conveyed a professionalism, an expertise, she didn't feel she possessed.

"They're all yours, Isobel," Kathleen said with a resigned smile, and touched Isobel's arm as she left. "I'll be back in forty-five minutes. Nice meeting you, Elika—am I pronouncing that right?"

"Perfect," Elika said, and rolled her eyes slightly at Isobel once Kathleen had left.

Isobel grabbed Elika's hand, more to support herself than to guide her friend, and led her to the front of the room.

"Okay," she said to the girls softly, almost too softly, "why don't we begin with our check-in? Let's put all the chairs in a circle, at least as much as we can."

The girls scraped their squeaky chairs into a ragged semicircle along with Isobel and Elika. At the beginning of every session, Isobel liked to have each girl share a meaningful event that had happened since they last met. She gestured to a tall Latina girl who was chewing a piece of gum with gusto. "Marina, why don't you start?"

"I got a B on my midterm," she said proudly, "so my curfew is twelve now instead of eleven."

Isobel swallowed, trying to imagine herself in the eighth grade and staying out until midnight. She couldn't.

"Hey," another girl said, "let's hurry so we can get to her." She pointed to Elika.

"Okay, Tracy," Isobel said to the eager one, "what's up with you?"

Tracy shrugged and continued the litany of twenty troubled voices, some hesitant, some surly, all describing a parade of pain and exuberance, sadness and selfhood, in words that Isobel, at their age, never would have used:

"Not much going on. Nothin' ever happens."

"My weekend sucked. My mom left me to watch my little brothers, like, the whole time. And I was gonna go with my boyfriend, Danny, he's got this new car, 'cause he just turned sixteen, and we were gonna go to New Jersey, where his parents live, but no, her partying was more important. My mom, she's such a bitch."

"Shut up, girl! You want her to tell on you to Mrs. Sullivan?"

"Oh, Tanisha, for Chrissakes. She's cool, she likes us to say whatever we want, remember? Chill, and tell about your week."

"Okay. My week. Well, this one teacher, she and I, we been having some problems. She says I'm disruptive in class, always talkin' out of turn. Show some respect, she says. But how am I supposed to show it if I don't get any back, that's what I wanna know."

"For real. Who was it? Menninger? She doesn't pick on the boys about that manners stuff, does she, and they're a major pain in the ass. Hey, Moira, tell Ms. Siv—I mean Isobel—about what happened to you this week."

Sheepish, self-deprecating smile from a fair-skinned, punkish girl. "Oh, that. I got in-school suspension for telling Mr. Murray to go fuck off. Mrs. Sullivan almost didn't let me come here today, but I guess she figured I was such a nutcase I could use some help. Ha ha."

"Well, he deserved it. He's always staring down the girls' blouses in biology. He gives me the creeps."

"God. He's a teacher. He oughta know better."

"Teachers here don't know shit."

"Hey, hey, ya loudmouths. You forgot Shireen."

Everyone turned to face the far corner, where Shireen sat with her arms around her knees, eyes mournful, long, stringy blond hair uncombed. Shireen was the student Isobel had chosen to mentor one-on-one, and Isobel felt an aching tenderness for her.

"Do you have anything you'd like to share with us today?" Isobel asked her gently.

"No," Shireen whispered, as she picked a thread on her baggy blue sweatpants. "It's just been a bad week."

"Okay," Isobel said, "but be sure to let us know if you need anything, all right?"

Shireen gave a quick, bashful nod. To break the melancholy tension, Isobel stood, motioning for Elika to rise with her.

"Now, if we're all finished," Isobel said, "I'd like you to meet a very special friend of mine. Her name's Elika Muraski, and she's studying film and video production at New York University. I thought you might like to meet someone who's been through a lot but gone on to college and become successful." Isobel smiled and sat down as Elika gave a wry grimace at her accolades. "So, take it away, Elika."

"Hey, I like your boots," Marina called out before Elika could speak.

"Thanks," Elika said cheerfully, undisturbed by the interruption. "You can get them really cheap at Canal Jeans."

"So tell us about your movies," Tracy said, bouncing on her still-childish hands, which were encrusted with silver rings and friendship bracelets.

"Well," Elika said, "to understand that part of what I do, you've got to back up a little. I guess you could say I was different from the beginning—"

"I know what *that's* like," Moira said, rolling her eyes.

Elika grinned. "I was a Navy brat," she continued. "I was born in the Philippines, and we moved around a lot. I think I saw ten countries by the time I was ten—I've lost count by now. Living abroad taught me a lot of good things—how to respect being different, and how cool it is to be an individual. Then we came to the U.S. when I was about your age, 'cause my dad had retired, and he wanted to move back to the Midwest, where he'd grown up. I was used to studying at embassy schools, with kids from all kinds of cultures, and suddenly I was plopped down into regular old junior high, where there's so much pressure to dress right and talk right and like the right things, yeah?"

Marina nodded vigorously.

"Needless to say," Elika went on, "it was the pits. I was into grunge before it was trendy"—Moira gave her a thumbs-up—"and perceived myself as an artist with a capital *A*, plus I was just off the plane from Prague and had this wacky pretentious accent that was a mix of all the foreign voices I'd ever heard. I didn't stand a chance.

"I was teased like you wouldn't believe. I was too smart and focused for the real hell-raiser kids, and too weird and mouthy for the preppies. Teachers thought I was a show-off, and I got so tired of their judging me that I said to myself, *What the hell? They want a loud, obnoxious artsy-fartsy girl, I'll give them one.* I bragged about watching 'brilliant' French films I'd never seen, and insulted everybody in earshot for not being worldly and cultured enough—including the principal. I had a few in-school suspensions of my own.

"My final year there, though, my parents sat me down and said, 'Look, Elika, we know you're having trouble adjusting, and we want to help you, but you're screwing up your own future if you keep this up. We know you're too intelligent and too unique to do that to yourself.' I told them I wanted to apply for a scholarship to a super-elite arts academy in Michigan for high school. They made me a deal: If I got the award, and I had no more bad behavior reports the rest of the year, I could go.

"Well, those nine months of school were miserable. I kept totally to myself, didn't say a word in class—everyone thought I had had a personality transplant over the summer—and at night I'd go home and paint and listen to gloomy music and think, poor, pitiful, misunderstood me. But you know what? I survived with a perfect conduct record and got the scholarship to the academy.

"Interlochen was great. Finally, I was with kids who were as crazy and dedicated as I was, and with teachers who respected us and believed we were talented. But there we had expectations of each other, too—it was like a contest to see who could be the most freaky, as well as strong in the arts. I liked to think I was good at both.

"My senior year, I met this guy named Lake. Yep, that was his name, no kidding. He had this English accent that I loved—I'm sure now it was an act, but back then it made him sound so adorable—and he wore a long black trench coat and drove a beat-up old Audi. He smoked clove cigarettes, and had a black light in his room, and listened to shortwave radio to keep up with the latest techno remixes coming out of London—oh, my God, Lake was *all* that." The girls giggled. "We hooked up around Christmas and thought we were the slickest couple on campus.

"Two days before our graduation, Lake and I did a really crazy thing. We packed our clothes and CDs and art supplies in the Audi's itty-bitty trunk and left our little school town. Didn't tell anyone, not even our parents, who were driving to Michigan to watch us graduate even as we left. Oh, we got our diplomas and all, but . . . My mom still gets tears in her eyes, remembering how she sat there while the class filed across the stage, wondering whether I was alive and okay. She doesn't like to talk about it much.

"Meanwhile, Lake and I drove cross-country. We got engaged in Wisconsin. He gave me one of the plastic rings little kids get out of the machines at the grocery store, said he would buy one of those groovy claddagh rings, the silver Celtic ones, later. We thought it was so tacky and great. We didn't know anything about marriage; we just liked the idea and the sound of it. 'Perhaps you'd better call your mum,' he said, in the snooty accent. 'Perhaps I shall,' I said, imitating him. I got out of the car and went to the pay phone outside the supermarket. I was floating, I felt so happy.

"My mom screamed when I called her, wanted to know where I was and when I was coming home. I kept telling her, 'Ma, I've got to do my own thing, you've gotta accept that,' and she just kept pleading for me to stop. I finally hung up on her. There I was in the pouring rain somewhere south of Madison, in my shiny silver raincoat with my big old plastic bubble ring, thinking I was the shit, totally invincible.

"Our trip was fun, but looking back, I'm shocked at how I made it through. We did a lot of stuff that wasn't safe. We slept in the car, or sometimes on people's lawns late at night, if the weather was nice. We smoked and drank constantly. I gained a little weight, 'cause of all the alcohol and living on fast-food crap, and one day I got back into the car after throwing away our McDonald's trash, and Lake said, 'My goodness, Elika, two weeks on the road have not been kind to your figure.' He liked his girls to be walking Euro-pencils, skinny waify heroin chicks, tailored, with the black eyeliner and stark faces and blunt-cut hair. He was a big stupid poser, but I really loved him, and I thought: Damn it, I've got to do something."

Isobel saw Shireen wince and turn her head to gaze listlessly out the window.

"So," Elika said, "I went on a mission. For the rest of the trip, I lived on cigarettes and coffee and diet pills. By the time we got to Arizona, I had lost twenty pounds. Lake thought I looked gorgeous but, girlfriends, I was sick as a dog! I got out at the gas station in Tucson to fill up the car, and the smell coupled with the horrible dry heat made me pass out. One minute I'm checking the gas pump, the next I'm all woozy and staring at the dirty ceiling tile in the emergency room, with a needle in my arm pumping fluids into me. They had to call my parents because I was still under eighteen.

"My mom flew out the next day. I remember her standing in the hospital hallway, like an Amazon, and the firmness in her voice. 'Elika,' she said, 'I have had enough.' As soon as the doctors let me out, she got me on the first plane home.

"The next few years were hell. I lived with my parents because I was too depressed to get a job. I had a diploma from a fancy high school, but nothing else to show for myself. I'd get alumni newsletters from Interlochen, full of articles about so-and-so on Broadway, my former roommate dancing in a professional ballet company, Lake's old girlfriend getting her first gallery showing— man, that one tore me up. I felt like such a loser, sitting like a big lump on the couch, watching game shows all day.

"What turned me around was my little sister, Noura. She was just going into junior high school then, and having a hard time— things were pretty tense at home, 'cause my mom and I fought nonstop. I saw Noura getting a tough attitude, you know, like, 'Why do I have to do any work, look at Elika, she doesn't do crap.' That scared me, because I didn't want to do that to her. Me messing up was one thing, but my baby sister, that was another story. So I resolved to get my act together, if only for her.

"Let me tell you, it took a while. Things went real slow. I got a job waitressing in the evenings and eventually made enough to move out into a little place—I mean, *really* little, the tiniest, grungiest studio you can imagine, but at least it was mine, rented with my own paycheck. When I started feeling better, more sure of myself, I got a side job teaching art to kids. Doing that reminded me of my old focus, of what I had wanted to do all along. I decided to dig out my old portfolio and apply to NYU for film and video production. I never thought I'd get accepted, but I did."

Isobel watched her friend stand tall and strangely elegant in her own Gothic way, face open and alive, hands gesturing warmly to the girls who sat slumped in their chairs, bodies relaxed but gazes intent. She's terrific, Isobel thought, but why can't I reach them like she can?

"Elika," she said, checking her watch, "we've only got a few more minutes, so I'm wondering if you've got any closing advice for the girls?"

"Well," Elika said, rocking back and forth on her high heels, "I don't want to sound like one of those boring 'motivational' assemblies where they drone at you, 'Believe in yourself and anything is possible,' blah blah blah." Moira snorted. "But I guess what I'd say is this: I know your teachers and your families are probably giving you a hard time about having a better outlook and obeying authority and all that good stuff. And I'm sure you're probably thinking, Yeah right, you don't know what it's like to be me, or how unfair things are. But please, do yourselves a favor and pick your battles, okay? 'Cause there's a fine line between fighting for what's right and fighting against what could help make things go right for you, ya know?" She smiled. "Oh, yeah . . . this is gonna sound totally whack, but trust me, your parents are not always your worst enemies. Take it from someone who was convinced they were. So be good to yourselves, and hang in there, alrighty?"

Elika sat down, and the girls burst into what Isobel sensed to be genuine applause. "Okay," Isobel said, "we've got a couple seconds before Mrs. Sullivan comes back, so why don't we quickly break into our mentor groups."

Their spell broken, the girls returned to their grumbling selves and paired up with their college-age partners. While they chatted, Isobel hugged Elika.

"You, my friend," she said, "can take over my job anytime."

"Thanks," Elika said, voice scratchy, "but first I think I'll go search for some water. Even my famous big mouth isn't used to all this action."

"There's a fountain down the hall to your left," Isobel said. "I've got to find Shireen."

Isobel discovered her far away from the other, more boisterous girls, seated on top of the heater with her cheek against the cold windowpane. "Hey, Shireen," she said. "Mind if I join you?"

Shireen shrugged, gave a meek gesture of affirmation. Isobel sat beside her.

"Did you like the speaker?" Isobel said.

"She was good," Shireen said, her voice lackluster.

Isobel stared at her hands in her lap, not wanting to push but longing to unearth what was troubling her young charge. "Listen, Shireen," she began quietly, "I don't mean to pester you, but I couldn't help noticing you seemed really down at check-in. Are you sure there isn't anything I can do for you?"

Shireen turned to face Isobel, turbid but unblinking. "You wouldn't be able to help," she said.

Isobel got the sense she was being tested. "We won't know until you try me," she said.

With a sigh that sounded as if it should erupt from the throat of a middle-aged woman, Shireen tipped her head back against the windowsill. "It's the boys," she said.

"Which boys?" Isobel asked. "The ones in your class?"

"No," Shireen said, exasperated, as if Isobel should know better. "In the hallways."

Isobel swallowed. She knew intuitively what was coming, but she still had to play along and query. "What are they doing that bothers you, sweetie?"

Shireen closed her eyes. Her pale hair spilled over her tight face. "Saying things. And laughing."

"What kinds of things?"

"About . . . about how I'm a whale. How they want to harpoon me."

Isobel felt her teeth clench. "Shireen," she said, "would you look at me, please?"

Shireen's eyes flickered open again.

"They have no right to treat you that way," Isobel said. "That's harassment. We had a program on that a few weeks ago, remember?"

Instantly she regretted her tone of voice. She sounded, she realized, like a teacher trying to sound perky while secretly admonishing. No wonder I can't reach these girls, she thought.

"Yeah, but they don't try to feel me up or anything," Shireen said dully. "And besides, they're right, because I'm . . . you know . . ." She lowered her voice to a whisper. "Fat."

"Listen to me," Isobel said. "It has nothing to do with what you look like, or whether or not the boys touch you. If they treat you on purpose in ways that make you feel uncomfortable, it's wrong."

"I guess." Shireen toyed with one of her shoelaces. "But there are teachers right there in the hall when they do it, and they never stop them."

"Have you ever told a teacher about it?"

Shireen nodded.

"And they didn't do anything?"

She shook her head. "There are so many kids," she said. "They can't keep track of us all. As long as no one's beating anyone up, the teachers stay out of it."

Isobel ran a hand through her hair. "Would it be okay," she said, "if I talked to Mrs. Sullivan to see what she could do?"

"If you want to," Shireen said. "But don't make a big deal about it, please? 'Cause if the guys find out, that'll just make it worse. I'm scared to walk to class as it is. Sometimes I take the long way around, and I get late slips. A lot of them."

"Maybe we can get those waived," Isobel said. "I'll let you know as soon as I can."

Shireen gave a short jerk of her chin to show that she'd understood. She crossed her arms over her chest, as if to hold herself together, and drummed her heels on the heater. "See you next week," she said as if by rusty reflex.

Isobel saw Kathleen reenter the room. She loomed, a prim yet lanky figure in a sensible khaki skirt and wire-rimmed glasses. Isobel stood and strode over to her. "I need to make an appointment with you this week," Isobel said.

⌒

"You were wonderful," Isobel said later that night, while she and Elika ate linguine with pesto, seated on velvet couches in a favorite restaurant off Prince Street.

"Stop," Elika said. "I was not."

"You were. Didn't you see how they clamored around you at the end?"

"Asking when my movie was coming out, which is probably never, yeah. I did think that was cute."

"You're a natural speaker. And I really liked how you mentioned the rough spots. I think that was good for them to hear, that they don't have to take the traditional overachiever path, like me, to find success."

Elika twirled her pasta around her fork. "You think I made an impression?"

"When do you not? Elika, *yes*. The girls asked if you could come back again, and even the guidance counselor said she was glad you spoke."

"There's a relief. At first she seemed rather taken aback."

"Maybe it was your outfit."

"It's always my outfit." Elika's features softened in the glow of the candle at their table. "That's good to hear. Because I did this as a favor, but I wanted to encourage them, too."

"Your strength never ceases to amaze me."

"Isobel," she said slowly, "what you see as my strength comes after years and years of uncertainty and impulsive decisions. It's not a quality you suddenly get hooked around your wrist like a bracelet."

"I know. But I can't help being both admiring and jealous."

"All in good time. How about a drink?"

"Great idea. Something fruity." Isobel gestured toward their waiter as he walked by, but he ignored her. Elika did the same on his next round, and he came over immediately.

"I'm afraid I need a little more kick than fruit," she said. "A vodka and tonic."

"And a Midori sour," Isobel said as he wrote down Elika's order.

Later, as she sipped her drink, Isobel said, "I think I will take part in your documentary, if you'll still have me."

"If I'll still have you? Of course."

"You've done so much for me, it's the least I can do."

"Isobel. Thank you. And there's no rush. I don't plan to finish until the summer."

"I can start whenever you want. I figure it'll take my mind off my own work."

The waiter deposited their check by the candle, and Elika got out her kilim wallet.

"No," Isobel said. "I'll get it."

"You don't have to do that."

"I want to. Think of it as a commission for all your fashion help."

"Thanks." Elika took a final swallow of her drink and stood. "Three cheers for hedonism. Let's take a cab."

༥

When Isobel returned home, she found a message on the answering machine from Colette back in Staplin. Elika left her alone to return the call, and Isobel curled on the futon with her knees tucked under her, waiting to hear the voice of her childhood best friend.

"Hey, woman of mystery," she said when Colette answered. "I haven't heard from you in ages."

"Well," Colette said, "I've got some great news."

"Really?" Isobel said, thinking perhaps she'd aced a midterm. "Do tell."

"I'm pregnant," Colette said.

Isobel pulled the ivory afghan down from the back of the futon and wrapped it around herself, as if chilled by the words. "What did you say?"

"I said I'm pregnant."

"This wasn't a planned thing, was it?"

"Not . . . not really."

"What will you do? You aren't going to have the baby, are you?"

"Yes. I'm due in August."

"And what about Brian?"

"I'll marry him."

"Do you want to?"

"We've talked about that for a long time. It'll just be a little sooner than expected."

"You don't have to do any of this."

"I know."

"You like the idea of marriage and motherhood at twenty-four?"

"It wasn't my first choice, but I've decided to be happy with it."

"And what year are we living in?"

"I've always wanted children. I've always wanted to get married. Yes, it's happening fast, but—"

"What about school?"

"I've only got two more years to go for the dual master's degree. I can go back."

"You said you wanted to get a doctorate. You said you weren't going to stop for anybody. The two of us against the world, remember?"

"Academics is not my entire universe, Isobel."

Colette's voice sounded gentle and patient as ever, but tinny and crackling, as if gleaned off a radio-station broadcast from a faraway land. Isobel heard a couple yelling in the apartment below, either in tense argument or gleeful joy, she couldn't tell which. A bird chirped on the other end of the line, its simple, pastoral call almost shocking in its clarity. In that moment of dissonance, Isobel felt utterly alone.

"But you've got other options," she said lamely.

"I love you to death," Colette said, "but you have to understand that we aren't in the same symbiosis anymore. I have different priorities."

Isobel sighed.

"Look, I'm not joining the cult of domesticity," Colette said. "And I need to know that you'll support me."

Isobel thought of her in a tiny, cramped apartment in Staplin, walking the floor at midnight in a pink terry-cloth robe, a screaming baby on her shoulder, cloaked in the scent of spit and panic.

Either I jump off the cliff with you or I lose you, she thought.

"Absolutely," she said.

๙

After she got off the phone with Colette, Isobel called Gavin and asked him to come over. She craved touch, free of obligation, nothing more. Pleasantly surprised, he reminded her that he and some friends from the office had tickets to a concert that began at eight, but promised he'd stop by briefly on his way there.

When he arrived, she bounded up to meet him at the door.

"Hey, hon," he said casually, still in his work clothes. She wrapped her arms around him and kissed him hard on the mouth. "You went for pasta at that place in SoHo again, I take it."

"You're disgusting."

"I try."

"You succeed brilliantly."

He grinned. "What did they put in that pesto tonight, anyway?" he said. "I've never seen you quite like this."

"Who knows?" she said, shrugging. "Maybe basil is some secret cure for sexually repressed girls who study too much."

"I love you," he said.

She glanced around the gold warmth of her dirty kitchen. This is what I want, she thought. To be loved without needing to be.

"I love you, too," she said, "but don't get any crazy ideas, all right?"

᷇

Kathleen was able to see Isobel after school that Friday afternoon, as long as they kept it short. Isobel arrived five minutes late
and stood, shaky and disjointed, in the doorway of Kathleen's office, which was no bigger than a closet.

Kathleen glanced up from a stack of manila folders, glasses
perched on the edge of her nose. "What can I do for you?" she said.

"Um," Isobel said, "it's about Shireen, and—"

"Please," Kathleen said, "sit down, so we can talk about this
properly."

She gestured toward a folding chair pushed up against the wall,
and Isobel sat meekly.

"Shireen Davis," Kathleen said. "She's quite a puzzle. Nice girl,
very quiet, no discipline problems. Her grades have always been
mediocre, but lately they've slipped further, and she's received a
lot of demerits for tardiness."

"Yes, well, I think I've found something of an explanation,"
Isobel said. "During this week's mentoring session, Shireen revealed to me that a lot of boys have harassed her in the hallways . . . saying explicit and cruel things to her, especially about
her weight. She told me it would be okay if I spoke with you about
it, as long as you didn't make it a 'big deal'—those were her words."

Kathleen sighed. "Unfortunately," she said, "I couldn't make a
big deal out of it even if I wanted to."

"There's got to be something you can do," Isobel said. "Shireen
said this has happened in plain view of teachers who took no action. Other girls have reported harassment in class by their in-
structors, too. Granted, that's a whole other issue, but—"

"I know it's a huge problem," Kathleen said, "but you have to
understand her complaint in the greater context of this school.
We've had to install a forty-thousand-dollar metal detector this

year, out of fear of student violence—mind you, in junior high! Do you realize what that does to an already strapped budget? Small private schools have the luxury of training workshops and awareness assemblies. We don't."

Isobel averted her eyes. "I understand you've got limitations," she said quietly, "but you may want to take a look at how they're affecting your students. Many of the girls seem cynical and resigned because they feel like the school system doesn't listen to them."

"Of course they're going to feel that way," Kathleen said, frustration tinged with irritation creeping into her voice. "That's the studied pose of adolescence."

"I don't agree," Isobel said, so quickly and forcefully she surprised herself. "In fact, I think they've got a point."

Kathleen rested her chin on her hand. "Look, Isobel," she said, "I don't want to give the impression that I don't take you seriously, or that I don't care. I cannot thank you enough for bringing your project here, because honestly, without you those young women would have fallen through the cracks. You're young and enthusiastic, and that's great. That's where we all start out, but when you've been here for twenty years like me, you start thinking in terms of priorities and realities."

"I'm not saying you shouldn't," Isobel said, "but Shireen, and the other girls who say they've been harassed, need support from an authority figure, someone in the administration who's here all the time. I had a teacher as a mentor in high school, and she literally changed my life."

Kathleen set her glasses on top of her desk with an exasperated clink. "And where did you go to school?" she asked.

"A small junior high in rural Pennsylvania."

"I rest my case."

"Kathleen," Isobel said, "I don't want to ask you to do anything for these girls that you aren't prepared to do. However, I did tell

Shireen I would ask for your help. Do you know why she gets so many late slips? She takes the long way around the building to avoid the boys in the hallways. Now, what can I tell her at her next mentoring session that might make her feel more secure at this school?"

The vehemence, bordering on bitterness, in her own tone made Isobel feel as if some darker, harsher woman were speaking through her in a desperate act of ventriloquism.

"Tell Shireen," Kathleen said crisply, "that I will ask her teachers to excuse her lateness and keep an eye out for any trouble. You're idealistic and full of energy—more power to you, Isobel, but remember that you can't save them all. You just can't."

❧

"She blew me off!" Isobel shouted a few hours later, in the back of a cab with Gavin, on their way out to dinner. "And even worse, she did it to Shireen!"

He put his arm around her. "It sounds like she was being honest about what she could and couldn't do, that's all."

"Nothing's going to happen," she said. "It won't change for the girls. It's the same as when I was growing up."

"Honey," he said, "you're being awfully fatalistic."

"Maybe so. I would think at the very least Kathleen would take action out of fear of liability, of some parent suing the school."

"Isobel, those parents probably don't care enough to get into a lawsuit."

"You're right," she said, and, at the thought, banged her fist against the window. He cuddled her head against his shoulder. She tensed, his tenderness grating on her.

"At least you can say you tried," he said, and brushed her hair back from her face.

"Yeah, I can put it on my fucking résumé."

Gavin drew back a little, surprised at her language. The fact that she had shocked him pleased her. Even the cabdriver turned around to give her a look of wary curiosity.

"Why don't I just tell him to take us home," Gavin said. "I mean, if you're going to be like this, we might as well—"

She sat up straight and pulled away from him. Her hands trembled. Her jaw clenched. "No," she said. "I'll go. I'll be fine."

Trust me, she thought, because I don't.

≈

That night, while Isobel slept, the girl returned to stand again in the darkened room at the foot of her bed. Her eyes were dull yet accusatory; they asked for something Isobel couldn't give. Her round face looked a bit like Shireen's. She stared directly at Isobel, glowering, and said, *See, I told you you wouldn't be able to help me.*

And then, on the following Tuesday, the next-to-last session, there was Shireen herself, slouched on her perch by the window, memorizing the dirt under her fingernails so she wouldn't have to make eye contact, painfully forlorn. Isobel sat on a chair in front of her, made small, like a supplicant asking forgiveness. "I talked with Mrs. Sullivan," she said.

"Yeah?" Not a shred of hope or eagerness resounded in Shireen's voice.

"She said she'd see that your teachers knew about the situation."

"They already know."

"That's what I told her. She says that's the best she can do."

"She's a liar." The words exploded from Shireen's lips, the most animation Isobel had ever seen from her.

Isobel sighed. "I don't agree with her, either," she said, not sure whether she had taken too much of a risk by sharing her opinion. "But I tried."

"It's okay," Shireen said, shoving her hair out of her face. "I figured you wouldn't get anywhere. It's cool that you asked, though."

"Thank you," Isobel said softly. It was the most recognition she had ever gotten from her silent, stoic mentoring partner. "She did tell me she'd make sure you didn't get any late passes from now on. That's some good news, at least."

"I guess."

"It must make you feel a little safer, huh?"

Shireen didn't respond. She leaned back against the window. "Hey, Isobel?" she said.

"Yes?"

"Do we have to keep talking?" She closed her eyes. "Everybody wants me to try to say more, but somehow it doesn't seem worth it."

Isobel placed her hand over Shireen's. "It's okay, sweetheart," she said, her voice quaking. "Just sit here and hang out for the rest of the period if you want to."

Shireen looked relieved.

Isobel stood. "I'll be right back," she called to the other groups. Then she ran out the door and into one of the stalls of the nearest restroom. She flailed out, her mouth pulled back into a silent scream as she struck at the walls.

☙

When she arrived home after the end of the session, Isobel called her mother at work.

"I don't know how much longer I can keep going like this," she said.

"But you only have another month."

"That's part of the problem. Worrying and waiting."

"There's just so much you can worry about. You handed in your dissertation, which you've put massive effort into, and the review-ers will read what you've done, and then you'll prepare yourself the best you can to explain it."

"You make it sound so easy."

"I can't tell you whether it is or it isn't, because I've never been there. But I know how hard you work, and how bright you are. I have faith in you, Isobel. What else can I say to calm your anxiety?"

"I don't know."

"Maybe you should quit doing that program with the girls if it's making you obsess more."

"Mom!" Her voice rose to a shriek. "I can't desert them like that!"

"I'm not suggesting you desert them, but you might pass the heavy organizing duties on to someone else."

"No. I couldn't."

"Just a suggestion. Hold on." Isobel heard her whisper to a colleague in her office. "I have to go. Alan wants me to type a dep-osition."

"Okay."

"I hate to see you so overwhelmed, though." Her voice bright-ened. "I wasn't going to tell you this, but maybe it'll give you something to look forward to. Nick and I thought that since you've never been abroad, we'd send you to Europe for your gradua-tion present. Nothing glamorous, but all expenses paid. How does that sound?"

"That sounds terrific. But the money—"

"Don't worry. We've got it worked out. When you get bent out of shape, just think about the prospect of a nice, relaxing trip this summer, okay?"

"I'll try. And thanks."

Isobel hung up the phone and sat there for a moment, temporarily elated. Then she remembered she had only one session left, and her mood fell. She wondered if her mother was right, if perhaps she did need to divert herself more.

She found Elika seated in front of the television, eating pistachio ice cream straight from the container. "I'm just having a little mind-numbing before I go splice some more," she said, mouth full. "Want some?"

Isobel shook her head and joined her on the couch. "I hope you're prepared to splice your roommate," Isobel said, "because I'm ready."

"To do the documentary? Fabulous." She plucked her hot pink organizer off the coffee table and flipped through its pages. "How's Saturday? I'll try to do as much as I can then, but I like to shoot people more than once—"

"Just to make sure they're dead."

"No, smart-ass, because it can get pretty exhausting, both for the directing martyr and the subject."

"Self-preoccupation usually is. Maybe I will have some of that, Elika."

"Self-preoccupation or ice cream?"

"Both."

"Grab a spoon."

❧

That weekend, Isobel watched as Elika and her production assistant lugged two huge lamps and a tripod into their apartment. Elika adjusted her camera, then surveyed the living room. "It's awfully bright in here; you're going to look washed out if we aren't careful. Maeve, let's get a light reading."

"Would you two like something to drink?" Isobel said.

"That would be wonderful," Elika said.

Isobel went into the kitchen and poured two glasses of lemonade. Her hands shook. She carried a tray back in to find the shades drawn and the lamps suffused in deep gold.

"Why don't you sit over there?" Elika said, pointing to the old bentwood rocking chair that had belonged to Isobel's mother.

Isobel sat with one knee drawn up and stared into the camera.

"Are you comfortable?" Elika asked. "You look tense."

"I'm as comfortable as I can be, given the inherent artificiality of the situation," Isobel said.

"Well, if you get tired or want to stop, just tell me."

Maeve pinned a microphone to the collar of Isobel's white blouse, then joined Elika by her tripod. "We're ready," Elika said. "Why don't you start by introducing yourself?"

Isobel took a deep breath.

"My name is Isobel Sivulka," Isobel said. "I'm twenty-five years old and a doctoral student at NYU."

"Okay," Elika said, "I'm going to start with the same question I ask everyone initially. I know it sounds incredibly simplistic, but we'll delve into specifics later. If you had to give me a short description of how you see yourself, what would it be?"

"Disconnected," Isobel said, so quickly she stunned herself. "Wandering around in my own head, afraid of my own flesh."

"That's a very lyrical, very abstract idea. Can you give me a concrete example?"

"My entire life," Isobel said.

❧

On a Tuesday in mid-April, Isobel came home from the last mentoring session of the year and sank to the floor. She rested her head in her hands and thought of her twenty girls clustered in an unused classroom, long legs coiled around the backs of chairs, wild, wavy hair obscuring their keenly alert faces, sneakered and platform-heeled feet propped on empty desks. She and the other mentors had thrown them a party, with punch and candy and badly burnt cookies. They had presented the students with coyly multicultural pins that read LISTEN TO GIRLS, handed out photo-copied lists of their home addresses in case they were needed over the summer, and wished them well. That was it. That was all that Isobel had given them before she took the subway home.

And Shireen, diffident, slouchy Shireen, had let her arms hang listlessly at her sides when Isobel had hugged her goodbye. "I'm glad to be going to high school," she'd said. "I'm sick of this place."

"I know you are," Isobel had said, knowing also that she had failed her.

Isobel got up now and called Natalie's office. The phone rang three times. *She's usually in on Tuesdays,* Isobel thought. *I wonder why it's taking so long, she's got to—*

"Natalie Hoffield." Natalie's voice was crisper than normal.

"Hi, it's Isobel Sivulka."

"Hey. What's up?"

"Are you busy?"

"Actually, I am. I've got a student with me right now, but if it's something quick, go ahead."

"Well, I had the last mentoring session today, and . . . I don't want to do this."

"Your defense? Come on. Your research is meticulous, your thesis itself is stunningly written, and you're more than articulate enough to field any tough questions you might get."

"I'm flattered that you think so, but . . . Natalie, I've chased this all my life. I need to get off automatic pilot and let myself crash, just once."

"Listen, I'm all for rejuvenation, especially given the two years you've just had, but what would happen if you bailed out this se-mester? You'd prolong your anxiety the whole summer, pay the matriculation maintenance fee next fall, and go through this all over again in order to graduate in December. Is a month of relief worth that?"

"I guess not, but I've pushed myself so hard that I've got time to work with."

"I'm sure you do, but I'd hate to see you sabotage yourself like this under stress."

"Could I come see you this afternoon? If you're free later?"

"I'm sorry. I can't. I'd work you in somehow, but my son has a cold, and the baby-sitter can only stay so long, and I have relatives coming in from Connecticut for the week, so—"

Isobel longed for the boundless empathy and patience of Ms. Johnson, her high school mentor. "You're sure?"

"Isobel, I don't mean to sound blunt, but I'm your academic adviser, not your therapist. I'm not in a position to constantly nudge you toward the insight that will make you feel calmer about this project. If you want to come see me Thursday or Friday, leave me a message tomorrow with what times are good for you, but right now I really have to get back to my student who's here. Okay?"

"Okay," Isobel said.

After she hung up, Isobel went to her desk, pulled her address book from a drawer, and found the entry for Ms. Johnson. She stood long enough to grasp the phone and knelt again to dial. The phone rang once, twice, three times, four. An answering machine picked up, with a man's affable voice informing her that she'd reached the Kearney residence, while a small child squealed in the background. She tried to remember the last name of her mentor's husband but couldn't. The machine screeched its prompt at her.

"Hi," she said, voice hoarse, "my name is Isobel Sivulka, and I—I'm not sure if I have the right number, I know it's been a long time, but I'm calling for Ms. J.—I mean, Sylvia Johnson. I'm a former student of hers, from Andrews, and, well, I'm in Manhattan now, but I'm working on this graduate study of young girls, and I would really like to—to talk about it, to get some insight, and Sylvia, I guess I just want to talk to you. Could you please call me?"

She rasped out her own number, thanked the disembodied voice of Mr. Kearney, and closed her address book. She put the phone back on its hook. She hung her blazer in the closet and filed her folder full of mentoring notes in her desk. She took off her shoes, her blouse, and her good linen slacks, and pulled on an old, washed-thin T-shirt she'd kept from the school she'd attended as an undergraduate. Then she crawled into bed.

Chapter Seven

Reykjavík

*T*he Tuesday morning after Kjartan had gone to Akureyri, Isobel was sound asleep when the phone rang. She batted out to answer it while, blurry-eyed, she checked the clock. It was four-thirty.

"Isobel *mín*, it's so good to hear you again."

His voice was slurred and husky. It made her want to worm out of her drowsiness and move in sibilant ways she never knew a body could.

"Do you want to see me?" he asked.

"Yes," she said.

"Come over, then."

"But—"

"Leave right now. Don't worry about how you look. Just put on your shoes."

She hung up, washed her face, and brushed her teeth. I can't believe I'm doing this, she thought as she wiped a daub of tooth-paste roughly from the corner of her mouth. She put on a pair of jeans, a long white cotton blouse, and a pair of turquoise slides that she'd gotten to match her dress on her day out with Kristín and Ásta. Isobel propped a book in the door and ran down the front steps, almost twisting her ankle. The sun had just risen, and the sky shimmered like saffron-colored silk. Isobel felt like singing. When she reached Kjartan's street, she saw a taxi pull up at the house next to his. A man got out, his back hunched from the strain of carrying two large suitcases. Above his head, an infant's cries poured through the open window.

Isobel knocked on the door. No answer. Then she noticed a note that read, in schoolboy scrawl: *Isobel, it's open.*

She went inside, dropped her purse on the couch, and sat on the edge of the bed. Kjartan lay there on his back, still in his clothes, passed out. Isobel leaned over him. He smelled slightly sweet, but with a sickly undertone. On her usual side of the mat-tress, there was another stain, pale and new, that looked like vomit. You would disgust me, she thought, if I didn't want to taste your mouth so much. She stroked his hair, damp with sweat.

Isobel took his hand, threaded her fingers through his, and gripped hard. Kjartan twisted, moaned, swung at her with his free arm. She grabbed his other hand.

"Don't," she said. "It's Isobel."

His eyelids scraped open. "Sorry, baby," he said. His voice sounded like he had a mouthful of gravel. "I didn't realize it was you."

She smiled. "Well, here I am," she said. She crawled onto the bed and settled on top of him. Her hair fell in a russet-colored frame around his face.

"Here you are." A creaky, hollow laugh escaped his throat. He touched a finger to her lips. "Dream girl."

She kissed his fingertip. "How much did you drink last night?"

"Not much, for me."

"Which is what? A whole bottle of vodka?" She had meant her query as a joke, but it came out brittle, almost hostile.

He opened the top button on her blouse. "Oh, my darling," he said. "You have no idea."

Kjartan's hands shook and fumbled as he tried to undress her. "No," she said. "Let me do it." She yanked off her jeans and let them fall to the floor, not caring. She pulled off his belt. He lifted his hips just enough to wrench off the necessary clothes. He put his mouth against her ear. "You've missed me, Isobel," he said. His trembling hands clenched the small of her back. While she came, she rested her head on her forearm and sank her mouth into it, as if that would silence the desirous howl that eclipsed all other sounds.

She rolled off him, and he watched her with sad, distant eyes. "What's wrong?" she asked.

Kjartan struggled to sit up. Isobel draped her arm around his back and adjusted the pillows for him. Still he slid down, head on her chest.

"Nothing, baby," he muttered. "Nothing you didn't just cure."

"I'm serious," Isobel said. "What happened?"

He began to sob, the shaking, messy tears some men cry when they're drunk. Isobel stroked the back of his neck and listened to his barely coherent tirade. The weekend had been a disaster: he and his ex-wife quarreling, the children more interested in their new stepfather than in him. Women were the crueler sex, he said— "except for you, my lovely girl, you know that . . ."

"Shh, shh," Isobel said, and rocked him until they both slept.

᙭

Around lunchtime, she convinced him to hobble over to the couch, where he sat, dead-faced, in front of the television. In his minuscule, dirty kitchen, Isobel made them coffee and vegetable soup and put extra crackers in his, as if he were Ásta's age and that would delight him. She placed the cups and bowls on a rickety tray, carried them out, and set them on the metal table before him. As Isobel bent down, Kjartan twisted his fingers through her hair.

"We take good care of each other," he said.

She sat beside him, and they watched a children's cartoon, followed by a risqué music video.

He sipped a little of his soup, then set it down. He picked his wallet off the table and pulled out a picture, handed it to her.

"That's them," he said. "My boy, Guðjón, and Ingibjörg. She looks a bit like you." He pointed to a somber girl of about seven, her dark bangs cut straight across her pale forehead. "With the long, narrow face. Don't you think?"

Isobel saw no resemblance between her and Kjartan's daughter, but to appease him, she nodded.

❧

Isobel stayed with him until that evening, when he had to go to work. They drove over to the restaurant in his small, boxy black car. "I can walk from here," she said.

Kjartan took her hand, rested it against his unshaven cheek. "Thank you," he said. "For everything."

"You'll be late if you don't go in now," Isobel told him.

❧

When she got home, Isobel took off her white blouse and sat on the bed, turning the thin chambray fabric over and over in her hands. It smelled of perspiration and smoke, and bore discolored patches from moments she didn't want to think about. She took it to the kitchen and threw it in the trash.

Letting the Body Lead

On the table, Isobel glimpsed the package that had arrived the night Kjartan had stayed at her flat. She had assumed it was for Magga or Einar, from one of their foreign friends, but it was addressed to her. She opened the parcel cautiously, careful not to rip it. Inside she found two pages of precise, curved handwriting. The monogram on the stationery read SJK. Sylvia Johnson-Kearney.

Isobel shoved the letter back in its envelope, as though it might burn her if she held it for too long. She was glad Sylvia had written, but she didn't want to read her words, not now, when she felt like a wet washcloth wrung out too many times over a hot forehead.

❧

He called her early Wednesday evening. "I'm taking you out," he said.

They went to an Italian restaurant with long white tablecloths and a map of the Mediterranean painted on one wall. Kjartan ordered them garlic bread and pasta with salmon, and each time Isobel so much as glanced at her water glass, he motioned to their waiter with a brisk *"Vatn með klaka, gertu svo vel!"* ("Water with ice, please.") As they ate, Kjartan pointed out people he knew at other tables, and did imitations of them that were so funny Isobel almost choked.

He gallantly paid the bill, and as they walked out, he hooked his arm firmly through hers. Isobel smiled up into his face, and his eyes were bright and clear again.

❧

After he brought her back to Magga's, Isobel retrieved Sylvia's letter and sat on the couch with it in her lap. Kjartan had sobered up, Isobel possessed more energy, and she felt ready to read its contents, which were dated the night she had met him:

June 28

Dear Isobel,

Where do I begin? With an apology, first of all. I've got a new job in school administration, which keeps me pulling my hair out seventy hours a week, but is no excuse for not returning your call in a timely fashion. I'm so sorry to have missed you, but your roommate (Erika?) was kind enough to give me your summer address once I explained to her who I was. She sounds like quite a character!

Your journey to Iceland brings up a patchwork of emotions for me, some of which are my own personal baggage, but many that are relevant to my concern for you. Isobel, I remember you as a thoughtful student at thirteen, sitting on the heater in my classroom, talking with me so long that I had to write you a late pass to your next class. I remember you tripping up the front steps of my apartment building in that ridiculous, charming black hat. I cannot forget you at seventeen, run-down, a little sullen, convinced nothing could stop you as you sat, drawn-faced, on my damp lawn. But I do not know the woman you have become, save for her timid, confused voice on my answering machine, so haunting I cannot delete it.

Isobel, I feel as if I have failed you, am still failing you now.

I was young when I first began teaching—too young and too full of my own pain to stop dancing inappropriate waltzes, to tunes too fraught with intimate detail. I took you in, and then pushed you away after Tasha was born. A mentor of parallel extremes, when all along I should have walked the solid, narrow path, which may not have helped but definitely would not have hurt.

Now, as I write this on a simmering small-town evening, my husband clears the table and my daughter skips through the yard. When she was younger, and I rocked her to sleep, she would reach up for me and probe the outline of the scar that lingered, years later, on the edge of my mouth.

I vowed then never to burden her with its jagged history, the way I did you, and never to tell her what she did not need to hear.

And, you may ask, do I ever look up from the desk where I sit, stare at my neatly plotted, bland neighborhood, and long for those days when life was ripe with intrigue and possibility but far from safe?

Yes. Absolutely.

I think of you, Isobel, in that city like something out of a dream, a tempting place in which to be bright and attractive and young. Maybe you're a little lonely, a lot overwhelmed. No doubt foreign life excites you, so I won't sully the moment with lectures. Just think about this:

Being a woman in a body, and letting that body lead, is an act of blind trust. Trust in what you want and deserve, and in your power to speak for it.

I have faith that you'll speak loudly.

Much love,
Sylvia (Ms. J.)

When Isobel finished the letter, she folded it and sat without moving, stunned. I'll be okay, she thought. He hasn't hit me.

∽

When she arrived at his place that Friday, Kjartan had a bottle of wine on the table, already chilled. "Look what I found for you, my girl," he said, and encircled her shoulder with his arm as she sat on the couch. "A German vintage, with your name on it. Only it's not spelled properly, it's *Isabelle*. Shall we have a bit?"

"Sure," she said, even though she didn't particularly want any. She leaned her head into the crook of his neck.

"I got out the good glasses, just for you," he said, and poured the wine into two goblets. The liquid was a burgundy hue, not merely the hated color of her hair, but now also that of the flush that spread across her face, and of the blood that surged, dense and warm, down her back, across her belly, and between her legs. She could feel every vessel that it plunged through quiver. She felt drunk already.

Kjartan raised his goblet and handed her the other. "*Skál,*" he said. Glass clanged against glass.

"*Skál,*" she said. She took a sip. It tasted rich and deep and smooth, with just a hint of a burn that satisfied her.

"As good as its namesake, yes?" he said, and smiled.

She nodded and set her glass on the table. Leaned forward to put her arms around him. His drink sloshed against her, soaking to her skin. He unbuttoned her damp blouse and put his mouth to the moisture between her collarbone and her breast. She slid out of her shoes and wrapped her legs around his waist. She wanted to anchor herself to this feeling, wanted to find in his pliant body a vibrant echo of her jarring pulse.

"Well, this is quite a surprise," Kjartan murmured with a little laugh as he lifted his head. She wanted to say: *No, you don't under-*

stand, it's more than that, either part of me has opened up or I'm falling apart, can't you feel how my bones are shifting, how I'm changing? But when she opened her mouth to speak, she had to draw in her breath sharply as he sucked on her earlobe.

With one hand, he steadied her shoulder, while with the other he pushed her back onto his knees, just far enough that he could slip his fingers under her skirt and into her. She tipped her head back and felt herself tumbling into dangerous black space as he pressed against what felt like the hardest, deepest place in her to reach, but a lovely one, too, the last tiny baby in the set of *matrioshka* dolls. The stinging sensation both thrilled and terrified her. Her neck tensed. She closed her eyes. His knuckles twisted; his fingertips stroked with maddening gentleness, then lunged. She gritted her teeth.

"Isobel," he said. "My darling. Look at me."

Her throat felt tight. She let her eyelids flicker, just enough.

"You'd float up to the ceiling if I let you, wouldn't you?" he said.

As if in answer, she fell back onto the sofa cushions, swallowing her gasps.

"Relax," he said, and slid his hand from her shoulder to her breasts, to her hip, all the way down her extended calf to her ankle, as if to draw some long-dormant heat to the surface. She pressed her lips together until they almost grazed her teeth. Her legs shook. She came in explosive shudders, so intense her thighs and her throat hurt. She yanked his hand out, and he rested it against her cheek, wet thumb brushing her bruised lower lip. She let her tongue dart out to taste it; her mouth filled with blood and wine and tart homecoming. She shivered.

Kjartan picked her up and carried her tenderly to the bed, her legs dangling around his as he walked. She felt like some raw, loose-limbed new creature. He lay her beneath the duvet and crawled in beside her. She curled in a fetal position, underwear at her knees, sweat trickling down her back. He cradled her in his arms, rocking her ever so slightly, smoothing her hair, and Isobel thought of Ingibjörg, the dark daughter.

"Isobel," he said, "my girl whose energy they cannot bottle. You've got more passion than you give yourself credit for, do you understand?"

༷

In Reykjavík, there were children everywhere. Isobel couldn't remember ever seeing so many children in her life, at least not packed into such a dense labyrinth of streets, or prowling with such carefree audacity. They swirled around her, ruddy-faced and screeching, bright-colored cardigans tied around their waists, blond heads and red heads clustered in jaunty gangs.

To them, Isobel was a pale shadow of looming adulthood, yet another fair woman strolling down Laugavegur, maybe a tourist, maybe someone's solemn older sister. They paid her no attention, calling to one another in trilling voices both sweet and tough, but she watched them, could not take her eyes off their slender sprite-like bodies, could not fathom the ease with which they navigated the world in perky jumpers and baggy sweatpants. It was the youngest ones Isobel liked best, the little boys trying to show off on their tiny skateboards at Ingólfstorg, and of course the bundled-up infants, chubby faces and alert eyes peering out from underneath pastel sun hats in their procession of neon and navy carriages. The turn of pram wheels, a soft but constant echo in her head, made her think of Colette.

In July, when her period was three days late, the echo became a roar. No more window-shopping, then; Isobel's gaze was stuck fast to the children, the ones she wanted to keep, to steal, to unfurl like a flag, to uncurl like a fist, inside her:

Letting the Body Lead

The six-year-old with wispy hair who sat on the stoop of her house, clad in a velvet dress the same dark green as her front door, singing to herself and making birdlike gestures with her hands to accompany her song.

The eight-year-old in a fuzzy orange jacket and pants who carried her mewling black cat down a side street in the eastern section of the city.

The three-year-old who toddled in from the terrace of the French café on Austurstræti, her pale face painfully intense above the collar of her pink polo shirt as she tugged a waitress's sleeve.

Girls, always. Isobel composed names in her head, hybrids of Icelandic ones she liked—Sólveig, Guðny—and the names of women whose strength she wanted—Sylvia, Elika. She had a vague sense that both her assumption that she was pregnant and her fierce, almost obsessive longing to have a child were irrational, but still Isobel dove down into them like a warm bath scented with fragrant oil, her illusions opening like lotus flowers.

Colette, she wrote to her best friend on an imaginary postcard, *I'm sorry if I judged you before. Come here with me, raise the baby in this city of prams. We'll get a bright blue basement flat, put knickknacks on the windowsill, cook fish with lemon butter, snag Brian to baby-sit while we go out dancing on the weekends, and our daughters will be safe, I promise.*

Five days, and Isobel's head was a pink swarm. She went into a clothing shop downtown, clawed through the racks of quilted jackets, slipdresses, and oversized jeans, and tried not to look at the tiny plastic table full of toys in the corner that stood out like a sweet, gracious anomaly among the black lacquer and hip-hop music. It was silly, Isobel knew, this vision she had of herself and Colette in their silver hair clips and nylon running pants, pushing their matching strollers, stopping on the sidewalk for coffee on breezy afternoons—superficial, inaccurately utopian, but utterly hers.

She took a detour on the way home, down Skólavörðustigur, past a store full of bright yellow and orange baby overalls, its windows' half-price signs screaming ÚTSALA. As Isobel came into the shadow of Hallgrímskirkja, her stomach knotted. She heard a child wailing in the house on her left, and his mother's soft but sharp reproach. The combination of the looming gray basalt church and the little boy's hoarse cries chilled her. The wind picked up. She walked faster.

By the time Isobel let herself into the flat, her hands were numb. She went into the bedroom, threw her coat on the bed. Her gut contracted. She decided to take a shower before dinner, warm herself up. She ran the water, lifted her shirt over her head, unhooked her bra. Her breasts were swollen and sore. She unbuttoned her jeans, left them wadded in a heap on the floor. She was just about to part the curtain when she felt the blood trickling down her legs. Isobel lowered herself onto the speckled tile and rested her head in her quaking hands. Her stomach twisted. The child's wail rang in her ears.

✌

Isobel never told Kjartan about her maternal mania. Introspection stagnated. They existed together in the confines of one bleak room like a sealed bottle, where they ate, drank, watched television, fucked, and made the polite, excruciating conversation of two people from different countries who barely knew each other. Still, every time he touched her, her heart lunged.

"Isobel *mín*," he said one night, kneeling over her. "Do you love me, just a little?"

She closed her eyes. Nodded.

He came all over her neck.

ॐ

"Did you see the sunset last evening?" Ragna asked the next day, when they went for breakfast at a cozy pub on Hverfisgata. "It was brilliant."

Isobel nibbled at her bagel. "No," she said. "I missed it."

"You and your whirlwind romance," Ragna said, oblivious, and grinned.

ॐ

When Isobel returned home, she found two more pieces of mail addressed to her, a package and a slim note. "I've gotten popular, huh?" she said to Siggi, her neglected charge, and opened the package first.

It was a videotape from Elika, with a letter enclosed, written in purple ink on the back of a grocery list:

June 30

Hey you!

How's life in the North Atlantic? Hope you're having a bitchin' time and that you haven't trashed M. and E.'s flat, seeing as you're such a badass (ha!).

The big news on Planet Me is . . . the video's DONE, baby!

Seventy-two straight hours in the media lab, but here it is, transferred to PAL format for yer (expensive, I must say) viewing pleasure, just 'cause I'm good like that. Let me know what you think.

I am having lots of fun with the apartment to myself, and have turned your bedroom into extra wardrobe storage. (Just kidding!)

Miss you bunches!

Smooches,
The Directress

P.S. Did that teacher friend of yours ever get in touch with you?

Isobel smiled and moved on to the other note. By the violet-bordered, cream-colored stationery, she could tell it was from Colette.

July 8

Dear Isobel,

As you can imagine, things are pretty crazy right now. I hope you're getting the rest that you need—I expect a full report on Iceland (and these new developments in your love life!). In the meantime, I thought you'd like a photo of Laura Isobel, who's now home safe and sound. Longer letter coming once (if?) I get more sleep . . .

Love,
Colette

Isobel pulled the snapshot out and stared at it. Colette and the baby on Colette's blue floral couch, by the window, so that sunlight shattered the cohesion of the picture, sending black stripes of shadow across some places, white-gold rays over others. A bad photograph, but painful with joy. Colette had on a white sundress, her hair pulled back. Her mouth was wide and delicate, locked in a smile. She looked wan. Laura was a pink-swaddled blur in her arms. Thin fuzz of brown hair. Alert sapphire-colored eyes.

Isobel rubbed the fingerprints off the photograph with the edge of her sweater and tucked it under a magnet on the refrigerator door, next to one of Magga and Einar and their children on a camping trip. Doing so strangely satisfied her, as if she had bridged some gap between culture and culture, moment and moment.

∽

That evening, Isobel was about to make herself a snack and watch Elika's video when the doorbell rang. It was Kjartan, still in his work clothes. He stepped inside before she could even say hello, and gave her a kiss. "Here," he said, and handed her a wrapped piece of tiramisu from the restaurant. "I saved you this."

For all his offhand attitude and absentmindedness, Kjartan possessed an uncanny ability to respond to Isobel in ways that she wanted or needed but never asked for—strong hands expertly massaging her sore neck, a phone call when she was at her most alone and aimless. Such bouts of touching generosity depended solely, however, on his mood and how much alcohol he'd had.

"You're too sweet," Isobel said now. "And you're just in time for a film festival."

"Oh?"

"From my friend in New York," she said, leading him into the living room. "She made a documentary with me in it, and today she sent me an advance copy."

"Isobel the cinema star," he said. As Kjartan went to stretch out on the couch, he swiped at Siggi, who backed off and hissed. "I didn't know you were such a Renaissance woman, baby."

"You know nothing about me," Isobel said as she loaded the tape in the VCR. She had meant for her words to sound mysterious, jokey, but they came out flat and irritated.

Isobel settled on the floor and pressed PLAY on the remote. The video opened with a montage of photos from stages in each subject's life. Isobel cringed at a snapshot of her as a skinny, copperhaired four-year-old in a jumpsuit with a huge watermelon on its chest, but he didn't notice. The first in-depth interview was with another woman.

Kjartan yawned. "When are your fifteen minutes of fame?"

"I think I'm third," Isobel said. As the second interview drew to a close, her muscles tensed. The woman on the screen looked so poised, so articulate, and yet so normal; she laughed, she made lovely, broad gestures with her slender hands.

Then Isobel's own image smashed into her.

A slight, nervous creature perched awkwardly on the seat of a rocking chair, her eyes huge in the engineered gold light. She wore the same demure white blouse she'd thrown away after nursing Kjartan through his hangover, and even though grandiose, hyperintellectual words—*internalize, dissociate*—fell from her mouth, she looked like an eccentric, frightened child. *This scares me*, Isobel turned to say to him; *I don't want to be like this, but I—*

Kjartan sprawled with his lips parted, asleep.

༄

Isobel ate the tiramisu alone in the kitchen with the cat. Then she went back into the living room and lay on the couch on top of

Kjartan. Her annoyance blended with an odd craving for human touch, an eerie desire for comfort from the one who was the source of her hurt.

He groaned. She kissed him on the mouth.

"Coffee and amaretto," he said, opening his eyes, and smiled. He tucked her hair behind her ears.

"My crazy girl," he said. "Why do you put up with me?"

✌

Sylvia was right. There was no category, no precise theoretical framework, into which she could place those midsummer afternoons. Cigarettes clustered along the rim of an ashtray in a demented arrangement of smoldering flowers. Through the blinds, pale sunlight turned the walls tart as lemon. Planes took off from the Reykjavík airport, and the rumble of their engines thrummed so loudly that Isobel thought the room might ascend as she lay there, safe and yet not safe, in his bed.

✌

On one of those days, she sat at Einar and Magga's kitchen table, attempting to write out postcards for Sylvia, Shireen, Natalie, and her mother, whose international checkup calls she felt horrible for ignoring. She heard Kjartan get up from the couch and cross the room, and then she felt his hands on her shoulders. He leaned down, shoved her hair out of the way, and kissed her, hard enough to leave a bruise, on her neck.

"Your reports home can wait," he said, and slid the pen from her grasp.

"But I need to—"

He pushed the cards across the table, and turned her chin to face him. "What do you *want*?" he asked.

She stood without thinking. Slipped her arms and legs around him. Hung there while he took her into Einar and Magga's room and dropped her roughly onto the bed. I'm an addict, she thought. Bound to the elixir of being wanted, not by a solid boy like Gavin, but one of those dark lovely ones, like Andrew Kennedy, like Michael Culley. Like him. Kjartan's palm pressed against her throat, while his other hand lifted her skirt up.

Ég vil, she thought, *ég vil.*

"I thought as much," he said.

⁓

Afterward, she lay on her stomach, damp with sweat, feeling utterly pleased with herself.

"What are you doing Wednesday night?" he said.

"Nothing," Isobel said, her reply muffled by the pillow.

"Good, because I have a friend who works at the Grill at Hótel Saga, one of the best places in town, and he promised to get us in. Would you like that, Isobel *mín*?"

"Sure," Isobel said.

He kissed the small of her back. "It won't be long till you leave," he said. "I want to make you happy."

⁓

On Wednesday night, Isobel stepped into the turquoise dress and sandals and pulled her hair up in a wild but passable topknot. As she put on her lipstick and dabbed mango perfume behind each ear, she sang along with the radio to a pop song whose jaunty chorus espoused the virtues of *"súmar ást."* Summer love.

Kjartan had told her to meet him at six-thirty, but she arrived at six-fifteen. Isobel figured he was simply surprised by her early appearance when she heard him rasp, "Come in."

She found him in bed, his eyes bloodshot. He reached around her, caressed her waist. Damn it, Isobel thought, but even as she cringed with annoyance, she felt herself go moist and open.

"Nice dress," he said, as if he'd never seen it before. "Buy me a pack of cigarettes, Isobel? I'm dying."

ॐ

Isobel knew they weren't going by the time she reached the little shop on the corner. When she returned with his precious Marlboros, anger flickering like a lit match inside her, she tossed them on the bed.

"Isobel the philanthropist," he said, and propped up on one elbow. "I owe you, baby."

"Five hundred krónur, to be exact."

Kjartan patted the edge of the bed. Isobel sat beside him, gingerly.

"I'll make it up to you later," he said. For once there was no hint of innuendo in his words. He closed his eyes. "Go have a nice dinner, talk gender politics with your new friends. I'm so sorry."

For once he's right, Isobel thought. Remember Ms. J. on the hilltop? Let this be your moment, your time to stand and walk away from him, toward your deserving self.

The sun slanted through the blinds. His sad, slender fingers stroked her back. Her spine hummed with the softness of the motion, its tender desolation. Neither desire nor injustice moved her. Let me lie here, she thought. I'm so tired of fighting, word against flesh. I'm so tired.

Isobel slid off one shoe.

"Go on, baby. I won't be offended."

She kicked off the other.

"No," Isobel said. "I'm staying."

❦

Eleven-thirty. Isobel lay on her side of the wall, on her back. The room smelled like spilled liquor. He snored. The phone rang; she didn't answer it.

Instead she got up and climbed over him, not caring anymore whether she woke him or not. She sat naked on the couch and watched the evening news. Her favorite newscaster with the purple lipstick was on, narrating over a shot of Akureyri, where solemn little Ingibjörg, with the long, narrow face like Isobel's, lived.

She looked down at the unfamiliar curves of her body. It struck her as a little sensual, and terribly sad.

"Góða nótt," the newscaster told her.

Isobel blinked back tears.

"Góða nótt," she said.

❦

When the official broadcast gave way to an infomercial in English for a "revolutionary" new product that could shave your legs painlessly in minutes, Isobel heard him call out. "Isobel *mín*, come here," he said. "I need you near me."

The urgency in his voice brought her to that tantalizing cross-roads between mother and lover. She went to the bed, wriggled under the duvet, and wrapped around him. "Better?" she said.

Kjartan clutched her and nodded.

❦

Isobel slept soundly until seven in the morning. As usual, she was the one to awaken first, and she rolled over to kiss him a tentative hello. Kjartan swatted at her back. "Too tired," he said.

Half an hour later, though, he stretched and came back to life, all the while mumbling words of groggy, insistent desire. Isobel felt her body tighten with a sensation akin to annoyance, only edgier.

"Too tired," she said, only half mocking him.

"Isobel, please," he said. "It would be so good for me—I mean us."

His pitiful, hurried attempt to cover his flagrant self-interest would have made Isobel laugh, had she not been suddenly petrified.

"*Nei*," Isobel said.

"*Ju*," he said, draping one leg over her waist and settling, too hard, deadweight, against her hips. He held her wrists gently, stroking the thin bluish veins, quieting the pulse that hammered there. Her thoughts surged with a multitude of queries: Do I want this? Do I not want this? Do I—

It occurred to Isobel that she had no idea what he was capable of doing.

Her mouth opened like a baby bird's, wide, dumb, unsure whether it should speak words of affirmation or protest.

"Shh," he said. "It's okay."

Okay, Isobel repeated to herself, and swallowed. That's it, Isobel *mín*, my darling girl, look in his face and see yourself reflected, just like a mirror, and remember how, on one of those lovely shining nights when he could actually carry on a conversation, he told you he was especially sensitive, or "perhaps the best word in English would be *psychic*"? He knows what you want, he knows what's best for you, so just let your mind wander down the garden path with every thrust, toward all those shining moments: fine bones and fire hair and ivory skin, saved pieces of tiramisu, we take good care of each other, *vatn með klaka, gertu svo vel—gertu svo vel—*

Isobel closed her eyes. Saw the girl again, perched behind her, at the bottom of the bed. She could have been Ásta and Ingibjörg in a few years. Her eyes were huge, a little afraid, but wildly curious. In her head, Isobel struck out at her, all her fury at him oozing from her frenetic fists. *Leave me alone!* Isobel screamed, smacking her away, smashing her across the room. Then she slammed back into her own flesh, silent and sore, and her breath came in ragged gasps as her body betrayed her, responding to him with a sound midway between satisfaction (*oh but I didn't want this!*) and a hollow sob.

When he was finished, she lay with her back to him, curled in on herself. No delicate midnight revelation for this tourist, she thought. No majestic view of the city like my mentor had, just a sordid room with me in it, sticky and shaking.

"Isobel the pensive," he said. "Why so sad?"

She got up and began putting on her dress. She jerked the zipper up without his help. "I've got to meet a friend," Isobel said. It was a lie, but it was also what she needed: someone else. "I'll call you, all right?"

Isobel went straight to Ragna's. She was dirty, she'd left her bra tangled in his bedclothes, and it was early enough to risk rudeness, but Ragna was the only person who could make sense out of such senselessness.

Isobel had never been to Ragna's flat, but she knew it was on Freyjugata, a short walk from the pond. Ragna answered the door in a red satin robe, an earthenware mug in her hand.

"Isobel," she said, "you're just in time for breakfast, I—" Ragna stopped and looked at Isobel—her stark eyes, her clothes full of wrinkles—and pulled her into a fierce, one-armed hug. "Why don't we come inside?"

The flat was large and sunny, homier than Isobel had expected, and she wanted to collapse in its warmth. Ragna led her into the dining room, and sat her down at a huge, antique wooden table. "Make yourself comfortable," she said. "I'll get the breakfast things, and then we can talk."

Isobel watched as she journeyed back and forth from the kitchen, setting out plate after plate. There was *kleinur* and rye bread, *skyr* and yogurt, a hunk of cheese next to an elegant planer, Wasa crackers from Sweden, and a platter of fresh salmon. By the time she brought the container of orange juice, the electric pitcher that boiled water, and the packets of tea and instant cappuccino, Isobel had already started to cry.

"Have something to eat," Ragna said. "You must be hungry."

"I am," Isobel said, wiping her eyes. "I was supposed to go to the Grill at Hótel Saga last night, and I didn't, which is a shame, but not the real reason I'm bawling—"

Ragna rubbed Isobel's back.

"Ragna," Isobel said, "I have no idea what's happening to me. I'm normally very good with words, with tidy, well-planned conclusions, but jargon just can't save me this time."

Ragna leaned her elbows on the table. There was none of her usual bright chatter peppered with quasi-British slang; her face was alert and serious.

"Let it be messy, then, *elskan*," she said. "Don't try to be clever. Tell me in whatever words you can."

Isobel helped herself to almond-and-caramel yogurt, and gave her the bare, brutal facts of the past month with Kjartan.

When Isobel was done, Ragna put her hand over hers.

"He's very Icelandic," was all she said.

Isobel swirled her spoon in the bowl.

"Maybe he is," she said, "but I can't believe how stupid I was."

"You weren't stupid," Ragna said, pouring herself another cup of coffee. "Look, I met a man once who was just as charismatic, the only difference being that, when we disagreed, he liked to shove me into walls. And I married him and had his kid."

"But you didn't want to be hurt," Isobel said.

"*Nei*, Isobel, and neither do you," Ragna said. "So you're trying to be a tough, bad girl for a change? So you're living in a country where everything is wild and new? Maybe you're a little attracted to danger, like we all are, but that doesn't mean you deserve it."

"Even if I see him again?"

"Even if you see him again." She sliced off a piece of cheese. "How would you like to stay with me for a few days, until you get things more sorted out?"

"I would love to," Isobel said. "We'll have to get the cat from Magga's."

"Oh, don't worry about that," Ragna said. "He and Valdi are good friends."

"Valdi's your son?"

"Valdimar, *já*." She passed Isobel the sugar for her tea. "I have to get him in a few minutes, he comes home from his farm work today."

"Do you need me to come with you?"

"I think I'll manage." She smiled. "Why don't you get some rest?"

"Maybe I will. But could . . . could I take a shower first?"

"Of course. Wash your hair, use my computer for the Internet, do you whatever you like."

Ragna stood up from the table and touched Isobel's head tenderly as she passed.

᠊ᡬ

Clad in borrowed silk pajamas, hair damp, Isobel snuggled under the bright blue duvet in Ragna's guest bedroom. She listened to Ragna on the phone, her voice rising and falling, lulling Isobel.

Letting the Body Lead

She was already half asleep when Ragna came, dressed now, to the doorway. "Isobel," she said. "I'm leaving."

When Isobel woke, she heard a young boy's shouts and the perky blips of a video game, along with Siggi's trademark yowl. Isobel lay content and tranquil, hugging herself, as if she could become the careful, soothing lover she should have had.

Chapter Eight

Staplin, Pennsylvania

*I*sobel's pilgrimage to the North Atlantic had begun a decade earlier, fueled by pure idolatry. Her teachers liked to call her *gifted*, and when she was young, this epithet confused her; she expected someone to hand her a gift-wrapped box adorned with a fat satin bow. Later, she realized that in some ways this metaphor really was a fitting one—only the gift happened to be a trick, a neatly encased bomb that exploded in her face with a puff of black smoke.

As a teenager, she fancied herself an intellectual, but her earliest childhood memories were bright, visceral splashes: warm summer nights spent between cool strawberry-printed sheets at her grandparents' beach cottage in South Carolina, a shard of sun cast across a glass-topped table in her first house on Monroe Street. Colette claimed she could pinpoint her first conscious memory at the age of two, when she visited her mother in the hospital after her brother was born, clinging to her father's hand as they walked the white antiseptic corridor, clambering up onto the bed in a pink pinafore and knee socks to stare down into the red squalling face wrapped in a blanket and decide she hated it. Isobel, when she heard this story, gave it the same begrudging, jealous admiration she always bestowed upon Colette's precise, orderly tales, but secretly she knew it couldn't be true.

Her own youthful memories were vague blurs, joyous, panicked, like trying to view the world in all its stillness while you spin yourself dizzy.

❦

"You're amazing," people grew fond of telling her when she was older. Sometimes the word was replaced by other, similar adjectives. *Fascinating* was one, followed by *intriguing* and *inspiring*—all catchphrases for awe, respect, admiration. And distance.

The gulfs others created, she widened. Not meaning to. Regretting it.

And jokingly, lightly, lovingly, they asked, "How on earth did we get you, Isobel?"

How on earth did they get me?

How did I get to be myself?

Isobel, of course, knew the multitude of answers proposed to these questions. And yet she always came back to this: the little girl at recess in the mauve toggle coat with the pale face, the penny loafers, the tousled hair, a preoccupied grin on her face, a haunted look (of loneliness? ecstatic contemplation? it had been too long) in her dark eyes as she swung around the blacktop's basketball pole, oblivious (or was she?) to the shouts of children who surrounded her like savages.

Herself, at eight years old.

❧

By the time she was thirteen, she had been promoted into high school a year early, and her parents had gotten divorced. Both events happened the same summer, and she wondered if there was some warped connection between her own academic prowess and their marriage's dissolve.

She never asked. Instead, she simply watched that fall as her mother bought a ramshackle but potentially gorgeous Victorian house in a different school district, and got a slick secretarial job at the most respected law firm downtown. In the mornings her mother clacked about the kitchen in her heels and brand-new green paisley suit, pouring out two cups of tea and sprinkling cinnamon on two plates of toast as she hummed. Upstairs, her body jarred by the alarm, Isobel curled tighter beneath the quilts and shivered, not wanting to peel out of her nightshirt and walk across the cold hardwood floor, not wanting to dress in the gray late-September dawn and go down to meet her mother's pleasant face, calm with freedom.

They ate their breakfast among still-unpacked boxes at a rickety old card table—Isobel's father had taken the good table—and on folding chairs. Isobel's mother laughed as she dropped crumbs on her silk blouse and brushed them away. "This is kind of fun, isn't it?" she said. "Like an adventure."

"I'm going to miss the bus," Isobel said before she could meditate more on their present circumstances, and jumped up to put her plate in the sink. A moment later she was running across the wet lawn in her shaggy cardigan, books clutched to her chest, shoulders smarting with tenderness and guilty irritation at her mother's goodbye embrace as she dashed across the street, her sandals hitting the pavement just as the school bus pulled up to its stop.

Letting the Body Lead

She stepped on with the few other high-schoolers who hadn't yet gotten their driver's licenses, and a bunch of scrawny, mean-eyed seventh-graders. She took a place behind the driver and propped her feet up on the seat so none of the boys would sit next to her and harass her. She opened the book of Sylvia Plath poems she'd discovered in the library one day while the rest of the girls were painting their nails in study hall, and read as the bus wound its way through small-town streets and drab farmland.

❧

Isobel began her first year at Andrews High perfectly accustomed to meandering the corridors of her own mind for amusement. Her fragile, pensive face, coupled with her shyness and penchant for honors courses, instantly branded her a misfit of the worst caliber, far below the goth kids who could pull off insurgence with studied cool. She hated her new school; it was too huge, and she missed Colette.

The only consolation was first period, when, for forty-two blissful minutes, she had Ms. Johnson's class. Ms. J., as she insisted that everyone call her, taught advanced-placement psychology, a course for seniors that Isobel had entered with special permission. Ms. J. was young and funky and wore gauze skirts and earrings with dangly beads. She had traveled around Europe for a summer and spoke with a twinge of bohemian flair that sent bursts of vivid color splashing through the rigid monochrome of Isobel's youth.

She also didn't care that Isobel read other books in class, the way most teachers did; in fact, she'd lean down, peer over Isobel's shoulder, and say, "Wow. Remind me to check this out. Who's the author?"

"You don't care that I'm doing this?" Isobel asked the first time she'd been caught.

"You're still keeping a ninety-five average," Ms. J. said. "I love the fact that you're doing this."

Sometimes Isobel would stay after class and sit on top of the radiator for long talks with Ms. J. One morning Ms. J. said, "You're a very articulate young woman, Isobel. Have you ever thought of joining the school speech and debate team?"

"Not really," Isobel said. "I'm too shy, and I hear enough lawyer stories from my mother."

Ms. J. laughed. "I'm sure it's more than just pretend courtroom drama. Plus I think it'll help you be more assertive. There's a meeting today after school. Check it out."

"Maybe I will," Isobel said, "but now I've got to get down to geometry class before Mr. Lauer burns me at the stake for humanities heresy." Ms. J. grinned and wrote her a late pass.

༄

Isobel went to the meeting that afternoon in the library. She had pictured a gathering where the eager-voiced teenage intelligentsia would sit and talk, leaning forward intently, making wide sweeping gestures with their hands.

Instead she found a sullen group sitting on tables, their combat-boot-clad feet dangling as they raked nervously through their hair, either bleached or dyed black, and complained about how the "trendies" were taking over the school system.

Isobel sought out the coach, a man in a suit with a huge raised mole on the side of his neck, and told him her interests. He informed her that the school also had a speech team and that, given her love of poetry, she might want to try oral interpretation. She took her Sylvia Plath book and sat at a study carrel by the window, far away from the scary-looking students who, she was sure, looked at her with distaste for being a carrot-haired, quiet little freshman. Afternoon sun slanted over the pages she turned, and she was seized with a sudden, delicious pleasure at gold light, at words, at their order.

"Hey."

She looked up, halfway through "Lady Lazurus."

"Yes?" she said.

A guy stood beside her. He was stocky and fleshy-armed, with messy brown hair and huge earlobes and a cleft in his chin. He wore smudged jeans and a black T-shirt. He held out a small three-ring binder.

"Here," he said. "Buckley's obviously forgotten to mention to you that you'll need one of these, so here's an old book of mine."

His voice was wry, flat, completely indifferent to her.

"Thanks," she said, and took the binder from him, furiously attempting to hide the fact that she had no idea what it was for or what to do with it. His broad, sweaty hand brushed hers, and a peculiar mixture of repulsion and excitement stirred in her. Blood rushed to her fingers.

"It's to put your poems in, for when you read them," he said with the faintest hint of an impatient sigh. "You're Isobel Sivulka, right?"

"Yes. And you're brilliant."

He laughed. It was an explosive sound, like a sneeze, like a light-heartedly sarcastic remark on the verge of anger. "I'm Michael Culley." He pulled a chair over and straddled it. "You aren't by any chance the new girl who's managed to take upperclassman-only courses as a freshman, are you?"

She looked down. "That's me."

"I admire that totally. The administration here needs to get their policies fucked with a little. Not to mention Buckley."

"The coach?"

"Yeah. He's a great speaker, but basically a prick."

"Keep your voice down."

"Don't worry about it. He doesn't care what I say. He can't. I won him the district championship last year." His tone held no hint of smugness, simply cynicism.

"Wow," Isobel said.

"There's nothing to 'wow' about," he said. "I haven't got any talent. I'm just good at playing the games people want me to play."

"I'm not," Isobel said softly. "I see the rules from too many sides. I'm too passive."

"So you're Switzerland, huh? Neutral territory."

She imagined snowy white mountains, girls in dotted skirts, safety. The metaphor both pleased and irritated her.

"I take it Buckley did explain to you the whole mentoring concept," Michael said, "about each freshman on the team being paired with a more experienced member to show them the ropes?"

She nodded.

He stood up. "Well, you're mine," he said.

❦

After the meeting ended at five o'clock, the team wandered in a loose cluster toward the school's back lobby. Isobel stood alone on the bus dock, against the red brick wall, books pressed to her chest, warm, protected. The punks ambled across the parking lot, and she watched as they crammed inside a tiny black car with a smudged paint job, girls sitting on guys' laps in the backseat because it was so crowded. As the car screeched away, loud industrial music blaring, Isobel felt the familiar taste of revulsion and haughtiness build in her throat. She was seized with the desire to run after them, to lunge at the door handle and hang on tight until they let her in, to be a long, pale-haired girl with a cigarette between her skinny fingers, face tilted in beautiful angularity, to be all chains and nose rings and metal and protest, to sit in the lap of a boy grungy with wildness.

142

But they were a small black dot now, nothing more, turning right at the football field and then gone. Isobel glanced over by the door at a semicircle of girls in navy blue varsity jackets, wrists adorned with ridiculous ponytail holders, voices vacillating between peevish whines and excited laughter. Off in the distance, she could see Michael Culley pacing back and forth in the dying September sunlight, his own three-ring binder in hand, a hungry shadow, coatless.

The late bus pulled up, and Isobel got on, taking a seat near the front, as usual. She was about to open her book of poems and review her favorites when she saw Michael Culley filing down the aisle behind a lacrosse player.

Michael took the seat in front of her and leaned over so that he was a few inches from her face. "I saw you watching the counter-culture crew," he said in a conspiratorial whisper.

"You did?"

"Don't waste your time with them," he said.

"No need to worry. I prefer companions with multiple brain cells, thank you."

He laughed. "So what brings you to the inferno?"

"Excuse me?"

"This place. Andrews School for the High." He snorted.

"My mother wanted to relocate after my parents got divorced."

He leaned back against the window, face blank but tense. "Mine think it's a sin," he said. "That's the only reason they're still together."

The way he spoke frightened her, as if this were a story he'd told a million times before and felt compelled to tell again, with no hope of catharsis or comfort, simply telling, as if she weren't even there.

"And what do you think?" Isobel asked, voice tiny.

"I don't believe in the sacrament of marriage."

She sat in silence, unsure how to respond, rubbing a dog-eared page of her book with her thumb as the bus passed by a produce stand, a meat market, a trailer park.

He glanced down at her lap.

"Plath, huh?" he said.

"My author of the moment."

"She scares me," he said. "She makes me see things I don't want to see."

"Isn't that one of the goals of good literature?"

He smiled absently. "You're such a little pedant," he said.

Isobel clenched her jaw. She saw the flower shop coming up in the distance and raised her hand to stop the driver. She could feel Michael's eyes on her hands, her knuckles, as she gathered her stack of texts and notebooks quickly, too quickly. The binder he'd given her slid out of her grasp and onto the floor. She picked it up, dusted it off. His gaze met hers.

"See ya," he said stiffly.

"Are you getting off here, or aren't you?" the bus driver yelled.

"Bye," she mumbled, and hurried down the aisle, off the bus, and across the street. She kept her head lowered as she made her way down the alley, trying to block out the sight of the pale fleshy void that was his face. She thought instead of her mother, home from work now, belting out Aretha Franklin tunes in her bathrobe while she cooked pasta in the card-table kitchen. She broke into a run.

༂

Later that night, while they were eating dinner, Isobel asked her mother, "Do you believe in marriage?"

Her mother leaned back in her chair and laughed. "What a question!"

"Well, do you?"

"That's a tough one," she said, dragging her fork through her linguine. "I mean . . . I think marriage can be a profound and gorgeous thing that we shouldn't just throw out the window, but at the same time it can be a huge mess you've got to just get the hell away from."

Isobel nodded.

"Why do you ask, hon?"

"Just wondering."

"There's nothing you want to talk about, any questions you need to have answered about your dad and me?"

She had already been told that he had had an affair.

"No," she said. She looked out the window, at the blackened sky like a bruise. Thought of Michael Culley, of his fingers over hers.

꿏

The next morning in psychology, while the class was reading a piece on whether or not electroshock therapy contributed to Hemingway's suicide, Ms. J. came over to Isobel, sat on the edge of her desk, and asked her how the practice had gone.

"Rather good," Isobel said.

"So are you pursuing the lawyerhood route or no?"

"Hardly. Poetry interpretation."

"There you go! What poet?"

"Plath."

"Isobel, you amaze me. I wasn't reading Plath until college." She turned around to face a noisy group in the back of the classroom. "Did you find any philosophical minds to bond with?"

"Not really, although there was this one guy, kind of interesting. His name was Michael Culley."

"I have him in third-period study hall," Ms. J. said. "We've talked a few times, and he seems like an intriguing young man." She grinned.

❦

The speech and debate team's first tournament was in October—"a warm-up for the season," Buckley told them. "Nothing to be stressed over." Isobel reminded herself of his words as she stood shivering in the school parking lot at six-thirty in the morning. She and the rest of the group huddled under the awning of the bus dock, waiting for Michael Culley to arrive.

Buckley checked his watch. "Come on, damn it," he said. "We don't have all day."

"Michael always does this," Sarah, a surprisingly sweet girl wearing black lipstick and a punky plaid skirt, whispered to Isobel. "At least he's good."

Isobel felt dowdy by comparison in her corduroy jumper and ballet flats. "Does he eventually show up?"

"At the last minute."

Buckley opened the door to the small van he had rented. "Pile in," he said. "We might as well get ready."

"Shouldn't one of us keep an eye out for Michael?" Isobel asked.

He shrugged. "You want to?"

"Sure." She watched as he got in the driver's seat and all the others crowded in the back two rows. She felt awkward yet deeply important, standing guard in her grandmother's old camel-hair coat, black binder tucked under her arm.

At seven o'clock, a Ford Pinto from the seventies with badly scratched brown paint pulled up, and Michael Culley, wearing a black trench coat and scuffed boots, got out. "Well, if it isn't the welcome wagon," he said. His eyes were bloodshot.

"I . . . I told them I'd wait here for you," she said.

"Thanks." He touched her shoulder, and she thrilled. "You're too sweet."

She couldn't tell if the remark was meant to be sarcastic or not, but it made her smile as they climbed into the van. "It'll be a tight fit, Isobel," Buckley said. "And Michael, what part of six-thirty don't you understand?"

Michael scowled as he and Isobel squeezed in beside Sarah. Their trip to the small Catholic school sponsoring the tournament took almost an hour, but she had never been happier with such cramped quarters. The goth kids had brought their Walkmans and soft-sided cases full of tapes, so they were engrossed in music the whole drive. Buckley watched the road, and Michael stared straight ahead and said nothing, but Isobel didn't mind. It was enough to feel the pressure of his shoulder against hers.

Once at the tournament, the team milled around in the school cafeteria, waiting to be assigned classrooms and numbers. Michael took off his trench coat, and Isobel discovered his version of dressing up: black jeans and a dark blue oxford shirt. She looked at the rest of the group, and thought: How perfect for each other we must seem. Two eccentric nerds.

"You look nice," he said stiffly.

"So do you," she said. She felt her face turn the color of her hair.

"No, I don't," he said, voice distant. "I look like someone who got home from a party at three A.M."

"You party a lot?" she asked.

"More than you do, I'm sure," he said. "You'd better hurry, Switzerland. I think they're reading off the assignments for poetry soon."

Buckley, who had been rushing from table to table in a panic, now came up behind Isobel and Michael and placed a hand on each of their shoulders. "My real team," he said. Isobel blushed even more. "Don't worry," Buckley said to her. "It's your first time out. No pressure." To Michael, he whispered, "You have *got* to win us some points, big guy. Trevor has decided at the last minute to read the comics off Bazooka bubble-gum wrappers as dramatic interpretation. Jesus Christ. Can you imagine?"

"Par for the course." Michael rolled his eyes.

Buckley handed them each a sheet of paper with their schedules for the day. "Here," he said to Isobel. "You're speaker J152, and your first round starts in room 208 in five minutes. Go for it, Lady Lazurus."

She swallowed. Michael reached for her hand, squeezed it hard.

"Good luck," he said.

※

Her first round, she was terrified. All her competitors favored affected voices and heavy theatrics. The second round, she was up against the guy from her own team who read the bubble-gum wrappers, and she felt better. By the third round, all she had to do was think of Michael Culley sitting where the judge was, and her voice rang out, passionate and clear.

The team reconvened in the cafeteria for lunch, and to wait for announcement of the finalists. Isobel sat on top of a table and picked nervously at the sandwich she'd packed. Michael came over and sat beside her.

"How do you think you did?" she asked.

"Miserably." He stared down at his hands. She wanted to place one of hers over his larger ones in a gesture of consolation, but he didn't seem concerned or upset.

"I'm sorry. How come?"

"Oh, I would have done fine if it weren't for the sleep deprivation or the hangover," he said. "It was my choice, though, so I can't complain."

"Won't Buckley be mad?"

He shrugged. "Maybe."

There was a sudden hush in the room as the judges began tacking the lists of finalists to the walls, and then a stampede of students impatient to read the results. Michael hung back.

"Don't you want to see?" Isobel asked.

"I know the outcome already," he said gruffly. "Go on, check for yourself."

Isobel elbowed her way through the crowd and craned her neck to read the lists. She saw the heading POETRY and closed her eyes briefly before scanning the numbers. Second from the bottom was J152.

"You made it, Isobel!" Sarah said from behind her.

Isobel glanced at the list for drama. There was no sign of K119, Michael's number. She turned to accept a hug from Sarah and saw Michael in the corner of the cafeteria, his arms folded in defiance as Buckley lectured him. She waded through the crowd until she stood before them.

"I just don't understand how you could throw away such—" Buckley noticed her and stopped. "Isobel! Well done! I'm so impressed." He clapped her heartily on the back. "Michael, aren't you going to congratulate Isobel?"

"Good for you," Michael muttered, and walked away.

Buckley sighed. "I don't know what the hell's wrong with him," he said. "Come on, I'll walk you to your final round."

She was mute with disappointment at Michael's cold response as Buckley escorted her to her classroom. She took a seat next to her five competitors, most of whom were the theatrical girls. The judge was about to begin the round when Isobel saw Michael slink in and take a spot in the back. "Are you a speaker?" the judge asked sharply.

Michael shook his head. "I'm just here to support one," he said, looking at Isobel, endearingly sheepish, and gave her a thumbs-up. She felt her heart leap as she and the others drew numbers to determine their order. Isobel plucked a one from the judge's basket. Under any other circumstances, she would have dreaded speaking first, but this time she was eager to take her place before the blackboard. Standing before her small audience, she lowered her head, took a deep breath, and began. The words of Plath's poem exploded from inside her, starting sly and slow, only to climax with a desperate, morbid wail. "I do it so it feels like hell!" she shrieked, her eyes fixed on Michael Culley.

Within moments it was over. She gave a meek nod, said, "Thank you," and sat down. Five other histrionic monologues floated by. The judge wished them luck and dismissed them all, and then Michael came up behind her. He looked visibly shaken.

"That," he said, "was amazing. I didn't know you had that kind of force in you, Switzerland."

"Thank you," she said, smiling tightly, jubilantly, as she stood and they walked out. "I didn't either."

She reentered the cafeteria feeling as if she had already won, hopeful that she and Michael could talk more, but other than a terse report to Buckley that "She's probably going to win," Michael was back to his skittish, vacant self. Isobel sighed and got a Margaret Atwood novel that Colette had lent her out of her bag, but the room was too noisy to concentrate. "What do we do now?" she asked Sarah.

"Hurry up and wait," Sarah said, "until they announce the winners. It could be a while."

"In that case, I'm taking a nap." Isobel curled up on the table, using her backpack as a pillow. Before she drifted off, out of the corner of her eye, she saw someone (Michael?) drape her coat over her tenderly. The next thing she knew, Buckley was shaking her awake, shouting, "Awards time!"

Groggily, she filed with the rest of the team into the auditorium, where the ceremony was to be held. She looked up, surprised, to see Michael sit beside her. They waited through the closing announcements, the thank-yous, the debate prizes, the informative and persuasive speaking awards, until finally poetry was called. "Go on, Switzerland," Michael said, and shoved her to her feet.

Trembling, she joined the other finalists onstage under the hot, golden lights. She watched as two speakers received their certificates, and thought, I'll be fourth. Not bad. Then she watched as a third piece of paper was handed to one of the ultra-dramatic girls. Her mouth opened in shock as she looked at the three trophies, one of which would be hers, and then she had to cover her dropped jaw with her hand when two statues were presented and she was still standing. Her entire team rose to their feet and applauded as her name was called and she went forward to take her blue first-place trophy.

"You should come to my final rounds all the time," she whispered to Michael on her way back to her seat. He gave her a high five and, for one shining, glorious moment, held her hand, tight.

༄

"Your trophy is so cool," Colette said, turning it over in her hands and then placing it carefully back on Isobel's bureau. She had stopped by the next afternoon to get all the details.

"Thanks," Isobel said. "Winning it was fabulous. Better than sex."

Colette's eyes widened. "Like you would know." She sat on Isobel's bed. "Or maybe you do. Care to tell me about this boy Michael?"

"I don't know if *boy* is the right word," Isobel said, joining her.

"Ah. He's a *man*."

Isobel snorted. "No. He's just . . . different."

"You really like him?"

"I don't know. It's not like a crush. He's too off-kilter for me to get all giggly about. But I want to be around him. I want to find out more about him."

Isobel didn't know how to explain to Colette that she wasn't hungry for the inane privilege of making the slow, vapid stroll with some big oaf under the purple neon lights of the mall on Friday night, or for a broad-knuckled hand sweaty in hers in the movie theater line, the lunch line, the hallways. She didn't pine for flowers, or heart-shaped boxes of sickly sweet Valentine's Day chocolate. Her cravings hit bone.

"Isobel," Colette said, "it's a crush." She reached down and plucked a book of Anne Sexton poems off the floor. "Mind if I borrow this?"

"Be my guest," Isobel said. "I'm so glad to be around someone who actually reads for pleasure."

"You're kidding me."

"No, I'm serious. Andrews is an intellectual Sahara."

They heard Isobel's mother call up the stairs. "Girls? Any objection if I ordered us dinner?"

"Oh, we'd hate it!" they yelled back, dissolving into laughter.

"If I get married," Colette said, "I am never cooking. Ever."

"Me neither. But who said anything about getting married?"

"Yeah. We could just be spinsters."

"And live in a penthouse."

"With built-in bookcases."

"And get lovely looking guys to give us back rubs and feed us grapes."

"Oh, you mean like your boy who's not a man but isn't a boy?"

Isobel whacked her with a pillow. "Please."

"It'll be the two of us against the world."

"Naturally." Isobel sat up. "Come on. We'd better decide what we want before my mom decides for us."

❦

She was sitting alone at lunch as usual that Monday, picking at her ham and cheese and reading a Charlotte Perkins Gilman book Ms. J. had lent her, when she heard the slam of a tray on the table beside her.

"Hey, Switzerland."

She looked up. Maybe this is it, she thought. We can pick up where we left off at the tournament. She couldn't stop shaking. "Hi," she said.

He heaved his backpack down on the floor and rummaged through it for a notebook. "Can't talk much," he said. "I've got a philosophy class in twenty minutes and I didn't do the fucking response journal."

Isobel leaned over his shoulder and read as he wrote.

"That's a really good argument for ethical relativism," she said. "Not many people can make a persuasive case for it."

He shrugged. "It's not that great."

"You should write more, though. Why don't you keep up with the work?"

"It's ridiculous. Plus the instructor's a slave-driving asshole who won't even entertain religious ideals not grounded in the Judeo-Christian tradition."

"Well, then," she said.

She looked up again as she saw a tiny, slender brown-haired girl, wearing a pink sweater and a crystal necklace, enter the cafeteria. "Ciara!" Michael called, and waved. It was the most genuine, excited acknowledgment of anyone's presence she'd ever seen from him, and in her opinion not warranted. Ciara McClellan was in Isobel's honors English class, and she struck Isobel as being overzealous, her tight, breathless voice too eager, her hand popping up into the air to answer every question.

"Hi, Michael," she called as she glided over to the table reserved for her circle of friends.

"She's beautiful," Michael said softly.

"She's an airhead," Isobel told him, half lost in "The Yellow Wallpaper."

"No she isn't." His voice was sharp. "And I've got feelings for her that I don't know how to express."

"Why don't you talk to her more, then?"

"Because it's wrong. I'm seventeen and she's fourteen. Isn't that sick?"

"I don't think so."

Isobel waited, tensed for the sound of the lunch bell's ring, wanting nothing more than for the next shift of hungry, chattering students to pour into the cafeteria and push her out into the hall toward Latin class. And yet she also wanted to be a fresh, gleaming girl in rose-colored angora, an object of awe and beauty, no matter how ludicrous, no matter how vacant.

"You don't?" he asked.

"No. Age doesn't mean anything."

He shook his head in frustration and went back to his journal while she bit the edge of her thumbnail and watched Ciara McClellan.

⁓

"I took your suggestion," Michael said two weeks later. They were sitting in half darkness on the edge of two seats opposite each other, the only ones on the five-thirty bus that night in early November.

"My suggestion?" Isobel asked.

"Yeah. I called Ciara. We talked from nine last night until six-thirty in the morning. That's why I was almost falling asleep during practice today."

"Why such a long conversation?"

"We've discovered we're kindred spirits," he said, voice solemn.

Well, good for you, she wanted to sneer, but didn't, flattered that he was telling her something so intimate.

"Really," she said.

"Yes," he said quietly. "I wouldn't tell this to just anyone, you know. I trust you."

The words were like an elixir. She looked over at him. His eyes glimmered. She wanted to take his broad jaw in her hands. She longed to ram her fist into the soft contours of his face.

≈

The next day she stood in the hallway outside the cafeteria after she'd finished her lunch, waiting for the sixth-period bell to ring. Farther down the rows of lockers she saw Michael in his usual dirty jeans and T-shirt, and Ciara in her swirling rayon skirt and cheap mall-boutique pendant. They stood leaning with their arms around each other's waists, whispering. With one hand he gently stroked her neck. Isobel watched with an emotion rising in her throat too complex to be called jealousy. It had nothing to do with wanting Michael, or wanting to be Ciara, simply wanting to be wanted, to have *that*, that slow stroke of possession and tenderness and sheer, sheer need.

"Hey, Isobel."

She turned. Before her stood Nicola, another member of the debate team, clad in a leather jacket and a velvet skirt and the de rigueur pair of combat boots. "Oh, hi, Nicola."

"Listen, I was just wondering, how long does practice last tonight?"

"Till five-thirty, as usual, I think."

"Okay, thanks. And hey . . . I've been meaning to tell you, I think your dramatic-reading thing of 'Lady Lazarus' is really cool. Very wild and profound. Enough to make someone, like, want to go out and kill themselves or something."

The sixth-period bell rang. As Nicola walked away, Isobel looked down at her own scuffed tennis shoes, then back at Nicola's laced-tight Doc Martens. The shining leather, the delicacy buried behind militance, struck her as oddly beautiful. She put the thought of Michael and Ciara out of her mind and waited for the cafeteria crowd to engulf her.

୶

"Some guy called for you," Isobel's mother told her later that night when she came home from dinner with Colette and her family.

Isobel stopped, stunned, in the laundry room. "Really?" she said. "What was his name?"

Her mother leaned against the kitchen counter, rubbing her eyes. "Michael, I think. He sounded kind of strange."

"Strange how?"

"Isobel, you know I turn into a pumpkin after eight in the evening. I don't do nuances after working with attorneys all day."

"Well, did he leave a message?"

"Not really. Said he'd talk to you at school eventually. Did you thank Mr. Eberly for driving you home?"

"*Yes.*" Isobel headed up the stairs. "Just because I'm not a social butterfly doesn't mean I lack social graces."

୶

The following Monday she sat with a new tome from Ms. J., Kate Millett this time, and her sandwich, absorbed and happy because she'd talked to her father on the phone the night before and he'd promised they'd get together for her birthday later in the week. She was jarred by the scrape of a chair pushed back. She looked up.

"Can't talk, Switzerland," Michael said as he lifted a heaping forkful of food into his mouth. "I've got to get back to internal suspension in ten minutes."

"And why are you in internal suspension, might I ask?"

"Didn't hand in the philosophy journal two times in a row."

"Not a good thing, Michael."

"Stop talking like a mother. You have no right to do that. You're four years younger than I am."

"Three as of this coming Thursday."

"What-fucking-ever, but don't lecture me, all right? I'm not in the mood."

"Where's Ciara?"

He made a vague swiping motion with his hand. "Some art-museum field trip."

They sat in silence for a few minutes.

"I did something really stupid this weekend," he said quietly, between bites of hamburger. "I got drunk and was about to take a whole bottle of pills, but a guy at the party I was at poured them down the drain."

"Good," Isobel said, after she'd regained her composure. "You should be glad."

"No, it's not," he said. "Not for me. You don't know how much I'd love that release from this loneliness."

She looked over at him with a strength and sternness she'd never felt she possessed. "Don't be stupid," she said. "You've got the team. And Ciara."

And me, she almost said.

"Oh, come on," he said. "The team doesn't give a shit about me. I'm just award points to them. And Ciara—she's a diversion. Nothing else."

"Michael," she said suddenly, "would you be sitting here talking to me and telling me all this if you were alone?"

He leaned back in his chair, closed his eyes.

"Yes," he said.

✧

On Isobel's fourteenth birthday, two days before her school hosted its own tournament, the team got together for a final practice. Buckley sent Isobel and Michael, who had finished his journal with the help of Ciara and gotten out of suspension, off to an empty math classroom to work on their pieces. Michael sat slumped in a desk and watched her perform her now infamous rendition of "Lady Lazurus."

"How was it?" she asked, after she'd dashed out to the water fountain for a drink.

"It was fine, as usual," he said. "You might want to vary your voice a little more, but other than that I see no problems."

"Do you want to run through your play cutting, then?"

He rested his head on his arms. "No," he said, voice muffled.

Isobel sat on the edge of a desk, feeling rather like Ms. J. She listened to him sigh, and then to silence.

"Do you want to talk?" she said softly.

He jerked back up, eyes wild. Isobel jumped. "Do I look like I do?" he said.

"I'm sorry, I'm sorry," he said. He shook his head violently, then let it fall down into his hands.

Isobel got up and stood behind him. She watched his neck quiver and thought of a time a few months ago when her parents had been fighting every night. Her own mother had been slumped over like this, cheek to the kitchen table, neck muscles tight, hair spread out over a place mat. Putting away plates, Isobel watched, amazed, as her father came up behind her mother and massaged all the tension out of her taut shoulders, offering her that much, putting aside the fire and the anger. Isobel wanted to do something like that now, bestow just a simple touch, a shard of kindness. She reached out, rubbed Michael's shoulder blades, shyly at first, then harder, but still gentle. She kept one eye on the door, in case anyone should barge in.

He lifted his head. His eyes were wet.

"Switzerland," he said, and turned toward her, and pulled her into his lap.

"I—I—I didn't mean—" She bit her lip and stammered, "I mean, I did sort of in the back of my mind, but I don't know, I didn't—"

He pressed his lips to the edge of her temple. She had never felt anyone's mouth on her like that before.

"I don't think we—" she said.

"You're afraid of me, aren't you?" he said.

"What about Ciara, what about—"

In answer, he ducked his face and pressed his cheek against her shoulder. She closed her eyes. "Switzerland, Switzerland, stop trying to play the neutral zone," he said.

"I'm not! I think you need help, I think you've got way too great a mind to keep screwing up like this."

He yanked away from her. "So you've joined the student intervention team as well as the debate team, I see," he said.

"No, no," she spluttered, "that's not it, I mean, yes, it is, I care about what happens to you, but I like you, too, I don't know how to explain it—"

With one hand he stroked back her hair.

"Don't talk," he said. "Just stay here."

She trembled. Closed her eyes. Felt his mouth move slowly down the curve of her neck.

"It's—it's four-thirty," she said. "I have to go. My dad's picking me up. We're going out for my birthday."

She stood up, wiped him off her.

"Happy birthday, then," he said blankly.

"Thanks," she said. "Will you do okay without a practice?"

"I've gone without them before."

She put on her jacket. He grabbed her hand.

"Don't leave," he said.

She glanced toward the open doorway.

"I have to," she said, and pried her fingers away from his. "I get in early. You can talk to me first thing tomorrow morning. Promise."

❦

That night her father took her out shopping and bought her a pair of Doc Martens like Nicola's—"A hundred dollars for something I could've gotten for ten at army surplus?" he said, but wrote the check anyway—and took her to dinner. Over steak platters he asked, "So school's going well? Ready to bring home some more debate-team trophies?"

Her father had always been the one her family said she favored—pale, quiet, with a dusted collection of books—but now he seemed so distracted that they couldn't connect, like he was trying too hard to be jovial. She simply nodded, rubbing the spot on her neck over and over.

❦

She sat in Ms. J.'s class the next morning, wearing her make-shift punk outfit—the new boots, a pair of fishnet stockings she'd pinched from her mother's underwear drawer, a black pleated skirt that all her relatives used to find "adorable," and her favorite ragged cardigan. The boots hurt her feet, but they were worth it somehow. She'd stood in the front lobby all morning before class, next to the real punks and the bench they always occupied under the loudspeaker that blared the radio club's bizarre mix of music. Nicola and her gang were there, complimenting Isobel profusely on her garb, but she hadn't seen Michael.

He'll show up at lunch, she thought, and then we'll get up and go sit in a stairwell and have an earnest conversation and I'll rest my hand against his cheek and tell him he must live, he must stop this dumb charade, and then who knows what'll happen, maybe we'll go off to Europe like Ms. J., sleep in empty churches in the rain with only a quilt to cover us and a loaf of hard bread we'll break open with our hands and we'll talk of Kant and Heidegger . . .

"Isobel," Ms. J. said, "for the third time, sweetheart, what's the concept of the collective unconscious?"

⌇

When the team met that night to set up for the tournament on Saturday, Michael wasn't there, and Buckley had a tight, nervous expression on his face. "Mike damn well better be there tomorrow," he said. "He and Isobel are the ones who are going to win it for us." The punks for once looked concerned, and didn't even notice that he'd been dismissive of them.

Isobel's job was to go around to every classroom that would be used for the tournament, wash each blackboard, and write, WELCOME TO THE ANDREWS HIGH DEBATE INVITATIONAL. She was in the process of writing when she heard a message over the intercom for Buckley to take a phone call in the office.

While Isobel was filling up her bucket of water in the ladies' room, Nicola came in and found her. "He wants us to meet back in the library," she said.

Isobel followed her there and sat on top of a table with her. Buckley paced back and forth until everyone had congregated. "I've got some bad news," he said. "Michael Culley won't be competing with us tomorrow. His mother just called; he's in the hospital."

"What's wrong with him?" Nicola asked. "He seemed fine yesterday."

"They're running tests," Buckley said. "No one's really sure."

Kevin, one of the guys with a mop of unruly black hair and baggy pants, poked Isobel in the back. "What a fucking liar," he said. "You know as cracked as he is, he's gotta be in psychiatric."

Isobel put up her hand. "May I be excused for a moment?"

Buckley nodded. Not wanting to look too panicked, she strode quickly out of the library and then broke into a run. She raced to the nearest restroom, barreled through the door, and crouched on the floor near the radiator. Gasping, she jammed her knuckles in her mouth and thought: I am Switzerland, neutral territory, a little pedant, a girl in a dotted dress breathing nice clean air and never taking sides, a girl who's the daughter of a woman with hair the color of fire who can't burn with her own flame. And she wept.

꿍

When she got home that night, she found her mother standing in the middle of the kitchen with a gigantic box. "Isobel," her mother shrieked, "I got my new table! Remember the one you helped me pick out? Isn't it cool?"

"Prodigious," Isobel muttered. Before her mother could say more, Isobel went upstairs and closed the door to her room. In the growing darkness, she crouched on her bed and, shivering, took off her boots. She had blisters on her heels, warm with ooze. She winced as she tore off her stockings and balled them up. She unbuttoned her skirt and sat there, waiting to become.

꿍

She never spoke to Michael after that. Nicola, whose gothic garb hid a thoughtful benevolence, bought a card for the team to sign while he was in the hospital, and Isobel dutifully wrote, "Get well soon—Isobel," in her neat, tiny print, as if he would be home and fine in a week. She didn't tell anyone about what had happened on her birthday—not her mother or even Colette.

He came back to school a month later, and they saw each other in the halls occasionally but quickly averted their gazes. He had quit the debate team.

Later on, she would refer to the incident with Michael in the clipped, nostalgic tones of one who realizes the immaturity of her youthful angst yet still takes a perverse delight in recounting them. She would glimpse him out of the corner of her eye one afternoon after school in a grocery-store parking lot, while picking up milk and bread for her mother. The sun would glint on her newly cut hair. She'd be wearing a gauze skirt that rustled against her legs in the spring breeze; the plastic shopping bag swung in her hand. It was right after she had gotten her college acceptance letter. She felt invincible. She wouldn't even realize it was him until she'd turned the corner.

꿍

For most of her high school career, however, Isobel threw herself back into studying and worshiping Ms. J.

One day, after they had become close, Ms. J. invited Isobel over for dinner. She lived downtown, in a run-down area that most people in Staplin viewed with a perfunctory sense of paranoia, but which in reality consisted of plain but pleasant, shady streets lined with semidetached houses in various stages of renovation by the young couples who lived there. Isobel felt terribly grown-up as her mother dropped her off in front of Ms. J.'s building. "Now be careful, mind your manners, and don't wait outside for me," her mother said. "Shall I walk you up?"

"No, that's okay," Isobel said. Much as she adored her bright, garrulous mother, and much as she put her at ease, Isobel didn't want her going upstairs with her, handing her over to Ms. J., explaining things to her mentor in that calm, vaguely southern voice of hers, spoiling the private, adult moment by being her chirpy, quick-tongued self.

"All right," her mother said with a shrug. "I'll be back at ten."

Isobel ran out of the car and up the front walk, tripping a little in the long skirt her grandma had bought for her birthday, reluctantly, at Isobel's insistence ("Sweetie, why do you want to look like a gypsy?"), not caring even though she knew her mother was watching in amusement. Isobel had selected her outfit carefully that afternoon, choosing the most flowing, avant-garde elements she could find in honor of the evening with Ms. J.: a good rayon blouse that she used to wear to church, a silver bauble on a leather cord that she had gotten at the mall with Colette (even though it looked suspiciously Ciara McClellan–like), an old denim jacket a bit too tight in the elbows, a woolly black hat her father had given her, and of course her boots. The pieces weren't quite right together, she knew (*Stop grinning, Mom!*), but it was the best she could do.

She opened the front door and made her way up the grimy carpeted stairs to Ms. J.'s third-floor apartment. Ms. J. opened her door, wearing a pair of baggy red paisley silk pants and a big, fuzzy red sweater. She wore her hair swept on top of her head, and a pair of red glass earrings. Her face shone.

"Hey, Isobel," she said, husky-voiced, and kissed her on the cheek. "How are you doing?"

"Great, thanks," Isobel said. There, in Ms. J.'s tiny, radiant living room, the words didn't feel like a lie.

She looked around. The walls were covered in framed posters of festivals and museums from so many different European capitals it made Isobel's head spin. The furnishings were simple yet elegant: a couch draped in earth-toned tapestry, an overstuffed chair covered in olive velvet—clearly a lovingly restored thrift-shop find—a tiny table graced with a pot of herbs, and a huge, soft flokati rug. There was a large, jarringly high-tech stereo, but no TV, Isobel noticed with delight.

"Your apartment," Isobel said. "It's . . . *wow.*"

Ms. J. laughed. "It's dirty," she said. "Let's see if my pasta sauce is done yet."

Ms. J.'s minuscule kitchen was so small they could barely stand in it together. Isobel leaned against the counter and watched Ms. J. stir the tomato and basil, her wrist turning around and around. Isobel felt ridiculously happy.

"So how's the debating going?" Ms. J. asked.

"I'm thinking of quitting," Isobel said.

"Really?" Ms. J. reached over to adjust the temperature. "Isn't it enjoyable anymore?"

"Why do you ask?"

"Well, that's what's important, isn't it?"

"Yeah. Yeah, I guess so."

"You don't sound too convinced."

"I just . . . expected you to say what everyone else would say."

"Which is?"

"'Oh, but you're so talented at it, you're such a poised young woman, and it would look good on your college applications, et cetera, et cetera, et cetera—'"

"To hell with your college applications," Ms. J. said. "Your life is not meant to be lived so that you can write it down on a piece of paper."

"Then could you please run our high school?" Isobel asked.

Ms. J. grinned. "My dear," she said, "keep right on dreaming. They would have me fired before they let that happen."

She reached up into the cupboard for two large terra-cotta bowls. "So the debate team isn't working for you right now, huh?"

Isobel shook her head.

"Well, if you don't want to get into the deep dark details, I won't make you go there. But if you ever want to talk about it . . ."

Isobel's stomach clenched in panic. She wanted to talk about it, wanted to sit down with Ms. J. over the linguine and tell her all the deep, dark details about the goth crowd and Michael Culley, but the part of her entranced with the shining, beautiful world of the fluorescent galley kitchen said, *No. Don't burden her. Don't shatter this.*

"So," Ms. J. said, "are you ready for some pasta?"

They sat down at Ms. J.'s battered wooden table. She turned off the glaring overhead light and lit candles, and they sat there and ate in the flickering, pastel-tinged glow. Ms. J. didn't need the sort of nervously cheerful interrogation other adults seemed to fall back on when talking to Isobel. Instead there was a comfortable silence, punctuated only by the random selections of music on Ms. J.'s CD player—a string quartet, a woman folksinger, some throaty blues.

After lemon poppyseed cake for dessert ("I spent *all* day in the kitchen baking it!" Ms. J. said in her best imitation of a TV-commercial actress), Isobel asked Ms. J. if she could see her photographs of Europe. "Sure," she said, "but don't expect any Kodak moments, okay?"

She went into her bedroom to search through her closet for the albums. Isobel heard the sound of falling shoe boxes, and Ms. J. swearing, and laughed.

"Finally," Ms. J. said, coming back with two large albums covered in a demure floral print. "I keep these way in the back of my top shelf."

"Don't you like to look at them?"

"Well, sometimes, but I haven't in a while," she said. "After I got home, I really needed time to take stock of the experience and what it meant. I don't think I'll ever totally fathom that."

"Is it . . . is it okay?" Isobel asked. "I mean, will it bother you to look at them?"

"Oh, no, not at all," she said. She touched Isobel's shoulder. "But thanks for asking."

Ms. J. sat down beside her and flipped open the first album. "These aren't in any chronological or geographical order," she said.

"So you've always been nonlinear?"

She laughed. "You . . . you could say that. I was so exhausted from the trip that I just threw them in here and there."

Isobel paged through a few sheets full of photographs that looked like dimmer versions of postcard images: Big Ben, the Eiffel Tower.

"The major sights," Ms. J. said. "After a certain point, you learn to just put down the camera and trust that your memory will suffice. It's very difficult to experience another country with your eye behind a lens. 'Never mind the economic devastation of postcommunist Eastern Europe, isn't that architecture stunning? Time for a photo op . . .'"

Isobel giggled.

"What's this one right here?" she asked.

She pointed to a photograph of an even thinner Ms. J., her face drawn and skeletal, her eyes wide and stark with pain. She wore a magenta fleece pullover, its bright color making her dark hair—pulled back to reveal her thin neck—look even darker. She stood on what appeared to be a lush green plain, with a tall, reddish-haired man whose eyes gleamed with hurt and tenderness, his mouth a surprised scowl. His arm was draped around her shoulder, holding her close to him in what appeared to be a pose of intimacy but what Isobel sensed was a captured moment of bound, sad confusion. Ms. J.'s lipstick looked overly purplish—or was it a bruise on her lip?

Behind them the sky loomed, pale, devouring, gray.

"Where was this?" Isobel asked. "Who were you with?"

Ms. J. ran her thumb over the page's glossy sheen.

"That was in Iceland," she said, with a certainty in her voice she hadn't had when naming her other photos of obscure destinations. "With Brad."

"Was he—"

"He was my fiancé," she said. "We traveled together for three months."

"Was?" Isobel asked.

"Not anymore," she said. "We broke up in Iceland, actually."

"I'm sorry."

"Don't be," she said. "It had to end."

"Wasn't that hard? Leaving him and going off alone in a foreign country?"

"Sure it was," she said. "I look back at that time, and . . . well, it almost makes my body hurt, to think about how hard it was. Do you ever feel like that, remembering something?"

Dumbly, Isobel nodded. She watched as Ms. J.'s hand, poised to turn the page, shook. There in that glowing sphere of candles and jazz, Isobel reached across the table and put her hand over Ms. J.'s to steady it.

"We . . . we don't have to talk about this anymore," Isobel said, "if you don't want to."

Ms. J. squeezed Isobel's fingers tightly, as if to thank her, then let go. "You're so sweet," she said. "And I think you should know what happened. So you can protect yourself, so you'll remember to trust your feelings, no matter what bullshit people tell you. Promise me you'll do that?"

Again Isobel nodded. She watched as her mentor sat up straight, closed the photo album with a snap, and rested her arms on its cover. Ms. J. took a deep breath, looked intently into Isobel's face, and began.

Chapter Nine

Sylvia's Story

In order to understand my story, any woman's story, no matter what its resemblance is to mine, you have to go beyond the easy ideologies, the ignorant media sound-bite simplifications. I don't say this because I think you aren't capable of doing that; I know you are. I say this because you need to understand that there will be times when you think you hold the answers, you know where you're going and where you've been. Like I thought I did, with my women's studies degree from an experimental college, my self-defense courses, my internships on crisis hotlines, my academic feminism assigned a grade-point average, remarkably like that which you're probably studying.

I met Brad my sophomore year of college. He was very politically involved in the women's group at our school. Had he been anyone else, I would have viewed him as suspect, a mere antagonist, but because he was Brad—committed, charismatic—we hit it off instantly. We were at a stage in our lives when everything was gospel, yet everything was malleable. Add to that the mystique of college life as an era of never-again-found connections, the time to find a soul mate, and you had one lethal prescription.

Senior year, we got engaged. We graduated in May; he had a job working for the state welfare department, and I had a teaching position lined up—I did a secondary-education major as backup, because, hello, this was Staplin, no one was going to take a women's studies degree seriously. We had three months before we had to enter the real world, so we decided to do what all students do to escape it: backpack through Europe for a summer.

The first few weeks were glorious, giddy, full of heightened intimacy. Oh, we'd shared an apartment on campus before, but this was different. This was waking up to a maid singing in Italian as she cleaned, this was picnicking with bread and cheese along a riverbank in France. We were in love. Actually allowed ourselves to say the words, hand in hand on those cobblestone streets, free from analysis.

Once we hit the halfway mark, though, tensions surfaced. Traveling will do this to you—the downside of that heightened intimacy—so I brushed off his outbursts as a temper frayed from six weeks on the road. After all, he was my darling, my aware one who went to the marches with me, and wasn't I a little mercurial myself sometimes? Even when he screamed at me for walking alone down the street to a café we'd been to the day before, I blocked the correlations, that slippery slope from possessiveness to abuse. I couldn't rationalize his fury on the grounds of concern for my safety, so I made excuses. *We're in love*, I said.

Isobel, love is a powerful element, but it is not enough.

At the end of the trip, on our cheap flight home from Denmark, we decided to take a three-day stopover in Iceland. We were doing

some last-minute packing that morning at our hostel in Copenhagen, cramming things into each other's backpack, only he was
trying to be meticulous about it, folding his clothes with almost
neurotic precision. "Hey, come on," I said lightly, "we'll never
make it to the airport if you keep up like that." I took one of his
shirts, creased it sloppily, and fit it in the bag the fastest way I
could, never mind the wrinkles.

He lost it. "Do you mean to tell me that you just fucking threw
that in there?" he yelled.

"Yes," I said. "I didn't think it was such a big deal. I mean, we
don't have much time—"

I didn't get to finish the sentence, because he hauled off and
punched me in the mouth.

I don't think any training you've had in the field of domestic violence will prepare you for something like that. No calm, statisti-
cal constellation of figures and research and psychological data
can. Here you are, you reel, you sting, your mouth implodes, you
taste blood, you feel like you *are* blood, and there this creature
stands before you, this man you have loved and listened to and
trusted, and he spins out of control, he is a mutation of himself,
you wonder why you haven't seen the connections, you don't want
to see them, and so you hold your hand to your ruptured lip,
bruised and purple, and sink to the floor.

Of course he got down beside me, and kissed me over and over
again, and cried, and said he was sorry, and I wept, and said I was,
too, even though I had nothing to apologize for, and on and on it
went, that endless textbook cycle, only this time it was me, and him.

We flew to Iceland: gathered up our things and got on the plane,
just like that. We didn't talk the entire flight. The silence between
us was soft, raw. I read the in-flight magazine. Kept it over my face
the whole time so no one would see my mouth. *Atlantica*, it was
called. Three hours I spent, turning its pages. The people around

me must've thought I had a real passion for articles on the Nordic fishing industry. During the descent, Brad put his hand on top of mine.

We landed at Keflavík in a light mist. I looked out the window at the flat, bright ground and thought: I've flown to the moon. We shuffled down the aisle with our backpacks, and into the small, light-filled airport. My lip throbbed. Brad reached out an arm to steady me as we lined up at passport control. I wanted to absorb all of it, the wave of voices surrounding me, the signs on the wall, but I was stuck fast to the pain. The immigration officer barely glanced at my passport. "Are you an American citizen?" he asked. I ducked my head into the high collar of my fleece pullover and nodded.

We took a bus into the city, and I grabbed a seat by the window. The landscape outside looked like I felt: ragged, desolate. Miles and miles of green. Dark ocean water that churned along the jagged coast. The sky more huge than desire.

Less than an hour later, we saw the Reykjavík harbor. Little houses, happy colors. I closed my eyes. I didn't want to see joy, didn't want to see primary hues covering up dismal concrete; I wanted to sleep and wake up uncomplicated and in love. We were staying at a hotel on the outskirts of town. The bus let us off in the parking lot. Brad took my hand, and I let him lead me across the asphalt, my head bowed. I couldn't look at anything. I felt like a disconnected mess of nerve and tissue, all purplish-red, split open, setting off storms. We took the elevator up to our room, which was dark blue and comforting in its sterile, familiar arrangement of chair, desk, bureau, bed, television. I heaved my backpack onto the floor and sank down into the mattress. "I'm going to bed," I said.

"It's only five-thirty, Sylvia," he said softly. "Don't you want to get something to eat?"

I did, but I couldn't bear the thought of walking into the hotel restaurant together, of sitting silently with my hand over my face and pretending to be in vacation bliss; or, even worse, ordering food and sitting cross-legged on the blue duvet, eating alone with him in that tiny room. I shook my head.

"I think I'll go down and see what they have," he said. "You're sure you won't get hungry?"

"If I do, I'll just call room service," I said, more sharply than I meant to.

"Okay," he said. He stood over me, bent until his hands were on my shoulders, and kissed the top of my head. I was paralyzed, delirious with the promise of gentle touch. He just had a little outburst, I thought. We'll be fine when we get home.

After he left, I sat there on the bed in shock. All day I had tried not to think about what had happened; he had been too close, too warm, all tentative, repentant flesh. Now, in the bland blue room by myself, gravity came to me in the guise of four walls. I fought it. I plucked a brochure off the nightstand. "Hótel Loftleiðir," it said. On the back, it bore a photograph, obviously staged, of a newly married couple in a room just like mine, the bride laughing, still in her gown, her veil thrown back from her face in faked ecstasy as she perched on the chair of the seated, suited groom. I let the glossy scrap fall onto the carpet. I put my head in my hands and started to cry. That was the worst part of it, the assault of the possible.

After that, I got up and went into the bathroom and put on my nightgown and brushed my hair. I looked in the mirror and saw a twenty-two-year-old woman with red eyes, a swollen face, a mouth like a scream. *You're just exhausted*, I told myself. *When you wake up tomorrow, you'll look normal again.* I went back into the room and made myself some herbal tea with the hot pot. It was the same tea you find at home, in little packets, and after three months in Europe, that calmed me. I crawled into bed and propped up on pillows and drank it out of a plastic cup. It was hard, drinking out of only one side of my mouth, but the mildly flavored heat soothed me. I reached over and turned on the radio. They were playing jazz, sparse and mellow, sung by a girl with a flinty yet angelic voice, and the trills and long vowels of Icelandic were like a safe hand stroking my hair. It was the state station. Útvarp Reykjavík. I still remember that. The foreign words were like a secret code, as if already I knew that this country would be my way out.

I fell asleep not long after that. It was deep, escapist sleep, thick and heavy. When I woke again, Brad sat on the edge of the bed. The radio was still on, Bob Dylan this time. My cup with its limp tea bag stood by the lamp. The room had a golden shimmer. "What time is it?" I asked.

"Eleven," he said. His face shone with an innocent gleam. "You should see the city, Sylvia. It's perfect. Like something out of a dream."

I yawned. "Where did you go?" I asked.

"I went for a walk after dinner," he said. "It's amazing, so safe and clean. There are bookshops on every corner, and not only is it still completely bright out, but my God, the light, it's so soft, and then—and then to come back and find you here. I'm so lucky. I take it for granted, how lucky I am."

I watched him, joyful and luminous, perched on the mattress, and I felt scooped out, every full place in me hollowed with dull longing. This man, I told myself, is not the one who hit you. But he was.

"Come out and see it with me," he said.

"Brad," I said feverishly. "We have to get up early in the morning."

I wanted to say, *We have to talk about this. We have to think about this. Look at my face. Where are we going?*

"I guess you're right," he said, with a thin, lovely smile of denial, and crawled into bed next to me. He left a little space between us. A peace offering.

The next day, we took a tour of the south of Iceland. The Golden Circle, it was called, even though there was nothing golden about it. I remember eating breakfast downstairs with him, my hair hanging over one side of my face, the bruise made up as best as I could, the collar of my pullover zipped up again, all those strategic tricks. It was the best breakfast I've ever had in my life. Sour milk and granola and brown sugar. I had three bowls. I tried not to look at him. "You should try the yogurty stuff," he said. "They call it *skyr.*" He could be really pedantic sometimes. I wanted to kick him under the table. I wanted to tell him I would stay with him the rest of my life.

The tour bus was a huge, drowsiness-inducing monster, with tinted windows and dozens of English and German tourists trying to experience a country in eight hours, just like we were. We drove along the Ring Road. Another pale, overcast day. The world was all mountain and sky. "What's that one?" I said to Brad.

"Mount Esja," he said. "I wish we had time to climb it."

My body felt wrung out. Our first stop was a greenhouse, which was really an excuse to make us walk through a gift shop. I was still hungry from skipping dinner the night before. Brad bought me an ice cream. I felt like I was on a long-awaited first date gone wrong. The ice cream was terrific. My mouth went numb.

After that we went to Gullfoss, a gigantic waterfall. First they took us through a little museum, a room actually, with information on the walls. It was all in Icelandic, so we couldn't read it, but I remember the guide telling us that the museum was a memorial to a woman named Sigríður who had walked all the way to Reykjavík at the turn of the century to protest the destruction of the falls. She even threatened to throw herself in. And they'd been saved. I felt a strange affinity with her when I heard that. At that point, my mind was beginning to grasp the concept of desperate measures.

We went outside and climbed up the hill to stand on a ledge by the waterfall. It was cold, standing so close, but I wanted to feel the whipping air, the spray of droplets. I thought of Sigríður. How she had been willing to fling herself into the rolling foam, to let her body churn in the freezing current, all for the salvation of something so dear. Something that was now a photo opportunity.

As for me? I was a coward. I wanted back on the tour bus. I wanted warmth and security. Around lunchtime, we drove to the Hótel Geysir. They wouldn't let us see the geysers and hot springs until we'd had a twenty-dollar lunch. We ate in a huge dining room with wooden tables set for six, like a high school cafeteria. Under different circumstances, I would have liked the communal aspects of passing a tureen of soup, offering strangers the platter of salmon, joining in multilingual chatter, but at the time I felt too exposed. Finally a woman next to me, from Canada, asked the question. "I don't mean to be rude, but what happened to your lip?" she asked.

I looked at Brad, smiled as widely as I could. "Oh, *that*," I said, with a broken laugh. "I slipped when we were climbing Mount Esja yesterday."

That's how easy it was to lie. For myself, yes, and my own shaken sense of dignity, but also for him. For the gleaming myth of the happy, adventurous couple, the strong, sweet, enlightened boyfriend who never, ever smashes his fist into his beloved in a hostel in Copenhagen.

For the first time, I was truly afraid.

We went back outside, having handed over two thousand-krónur notes, and waited for Strokkur, the smaller geyser. The real one, the first Geysir, stopped working awhile back, because tourists had tried to pour rocks in it to make it explode. There we were, prowling around the rock, waiting for the overpriced spectacle, impatient and clutching our cameras, and as soon as we turned our heads and swore it wasn't going to do it, *bang!* there it went, a fierce, hot spray so huge and sudden it made us wonder how a bigger one could have ever existed. I watched Brad circle a hot spring, and thought, Is my entire life going to be like this?

In the afternoon, we stopped at a service station in the shadow of a volcanic peak. Brad bought Diet Pepsi and Toblerone. We ate the candy bar as the bus wound through Þingvellir, the national park, passing the hunks of chocolate back and forth, laughing a little. Our hands touched. The tour guide rambled about the North Atlantic rift. I thought about the words *fault line.* Brad stroked my hair back from my face.

They let us off the bus, and we walked up a hill until we reached the plain. It was craggy and green. Vast. Silent. A tiny white church stood, sadly perfect, in the distance. At the site of the world's first democratic parliament, we got a fellow daytripper to take our picture, and forced a smiling pose that became the photograph you later saw.

We went out for dinner that evening, at a restaurant off the main square downtown. The drapes and table linens were heavy. On the walls hung brass-framed oil portraits of famous Icelanders. We had lobster, with crème brûlée for dessert. A splurge. We didn't say much. I felt like I was bolted down. My breath was so tight. We were supposed to fly back to America the next afternoon. I didn't know what to do.

I couldn't sleep that night, even though I was tired from the tour. Light kept poking its way through the curtains, no matter how tightly I closed my eyes. I tossed. Three years, I thought. Are you going to throw away three years, or are you going to let this slide?

At two in the morning, I got up and paced around the room in my nightgown. I took out my return ticket and stared at its obtuse codes and markings, as if they held some clue. I counted the hours until I would be back in Keflavík, in that gleaming airport, flying toward a future spattered with love-words and brutal tantrums and a life uncertain. I watched him sleep. The ease of his breathing tormented me.

I decided to go for a walk. I put on jeans and a light sweater and took my wallet and room key. I took the elevator downstairs, feeling strangely devious, and walked out the front door. Outside the sky was deep with dusk. A light wind whipped my hair. Up on the hill, above the water tanks, the silver dome of a revolving restaurant gleamed in its slow, steady turn. Without thinking, I climbed. My feet skidded a few times in the steep earth, and I was out of breath by the time I reached the top. But I could see the whole city, its late-summer stillness, the lights from the harbor. My head swirled, full of broken remnants of the past two days: Sigríður's waterfall, Útvarp Reykjavík, *Atlantica*, a cup of tea, a blue duvet cover, his hand slamming into my mouth, his fingers stroking my hair. It was there, among the pale wildflowers, that I realized I had to leave.

I walked down the hill and back into the hotel, went upstairs and entered the room as quietly as I could. I took some stationery out of the desk and wrote him a five-page letter, which I put in an envelope. I took off my engagement ring, put that in, too. I felt like a melodramatic sleepwalker, dislocated from my own body. I felt torn up but relieved.

I put the letter on the desk and went back to bed, still in my clothes. I lay on top of the duvet, on my stomach, as far away from him as I could, with my face on my arms, and sobbed. Three hours later, I woke again, panicked that he had gotten up before me. I took a shower. I dressed carefully, in my one nice pair of slacks and a silk blouse. I put on lipstick. I carried out each motion as if it were the one thing that would keep me from breaking. I went downstairs to breakfast. I sat by the window and ate *skyr* and granola and waited. I told myself I had just saved my life.

He came down half an hour later. His hair was rumpled. I could tell he had been crying. "You'll change your mind," he said. "I know it's been a rough week, but we'll talk about this when we get home, and—"

"No," I said.

He sat down across from me, leaned his face in close to mine. "You *will*," he said.

We took the bus to Keflavík that afternoon in silence. When we checked in at the airport, we found that we'd been assigned seats apart from each other on the plane. His was directly in front of mine. I stared at the back of his head for almost six hours. He wrote me desperate notes, passed them to me through the crack between the seats. *I'll do anything,* one said.

It's not what you aren't doing, I wrote back. *It's what you did.*

After dinner came another: *I love you.*

I love you, too, but love doesn't excuse anything, I wrote.

And it didn't. Even after the arguments, the terse phone calls, tears in the customs line, a restraining order. In the end, I was a solitary traveler, picking her way across a crowded airport, weighed down by her backpack, willing to trade the pain of a slap for the pain of loss. Willing to go it alone.

Chapter Ten

Staplin, Pennsylvania

The rest of Isobel's high school life had been a blur. She walked the halls, marked off hours of regimented time: psychology, then math, then English, then history, then lunch, then Latin, then study hall, then electives, then back home again. In health class, she endured the annual sex-ed filmstrip, the one that made the boys out to be hard-edged with slimy intentions, immature yet cruelly calculating, their bodies tight with lust and their minds full of come-on gimmicks, the clichéd words of obligation slithering out of their mouths: "If you loved me, you would . . ."

Isobel paid the grim narrator no attention. She knew she didn't need to listen to his ominous words. She didn't have shining hair and rounded fingernails painted demure colors; she didn't wear tasteful floral skirts, not like the girls who sat behind her. They gleamed like streetlamps, with their perky lipstick and careless-appearing careful joy, most likely to succeed at masking their inner lives. While changing after gym, she had heard them by the next row of lockers, whispering about sneaking out to fuck their boyfriends late at night. Isobel had pulled on her clothes quickly, thinking: I am too erudite, too bland, too shy, too everything.

So she pretended she didn't care. Pretended she was above it all. She looked at the world with a dislocated gaze, grateful but slightly contemptuous. She sat in class and stared over the heads of the boys in front of her. The blackboard was all she knew. It yawned before her, perpetually washed clean. She banished the word *desire* from her vocabulary; if she spoke it, she was sure it would taste like dirt.

❧

During her sophomore year, her father decided to move to California with the woman he'd had the affair with. He sent Isobel and her mother strangely formal Christmas cards signed "Ben and Denise," and kept promising to mail Isobel a plane ticket to come visit, but never did. The relationship between Isobel and her father was like a small stone dropped in deep, murky water; it plopped to the bottom, sent slow ripples to the surface, and then floated away.

By her junior year, Isobel had taken every upper-level course at Andrews. She petitioned numerous times for permission to do independent work or take classes at the local community college—anything to calm her inertia, her restlessness. Even with Ms. J.'s glowing recommendations, she was refused. The school told her that, while she was one of its most "gifted" (that word again) students in recent history, they could not amend policy for only one student. One day in October, she came downstairs in her pajamas, blank-faced, eyes glazed, and muttered, "I don't know why I even bother to show up."

Her mother, still in her pajamas as well, even though she was running late for work, sat at the "classy" kitchen table, its top now marred by water rings and gouges. She set down her cup of black coffee, for her the equivalent of breakfast. Her initial bustling efficiency had wound down to a droll, good-natured sluggishness, and Isobel liked her better that way; she seemed more real, cut to the bone, a reminder of what was essential. "If you hate it that much," she said slowly, deliberately, "then don't go."

Isobel reached over to turn off the electric coffeepot, which her mother had left on. "Don't tempt me, Mom," she said. "You know I can't do that. There are laws that regulate how good little schoolchildren must conform."

"No, I'm serious," her mother said. "Go to college a year early. There are programs that allow you to do it. A woman I work with was telling me about it at lunch the other day, how her kid took her senior year of high school at the same time as her first year of college. It wasn't that hard to do, and this girl was nowhere near the superstar you are." She grinned. "Of course, I'm a bit biased."

"I wonder why." Isobel opened the refrigerator and peered into it. "You do realize there's almost nothing in here?"

"I'll stop on my way home, promise." Her mother stretched, stood up from the table. "So what do you think of the early-admission idea? Wouldn't that be a neat trick?"

"It would be unbelievable," Isobel said. "But don't forget, there's this little thing that's pretty essential in terms of getting through college, and it's called money."

"I know," her mother said, "I know. Let me take care of that. You just do the research, make the phone calls, get the applications—"

"Bribe Andrews so they actually let me get somewhere, jump through all those hoops," Isobel said, putting a piece of bread in the toaster. "No problem. It'll give me something to do in study hall."

Her mother passed her on her way upstairs, and Isobel stopped her to give her a hug. "You rock my world, Mom," she said.

Isobel's mother patted her back. "What higher praise could I ask for?" she said. "My baby. You're almost taller than I am now, you know it?"

"The academic Amazon," Isobel said as they parted and her toast popped up. "Don't remind me." At sixteen, she was almost six feet tall but still gangly, and hated her height.

"Oops, sorry. I'll try not to." Her mother caught a glimpse of the time on the microwave clock and dashed for the landing. "Jesus, Mary, and Leopold, the powers that be at the law offices of Steinberg and Connell are gonna kill me . . ."

"Don't trip," Isobel called after her, as she got out a pitcher of orange juice.

A few minutes later, she heard her mother yell down, "Oh darling daughter, could I possibly borrow your blue silk blouse?"

Isobel yelled back, "Oh Mummy dearest, of course, but only under the stipulation that it be worn just to work, and not for that *date* you have later tonight."

"You drive a hard bargain," her mother said, "but all right."

Isobel smiled to herself, buttering her toast, as the running shower eclipsed her mother's words. The business about the blouse had been mainly teasing—especially since the days of the nonexistent plane tickets, her feelings toward her father had been less than reverent, and she wanted desperately for her mother to be happy—but there was a part of her that tensed, waiting for something wild or horrible to happen during her mother's foray back into romance. "Don't give me any steamy details," she always said to her mother, knowing her warnings weren't necessary, yet still driven to dole them out. All the while, underneath her jokey front, the mean, biting truth, the ruthless rushing current, hissed: *Don't go having any glowing second adolescence.*

༤

"You aren't really going away to college now, are you?" Colette asked. They sat on the floor of Isobel's room one Saturday, school catalogues spread out around them.

"If I can get a scholarship," Isobel said.

"You don't want to stay here? It's only another year, and besides, do you know how boring it would be without you?"

"It'd still be the two of us against the world. I'd keep in touch."

"You'd better."

The phone rang. "I'll get it!" Isobel's mother yelled from below.

"It's probably her new boyfriend," Isobel said.

"Blecch." Colette made a face.

"Yeah, that's what I said. He's coming over for dinner tonight after you leave. My first meeting with the mystery man."

"How weird," Colette said. "Especially the thought of them—you know, having sex."

"Don't even go there." Isobel leafed through one catalogue. "Hmm, you can design your own major at this place. I ought to visit it."

"That's what I love about us," Colette said. "We aren't going to stop for anybody. We don't waste our time on that romance junk. We're gonna be ninety years old and in our rocking chairs out on the front porch, and you'll be on your third PhD, and I'll be griping"—she mimicked a quivering, elderly voice—"'Weeeell, Isobel, I just don't know whether to go for my sixth master's degree or spring for the doctorate,' and you'll have no teeth and be missing one eye and you'll say—"

"Go for the doctorate. Definitely." Isobel checked her watch. "Hey, what time is your dad supposed to pick you up?"

"Four o'clock."

"Let's go downstairs and look out for him, then."

In the kitchen, they found Isobel's mother in an apron, scurrying about with preparations for a pot roast.

"Wow, we just walked into a 1950s sitcom," Colette said.

"Who are you, and what have you done with my mother?" Isobel demanded.

"She's been abducted to Planet Date. Could you hunt for the good tablecloth?" her mother said, wiping a hand across her forehead. "I can't find it anywhere."

"Let me see Colette off first, okay?"

"Sure. Sorry you couldn't stay this time, Colette," Isobel's mother said as she opened the oven door and peered inside. "Ugh. It's scary in there."

"There's my ride," Colette said. "Good luck with your dinner, Ms. Sivulka."

"Thanks. And please, for the nine millionth time, call me Jana."

Colette gave Isobel a delicate hug. "Don't you dare pick a college the whole way across the country," she said.

"She'd better not," Isobel's mother said.

Isobel waved goodbye to Colette, then went into the dining room and opened the drawer to the china cupboard. "The tablecloth's in here, where it always is!" she yelled, spreading the lace fabric over the table with an irritated snap.

"You're a lifesaver." Her mother looked over at Isobel's messy hair and jeans. "Aren't you going to put on something nicer? I'm taking a shower and dressing up as soon as this roast is taken care of."

"Mom, I don't see why you have to turn perfectionist all of a sudden," Isobel said. "You might as well show this guy what we're really like."

"He's not some *guy*; his name is Nick. Could you at least comb your hair?"

"Oh, I suppose," Isobel said with an exaggerated sigh as she escaped up the stairs. "Just don't expect me to be charming, all right?"

✍

The doorbell rang at six. Isobel quickly ran a brush through her hair, stuck out her tongue at the mirror, and went downstairs barefoot.

"Isobel, this is Nick Lewis," her mother, now in a dress and heels and wearing her hair up, said. "Nick, this is Isobel, my . . . err, rather informal fifteen-year-old daughter."

"Almost sixteen," Isobel corrected. She thrust out her hand to the tall, solidly built man with a dark beard who stood before her. "And he's rather informal himself."

She gestured toward Nick's chamois shirt, corduroy pants, and old loafers. Her mother shot her a dirty look. Nick smiled.

"Actually, Jana," he said as they entered the now candlelit dining room, "I wasn't expecting this to be such a dramatic affair."

Her mother didn't respond. "Care for some salad?" she said.

Nick said little during the first course. Isobel munched her pine nuts and arugula loudly, while her mother chattered along brightly about nothing. "You're awfully pensive, Nick," she said.

"Just taking in the scene," he said, stroking his beard.

"Rather like Isobel," her mother said. "Ever since she was little, she's been the silent observer."

"Not a bad position to take," Nick said. "Although I find that quietness can earn you a reputation for being cold or snobby, when really you're just looking out for yourself."

Isobel stabbed a piece of gorgonzola cheese with her fork and thought, Score one for Nick.

Her mother stood. "Excuse me," she said. "Let me run to the powder room, and then I'll check on this roast."

Isobel and Nick sat in silence after she left. They heard the hall toilet flush. Nick leaned over to her and whispered, "Is this as awkward for you as it is for me?"

Isobel laughed. "We don't eat like this," she said. "Ever."

"I figured you didn't."

"Heck, we didn't even have a real table for a while. Could I have some of that raspberry vinaigrette?" she asked. He handed her the bottle. "Thanks for being honest."

"What?"

"You know. For not trying to make some stiff, pitiful conversation with the Surly Teenage Daughter of the Girlfriend, like 'So'"—she deepened her voice a few notches—"'your mother has told me a lot about you.'"

Nick rested his chin on his hand. She liked the way he paused before he spoke, thoughtful, as if what she said mattered. "Had I done that," he said, "I have no doubt you would have instantly seen through it. Although she has told me a lot about you."

"Yeah? Like what?"

"How you're going to college a year early."

"I hope."

"That takes guts," he said. "It's a brave thing to be that focused, to take a leap of faith to do what you need to." He took a sip of water. "Any ideas on life after college?"

"Graduate school?" she said cheerfully.

He chuckled. "A perfectly warranted answer to an obnoxious question I'm sure you're tired of hearing."

"Yes, but I'll let you live." She heard clanging from within the kitchen. "Need any help in there, Mom?"

"Got it under control. Barely."

"What do you do?" Isobel asked Nick.

"I remodel houses."

"You mean like the guy on the PBS show that comes on Sunday mornings?"

"Sort of. I oversee the aesthetic aspect—making sure the old houses are brought up to date while still keeping their original integrity."

"Good, 'cause you're in the right place. We could use a new one. Desperately."

"A new what?" Isobel's mother said, banging down the serving tray in the middle of the table.

"House," Isobel said, mouth full.

"Oh. Yes." She sat down, breathless. "By all means, Nick, if you care to take on this nineteenth-century money pit, be my guest."

Nick grinned at Isobel. "I think I've got my hands full already."

I don't want to like you, Isobel thought, looking at him. *But I do.*

⁓

When she went for her college admissions interview that fall, at a small liberal-arts school just outside of Baltimore, Isobel wore the same blue silk blouse her mother had worn on that first date with Nick. She and her mother got there with time to kill, so they stopped at a little Italian café and swirled crostini in olive oil and drank overpriced sodas made with Torani syrups—or rather, her mother did. Isobel was so nervous she could barely swallow, much less eat. She sat and fiddled with her napkin, praying silently: *Dear God who in my more agnostic and contemplative moments I am not sure exists, if you let me get into this school with a nice little scholarship and maybe a work-study grant, if you're really generous, I will be the biggest believer you have ever seen. I will stop biting my nails, I will never fall asleep at Christmas Eve service like I did last year because I was so tired from studying for end-of-term exams, I will stop making irreverent jokes, I will—*

"I'm sure you've got nothing to worry about," her mother was saying. "You'll do fine. Even Nick said so."

Isobel's mother peered into her face, hazel eyes alert, probing.

"Honey," she said, "you look like you're about to faint. Are you okay?"

∞

Isobel must have managed to recover her composure enough to give a more than adequate interview, because that March she got not only an acceptance letter but also another piece of seal-embossed stationery that informed her she had received a full scholarship.

Nick took them both out that night to celebrate. It was a real celebration, not like her father's timid, fumbling attempts that crackled with tension. They laughed so hard over the dinner table (and the glass of red wine her mother had permitted Isobel to have) that they feared they would be kicked out of the restaurant. "Fortunately, I have no connection to these uncouth elderly creatures," Isobel told the waiter with a bad British accent, and that made them all laugh harder.

Despite her initial narrow-eyed suspicion, she found her jangly angst calmed by soft-spoken, soothingly deliberate Nick. She loved the way he walked slowly, the way his footfalls echoed solid and pure on the creaky floors of the house on weekends, the way he sweetly acted as though he didn't realize she'd borrowed one of his huge plaid flannel shirts. He was quiet, like her father, but centered beneath his whispery surface; there were no brewing signs of trouble. He promised her mother he'd refinish the top of her beloved table—icon of independence—and though it took him several months, he did it. After years of broken promises, wary Isobel could have kissed him for that.

"You've got to keep him, Mom," Isobel always told her mother on Sunday nights after he left.

"Thanks for the ultimatum," Isobel's mother said, laughing, as she ran her hand over the smooth, unblemished tabletop. "I'll keep it in mind."

One night in mid-May, though, Isobel was writing the last essay of her high school career in the kitchen, the windows wide open to let in the mild evening breeze, when her mother came in, a tight little smile on her face. "Check this out, Isobel," she said.

Isobel leaned over as her mother opened her purse and dug through it. A nail file, her wallet, her makeup bag, and a Chinese carryout menu spilled onto the table before she found what she was looking for. She handed Isobel a small velvet box. Isobel opened it. It was a massive diamond set in elegant gold.

"For me?" Isobel said. "Aw, a graduation present, you shouldn't have."

"No, goofball, an engagement ring," her mother said.

"Jesus, it's huge," Isobel said. "Way to go, Nick."

"Watch your language," her mother said, but her tone was light. "Isn't it wild?"

"It'll take your hand off, Mom."

She grinned. "I know. We're going back to the jeweler's together, to get something more subtle."

"That's terrific," Isobel said. "Really."

"See what great things happen when you're a good girl and let your mother raid your closet?" Her mother gave her a tight squeeze.

"Ha, ha." Isobel turned back to the book and paper in front of her, erasing a line.

"The infamous final essay, huh?" her mother said.

"Yes, thank God. One more paragraph to go."

"Well, I'll let you get back to work. I think I'll go call your grandma and let her know the good news."

"Is she gonna give you her routine about how Nick absolutely saved your life?"

She snorted. "Probably. That's me, the damsel in distress, waiting to be rescued."

"Good luck."

∾

Her mother and Nick were married in June, in a small civil ceremony that, thankfully for Isobel, did not require her to wear a bridesmaid's gown or high heels. That summer, before she left for college, Nick offered to build a bookcase for her dorm room, to hold only those most special titles from her growing collection, which now encroached upon her bed, her bureau, and the entire floor. He insisted, as much as anyone with Nick's temperament could, that she at least help him build it, so that she could get a sense of how things were made and how to repair them. "You're a highly independent girl, I can tell," he said, with a knowing smile, "and I'm sure this could come in handy."

They put it together on a sweltering weekend in August, and it was one of the most enjoyable tasks that task-oriented Isobel had ever accomplished. Nick sawed the wood in his basement workshop, but she pitched in on almost everything else. She loved the sturdy but pliant feel of a nail beneath the hammer. Here was an act all physical and pragmatic, useful yet dirty. She painted the entire bookcase herself, sitting on the floor of her bedroom with the windows open and a box fan whirring as she hummed, happily absorbed. She had chosen a weathered, almost denim-blue paint as a base, and then with a fine brush drew cranberry-colored flourishes—a touch of whimsy, she thought—for contrast. It was a small bookcase, very low, with only three shelves, so she was done in time for a late supper. She ate her sandwich on a tray in her lap, as if she were little and on her grandmother's screened porch again, paint flecks and wood shavings in her hair, her T-shirt stained, sweat trickling down her back, her fingernails crusted.

After a much needed shower, she lay satisfied and sore-limbed on her bed, and wrote her father a postcard to give him the date she would be leaving, as well as her college phone number and post office box. She took pains *not* to address the card to Ben and Denise; she had no idea, at this point, if Denise was even in the picture.

Right after he received her note, he left a breathless, excited, trying-too-hard message on the answering machine: "Isobel, sweetheart, I'm so happy for you, I'd love to fly out to help you on your big day moving in, so if you need me, just give me a call, okay?"

In his haste to make offers and amends, he had forgotten to give her his current phone number.

So it was Nick who drove down in his battered old van with her and her mother, and Nick who carried the bookcase up the stairs of the fieldstone building that would be her new home. She arrived before her roommate and chose the bed by the window. There wasn't much for her to set up: her navy blue comforter, extra-long twin size, bought expressly for the occasion, a clock radio, and a jewelry box on the bureau next to two framed photos: one of her and Colette on a day trip that summer to see shows in New York City, and another of her mother and Nick at their wedding. A quick but careful lineup of clothes and shoes in the closet, and she was done. Her normally laid-back mother peered around furtively, convinced they couldn't possibly be done so soon. "Are you sure you haven't forgotten anything?" she pressed. "Because if you have, we can always run over to the—"

"Jana, let her go," Nick said, drawing his wife close. "She's in her element."

Isobel sank down onto the bed and stretched her arms out wide. "I'm in paradise," she said, leaning back, and promptly bumped her head on the radiator.

Then she fiercely hugged them both goodbye, reassuring them

that yes, yes, she was okay, really. After they left, she curled up on the new comforter, hugging herself, while she listened to the hall-way sounds of banging doors, rolling suitcases, bickering parents, squeals of reunion and laughter.

☙

Dormitory life deteriorated sharply upon the arrival of her roommate. Meghan (pronounced with a long *e*, as she was wont to remind everyone she met) was a dance major, tall and leggy in a sensual, sinuous way that Isobel was very clearly not. She was also a chain-smoker—"I have to make weight check every week," she said cheerfully, as if she were a wrestler, "or else they'll drop me out of ballet and into modern"—and persisted in smoking in their room no matter how many times Isobel asked her, crisply but po-litely, not to.

Thankfully, Meghan spent most of her time at rehearsals, but when she was home, she talked on the phone incessantly, with a loud, shrieky laugh which Isobel was sure could be heard all the way back in Staplin. Sometimes Meghan brought in a gaggle of friends, and they would clamor on her bed, toying with one an-other's long, silky hair and gossiping, holding cans of diet soda (or, on the weekends, beer) in their slender, manicured hands. Most of the time, they wore leotards and the simple, beautifully Zenlike oversized black pants that seemed to be dance-department-issue, but on the Saturday nights they went to clubs, all hell broke loose. Clothes festooned the floor, the bed, the desk, and once even Nick's bookcase. The phone rang more than usual. Isobel, perched on her own bed as if it were a life raft in a sea of skimpy fabric, balanced her binder on her knees, and wondered why, if it took an hour to decide where to go and another two to ascertain what to wear, they bothered going at all.

On the nights when Meghan's crowd picked the Naval Academy

in Annapolis as their venue, it was worse. Dress there was semi-formal, which meant even more primping for the mere opportunity to swirl about under the lights to 1940s swing, feet pinched in heels, while a white-clad midshipman clenched your elbow. When preparations for that were in progress, Isobel made her way out toward the hall's commons room while she could.

Inevitably she would hear whispers before she closed the door:

"Your roommate, Meeg, what's *up* with her?"

"Yeah, she seems pretty stuck-up."

"Or at least pretty uptight."

"No, listen, guys, she's actually nice. She just *studies.* No, I mean, like, all the time."

Isobel was grateful for her roommate's defense, however backhanded, but as she entered the commons room and took a seat on its hole-filled couch, her face still burned. There, amid the smell of burnt popcorn and stale Corona and whatever had invariably just exploded in the shared microwave, she read the same words over and over, with the side of one hand roughly wiping angry tears from her strained eyes.

Usually a bunch of basketball players would come in at midnight with a fresh box of pizza and ask her if they could take over the TV to watch *Saturday Night Live.* She would acquiesce, a bit too sweetly, and stand with relief. "Oh, you don't have to go," they'd say, with gruff quasi-chivalry. "Don't let us bother you."

"No, that's okay," she'd say, hand on the doorknob, thinking of how delicious it would be to have her room quiet and empty again. "I've got to meet a friend anyway."

Even the lie felt good as she ran past the open door to the bathroom, where a line of graceful girls—some wearing clay face masks, some with their hair twisted up in towels—shuffled their delicate bare feet on dirty ceramic tile while they brushed their teeth and took off their eyeliner.

"Hey Isobel," one would usually call, "have you seen Meghan?" (Or Sarah. Or Cami.)

"No," she'd reply. "She went swing dancing." Or home to visit her boyfriend. Or I don't know.

Her room was at the end of the hall. She'd shove open the door with no need to fumble for a key; although Meghan loved to leave irritatingly precious messages on their dry-erase board like "Good night, Izzy! Love, your roomie," replete with smiley faces and hearts dotting the *i*'s, she was remarkably loath to lock up after herself. Intoxicated with solitude, Isobel would dive onto her bed, snuggle into her pillows, and stare with amusement at Meghan's side of the room. With the Calvin Klein ads, Christmas lights, taped-up photographs of her myriad of high school "best" friends, and a clay mobile of twirling multicolored fish, it looked "like a cross between an Indian restaurant and a toddler's playroom," as Isobel had put it in a long, descriptive letter to Colette. She watched the globs inside Meghan's turquoise Lava lamp shimmer and rotate until, still in her clothes, textbook open on her chest, she drifted to sleep.

੭৫

There were times, of course, when college was bliss. Weekdays, for instance, were fine, because then it was okay to sit by yourself and review your notes, or to sprawl on the grass and read in the fading autumn sun. Sunday nights were not as good, but passable, because then all the binge drinkers were catching up on the homework they'd been too hungover to remember was due Monday, and you felt a strange kinship as you all trudged to the library.

Not surprisingly, Isobel found that she did well in college. She had to work harder, but there was no more difficulty than there had been in high school, just a sharpening of focus, a necessary attention to detail that suited her perfectly. Her professors marveled at her, counseled her, listened to her ramble, pale face flushed, in their offices. She sensed in them an openness, but also a hovering aura of concern, as if they did not know whether to protect her or push her, help her or fear her, this overgrown child, barely seventeen, excruciatingly tall and yet somehow diminutive, nervously picking a hole in her sweater while she pleaded, staccato-voiced, to take a senior capstone course as a first-semester freshman.

Or at least that's what Isobel assumed they thought when they looked her way. She tried not to think too hard about what other people's perceptions of her might be; if she did, she might crack up. That was her biggest nightmare: cracking up. Having to go home for good, to forfeit this rare gift she had been given, and sit at a too small school desk in a too small town, a pretentious failure.

So she fought valiantly. Made herself talk just enough. Made herself smile, even at the students who, though trenchant and insightful in class, went shockingly vapid outside of it. She crisscrossed the campus—library, dining hall, student union, dorm—as if she had been training for it her entire life. She felt in a way like she had.

She went home for winter break feeling as if every bone in her body were a spike, ready to pierce anyone she touched or hugged or thought about loving. She knew she was falling, and caught herself as skillfully as Meghan might have landed from a tricky jump. She used a jar of her mother's foundation so no one would see the black circles under her eyes. She ate heartily, sometimes three bowls of the stews Nick liked to make. When her mother went to her weekly party with the other women in her law office, Isobel and Nick would sit on either side of the living room couch and read in front of the gas fireplace he had rigged up. She had decided to double-major in psychology and women's studies, so her book was usually Piaget or Irigaray; he was planning to build a new island for the kitchen, so his book was usually some variant on a home-repair encyclopedia. Their feet touched, clad in wool socks, a comfortable space between them. They were the esoteric and the mundane together, and it felt good. Every so often, she would glance over at him, and he would smile, probably thinking: That smart stepdaughter I have.

Nick, build me a body, she would think in return, because I can't feel mine, I don't know where I am in this one I already have.

༔

Her last night at home before classes resumed, she came back from a late dinner at Colette's parents' house and went up to her bedroom to pack. She shoved her suitcase into one corner to get a better view inside her cramped closet, and noticed a pile of wood shavings left over from building the bookcase. It made her think of the intense heat of that afternoon, the humid air dense with the sticky tension of creating. She folded her shirts one by one, placing each in the suitcase according to color, and, mind racing, thought: I want to be touched.

She returned to campus the next day feeling fevered and disoriented, and wondered if it was a harbinger of the flu. She surprised herself by actually hugging Meghan, who, upon hearing of her potential sickness, cried out, "Poor Izzy! See, I always told you that you worked too hard!" and plied her with honeyed chamomile tea and a box of fresh oranges she had brought from her hometown in Florida.

At five o'clock, still feeling jittery, Isobel announced that she was going to head over to the dining hall for dinner. Meghan surprised her by offering to come along. "Sarah and Jocelyn aren't back yet," she said, with sad, expressive eyes, and Isobel thought: Ah, there's a reason for your benevolence.

Letting the Body Lead

They got there just before the doors opened. There was a line in the lobby, and as they waited, Isobel noticed a boy standing to the left of her. He was tall and gangly, like her, with tangled ash-blond hair and a sensuous mouth whose sad passion leapt out from his gaunt face. Long, slender arms crossed over his chest, he wore a huge, baggy sweater, the same blue she had chosen for the bookcase, and a pair of faded cords. His chiseled features and ragged dress made him look like someone from another era, a bookish changeling, paying no attention to the neon-markered posters above his head that gleefully clamored to advertise club meetings and basketball games and ice-cream socials.

"Who is that beautiful creature?" Isobel murmured under her breath, quietly enough that he didn't notice, but loudly enough that Meghan did.

"Damn, Isobel." She giggled. "I didn't know you were into checking people out."

"No, it's not—it's not like that," Isobel said.

"I don't know, you look like you're blushing." Meghan grinned and pulled out her meal card as the line advanced. "I wouldn't mess with Andrew Kennedy if I were you, though. He seems a little scary."

"Scary how?"

"Really smart. *Too* smart. And just—creepy, like he might stalk you or something."

Isobel shrugged. She wasn't about to take Meghan's caveat on intelligence seriously. "Thanks for the tip," she said.

Just then she heard a telltale screech from farther up. "Meegs!"

"Nina?" Meghan squealed back, spotting one of her dancer cohorts, this one a vaguely Asian-looking, striking woman from modern. She turned to Isobel. "You don't mind, do you?"

Isobel shook her head; this was par for the course. "Go ahead," she told her. "I'll meet you back in the room later."

"Thanks," Meghan said breathlessly. "You are *so* sweet." She ran up to join Nina, and there were copious hugs and octave changes. Isobel turned back to look at Andrew Kennedy, who had fallen behind her in line, and watched him run a hand through his hair. Her own hands jumped. She thought, Let me. Pulled out her own meal card. Licked her lips. They were cold and dry.

❦

All through dinner, alone at her tiny table, she scanned the cafeteria for him, to no avail. She walked back to her dorm in the cold, without gloves or a scarf, glad for the biting air; it made her feel the outlines of herself more clearly, shocked her into sensation, sharp and clear. She sat down at her desk, tuned her radio to a classical station, and opened the books she'd purchased over break for the next term, hoping to get a head start. There now, she thought, that's better. She spun a pencil in her fingers as she read, and just as the clipped, faintly English voice of the announcer informed her that "We'll have a concerto by Dvořák later on, in a bit," she heard the lead snap. She stood, took a deep breath, and told herself, *You have to stop this.*

It was almost eight-thirty. Her roommate, she realized, probably wasn't coming back at a reasonable hour. Isobel reached up to touch the pastel-colored mobile and give it a swing; the blue and pink fish, mouths agape, twirled and twirled.

❦

Though she rarely saw him, and almost never outside of class, she thought of him constantly. She chastised herself for this, on the grounds that she was acting no better than Meghan, as if her roommate were some sort of moral yardstick. She diagnosed her pangs as mere infatuation, borne of her paucity of experience (Michael Culley, whatever he had been, did not count), but she knew that her obsession with this "*too* smart" Andrew masked something deeper, a bodily hunger. She began buying her sweaters even bigger, and got a pair of gloves to wear outside, to hide the raw skin on her fingers where she gnawed, and the raw skin on her forearms where she scratched, much as it hurt, just to feel and taste, under her comforter at night. In class, she caught herself drawing the outline of her hands with a pencil, as if she were back in kindergarten and making a construction-paper turkey to take home for Thanksgiving, only now it was not a bright, happy display fit for her mother to tack proudly on the refrigerator, but a deeply important reminder that *Yes, here I am, this is where I begin and all this ends.*

One night in late February, a Naval Academy night, Isobel walked down to the commons room as usual, stepped into the silvery gleam of the television, and found Andrew seated in her normal spot on the couch. She almost dropped her binder. She stared at the back of his head. He was close enough that she could lean over, silent as an unvoiced sigh, and duck down to press her mouth into the back of his waiting neck. *Come here,* she wanted to say. *Turn around. There's a cold clear moon out and a back waiting for warmth against it, and I know I look strange, but if you kissed my fingertips, their cracked edges would mend enough for me to touch you the way you deserve to be touched, I promise.*

Instead she walked across the room and pretended to scan the inside of the moldy refrigerator, as if it held what she wanted. Leftovers in Styrofoam? A jug of cheap wine? A carton of sour milk? She shook her head. She had to leave. It was not nervousness, no; it was not the anxious thoughts she might have expected, self-conscious queries of *What will I say? Does my hair look all right?* It was the desire, like a punch to the stomach, a slap across the face, stinging and hard, the knowledge of what she could do, what she might do, what she wanted.

She closed the refrigerator door, sighed in mock resignation and real sorrow. Without a word, she crossed the room again and left, then sprinted down to the end of the hall. On her way, she heard one of the girls call, "Isobel, have you seen Ashley?" but she didn't answer. She ignored the saccharine message scrawled on the door, let herself in, and took her coat from the closet. She needed to get out. She needed to walk. Deep in their pockets, her fingers balled into fists as she took the stairs and ran across the quad toward the student union. There was no one there in the basement post office, not at this hour, and under the dim fluorescent lights she jammed her tiny key into the lock of her mailbox, where she found a letter. She pounced on it, happy for a diversion. The return address label with its glossy sunflower informed her it was Colette. She tore the envelope open, grinning at its back, which read in large letters, "It's the two of us against the world, and we're winning!" She pulled out the sheet of purple legal paper and leaned against the wall, out of breath from her run, throat scratchy, as she scanned the almost calligraphic words written in blue ink.

Dear Isobel, it read, *this place is hideously boring without you. Things are looking up, though—our district (much less pigheaded than Andrews, thank God!) has let me take some classes at Staplin Community College—don't gag, I know, but some are actually pretty good. I've also met another senior there who's doing the same thing, and well . . . we seem to be an item. I would love for you to meet Brian over spring break—and don't worry, if he doesn't like you, I'll kill him . . .*

Great, Isobel thought, wanting so desperately to mean it, hating the sharp edge that drove into her over and over, that plunged the jealousy and spilled it to the surface.

It was her against herself, and she was losing.

She folded the letter roughly and put it in her coat pocket, then trudged home. She lay on her bed, listening to the classical station, waiting for the affected voice of the quasi-Englishwoman to soothe her into slumber. When she awoke again, the clock read one-thirty in the morning, and Meghan and her friends were crowded on the bed opposite, long legs draped over one another's laps, passing a bottle of vodka, their talk loud and meaningless. "Shh," one of them whispered, and pointed at Isobel, thinking she was still asleep. The girl's voice was husky and surprisingly sweet; her concern touched one of the few places in Isobel that was not raw and aching. *Come sit next to me,* she wanted to say. *I'll braid your hair. I'll sing about nothing. Let me rest my head on your shoulder. There's warmth by the heater. We can at least pretend we are friends.*

But she couldn't, and no one did.

∽

Just before spring break of her freshman year, Isobel found another letter in her mailbox, this one, surprisingly, from Ms. J. They had lost touch since Isobel had left for college, and Isobel's mother was never as good at providing hometown updates as she had promised.

Isobel read the letter as she walked to the library, savoring it. "Dear Isobel," it read, "there have been many changes for me lately. I resigned from my job at Andrews—the bureaucracy was more than I could take."

Way to go, Ms. J., Isobel thought, and read on.

"I also got married over the summer," Ms. J.'s letter continued. "Right person, right time—sometimes life gets serendipitous, you know?"

Isobel frowned. Her mother and Nick were one thing, but Ms. J.—spunky, iconoclastic—was another. She probably wasn't even Ms. J. anymore.

Isobel entered the library and sat down on one of the couches near the door to finish the letter. Ms. J. had invited her over for dinner when she went home at break. The letter was signed "Sylvia Johnson-Kearney," with a phone number and new address that Isobel didn't recognize. Isobel decided she'd call her, hyphenated name and all.

She went upstairs and quickly found a book on Kohlberg's theory of moral development that she needed for a midterm essay. There was a little time to spare before her next class, so she wandered about. She liked to pick sections she normally wouldn't browse, and today she chose foreign languages. Her college didn't offer Latin, which she had studied in high school, so she had to make another choice, and she figured she might as well get a sense of what she wanted. She knelt on the floor to skim the spines of the books on the lower stacks, and one book caught her eye, mainly because it appeared almost a century old. She opened it, gingerly, and discovered that it was an Icelandic-English dictionary. Iceland, she thought. Where Ms. J. went with her fiancé—

She sat cross-legged on the carpet to get a better look. Flipping through the pages, she squinted at the occasional bizarre letter that appeared to be a throwback to some medieval alphabet and found it was a textbook as well. Toward the end of the dictionary, she discovered the word *vilja*. Verb, meaning: want. She closed her eyes. The room felt too narrow, too warm. She hoisted herself to her feet, tucked the book under her arm, and went downstairs, her face flushed. She took out the book at the circulation desk and checked her watch as she exited the library. She had been too long; she was already five minutes late for her class. With an apathy that surprised her and yet didn't, she thought, Why bother? It was the first time in her entire six months at college that she had skipped anything.

She passed the humanities building, feeling mildly guilty but too numb to turn back as she passed the student union. She broke into a run as she reached her dorm, and raced up the back stair-well and into her room. She shrugged off her coat, threw it on the bed, sat at her desk without bothering to turn on the radio, and opened the book with shaking hands. She skimmed the first few pages of grammar explanations, then turned back to the word for desire. She pulled a legal pad from the large top drawer of her desk, grabbed a pen, and got to work on conjugating it:

Ég vil—*I want*
Þu vilt—*you want*
Hann/Húnn/Það vill—*he/she/it wants*
Þeir/Þær/Þau vilja—*they want*

Her gaze lingered on the first-person singular. She paged backward with a ferocious urgency, almost ripping a dusty page in her search for a negative, a word to blot out longing. In the *E*'s she found it. She took up her pen again and drew jagged lines through *Ég vil*. Above the blackened phrase she wrote *Ég vil ekki*, over and over, so hard the paper tore. At five o'clock, she heard a key in the door and swung her head up to stare straight at her blank portion of the wall, wondering why it looked so blurry.

"Izzy," Meghan called out, "I thought you were still in class, sweetie!"

Her roommate came up behind her, put a gentle hand on her back.

"Isobel," she said, using her full name for once. "Why are you crying?"

༚

She went home for spring break with the tightest, falsest smile that she could manage on her face. She endured a day out with Co-lette and her new boyfriend, Brian, and watched with a seething pain as their hands touched on the imitation-wood table of the mall restaurant where the three of them ate lunch.

The next evening, she drove herself down to Ms. J.'s in her mother's car. Ms. J. lived in a real house now, in real suburban Staplin, in a tiny development, far from their old school. Isobel was disappointed to see that the home was a predictable stone colonial with a basketball hoop in the driveway, but when Ms. J. answered the door in a simple black shift dress and French sandals, with her hair tied up and a silver chain around her neck, she looked just the same as she had a year earlier, except for the fact that she was about six months pregnant.

"You didn't tell me about *that* in your letter," Isobel said, with only half-joking irritation.

"Oh, I thought I'd surprise you," Ms. J. said. She kissed Isobel hello and led her inside. They walked through the living room, passing a green chenille couch, several fine-art prints, and, sadly, a television in a large cherry cabinet. In the huge, modern white kitchen, Isobel met Grant, Ms. J.'s husband, a stocky, good-natured man in a striped polo shirt, who was cooking dinner. He hugged her gently—"So this is the infamous Isobel"—and she felt her body uncurling in the warmth. His gentle irreverence reminded her of Nick.

They ate in the surprisingly formal dining room, with wine and candles. "I'll wash the dishes," Grant said afterward. "Why don't you two go take a walk or something?"

Ms. J. and Isobel grinned and took off instantly.

Outside, the March air was crisp enough to make a jacket feel comforting, but mild enough to make a short stroll a pleasure.

"So, how's domestic life suiting you?" Isobel asked.

Ms. J. snorted. "Please. My maternity leave doesn't start for another two months."

"Are you excited about her?" They already knew that the baby was a girl.

"Terribly. But I'm also scared, to be honest with you."

"You? You're so great with kids. You'll do fine."

"I sure hope so." Ms. J. smiled. "So what's up with you right now?"

Isobel fell quiet for a moment.

"Well," she said softly, "I got a grant for a project next year, and I went to a conference in Washington, D.C., in February . . ."

"Honey, I don't want to play pop psychologist here, and I don't want to pry, but this is not the real Isobel I'm hearing," Ms. J. said. "A terrific, hardworking part with some good ideas, but not all of her."

Isobel couldn't speak.

They turned around in the cul-de-sac. On a rope in a neighboring yard, a golden retriever barked.

"I get five hours of sleep a night," she finally said. "All my energy is consumed by my schoolwork."

They walked back to Ms. J.'s front lawn. They passed by the living room, where Grant sat reading in a chair by the bay window. Ms. J. took Isobel's hand, led her under a tree in the grass, and eased herself onto the chilly ground.

"Isobel Sivulka," she said. "What are we going to do with you?"

Her tone had lost its usual airy quality. She peered into Isobel's face.

"I can see the dark circles under your eyes," Ms. J. said. "You ought to take better care of yourself. All the parts of you, even the ones you don't want to think about."

"What do you mean?"

"Something my friends and I have learned over time," Ms. J. said, "is that when you leave adolescence, it's not a clean break, a sudden heaping of wisdom and comfort delivered into your lap. You don't leave behind the girls you were at fifteen, sixteen, seventeen. They're like those Russian nesting dolls, what are they called—"

"Matrioshkas," Isobel said, without a thought.

"Yes, they're like matrioshkas, one inside the other. Inside you. Waiting to be listened to, waiting for their desires, their hurts, to be honored."

"Which is all lovely and good," Isobel said, "but ever so much emotional indulgence when you've got a fifteen-page paper due Tuesday."

She was on an academic treadmill. Sisyphus pushing the rock up the hill toward a diploma. She shoved away her mentor's warnings, categorized them swiftly as New Age fluff.

Ms. J. rubbed her forehead. "I don't mean to lecture you," she said. "I'm just worried."

Isobel looked down, pulled at the lace on her tennis shoe. She cleared her throat. Her voice felt rough, unyielding, suffused with sudden, welled-up anger.

"You're a mother. It's your job," Isobel said.

❧

Isobel returned to school after spring break to find Meghan bouncing restlessly on her bed, a bowl of microwave popcorn on her lap. "Izzy," her roommate said, "you won't believe this!"

"What?" Isobel said, expecting some tale of petty woe.

"Your big crush, Andrew Kennedy," Meghan said, popping a burnt kernel into her lipsticked mouth. "Remember how I told you he was scary, like he might stalk someone?"

"Yes," Isobel said slowly, and sat on her own bed.

"Well, Ashley stayed here over break, 'cause she's in the nine-month housing, right, and he was staying here, too, I think he's originally from Seattle, so—"

"Meghan, finish the damn story, would you?" Isobel said, with a rudeness that jarred her.

"Okay, okay. You'll never believe it, but—he was following her all week, being super-creepy, so—they asked him to leave!"

"Leave campus?"

"No, leave the school. For good."

Isobel dropped her face in her hands.

"I know, Izzy," Meghan said, the syrup-filled banality of her voice proving that she really didn't. "I'm so sorry. But you don't need a freak like that. You'll find a nice guy. There are some smart ones at the Naval Academy. I mean, you have to be smart to get in there. We'll fix you up."

"Thanks," Isobel mumbled, and curled up on her bed. She turned her head toward the window, away from her roommate and her eager reassurances. This is how it goes, she thought. Me on my back, desolate. *Ég vil ekki.*

≈

When she went home for the summer, Isobel found a card in the mailbox from Ms. J. It was pink and adorned with a silky ribbon, and it announced the birth of Natasha. Isobel called immediately. The female voice that answered was hoarse and tired.

"Ms. J.?" Isobel said.

"Who is this?"

"It's Isobel Sivulka. Remember?"

"Oh, hi, Isobel." Isobel could hear a long, thin wail in the background.

"I wanted to say congratulations," Isobel said. "I got your card."

"Thank—thank you. Could you hold on for a second?" She

covered the mouthpiece with her hand, and Isobel heard her yell, "Grant, bring her to me, would you, please?" Then, "Okay, I'm back."

"I was wondering," Isobel said, "if you wanted to get together again."

"Sweetie, I would love to," Ms. J. said, "but it is crazy around here. We're spending most of our time getting adjusted to life as a family of three. I hope you'll understand."

"Sure," Isobel said softly. "It's no problem."

"I hate to cut you short," Ms. J. said, "but a certain hungry young lady is ready for a feeding. I'll keep you posted. Promise."

"Okay," Isobel said. She hung up the phone just as her mother came into her room with a basket of laundry.

"Who were you talking to?" her mother asked.

"Ms. J."

"That nice former teacher of yours?"

"Yeah." Isobel frowned. "I think her new baby has precluded friendship."

"Honey, raising a child is a full-time job. I'm sure it's nothing personal. Besides, why don't you hang out with someone your own age? Give Colette a call."

Isobel reached for the phone again and dialed Colette's number. "Don't forget to fold these," her mother mouthed, pointing to the pile of clothes.

"Hey, Colette, it's me," Isobel said when Colette picked up. "Are you free this afternoon? It's drudgery as usual over here."

"I wish I were," Colette said, "but Brian's taking me to the movies. Sorry."

Isobel sighed. "I'll talk to you later."

Everyone's changed, she thought as she folded the laundry. I'm the only one who's the same, locked in to my goals.

She resolved, then and there, to finish college as quickly as possible, to distract herself with as much hard work as she could stand. She took six courses a semester, filled her summers with electives, and graduated with a dual degree in three years, then fled to Manhattan for a doctoral program in psychology.

≈

As part of her full assistantship, the university gave her priority for its apartment housing in Greenwich Village, which pleased her immensely. It also stipulated that, in such accommodations, she would have to live with another graduate student, which terrified her. She and Nick arrived on a steamy afternoon in late August, with everything she owned tied down in the back of the smallest U-Haul they could rent. As she ascended the stairs, breathing hard, chest tight, with the blue bookcase in her arms, she saw a tall, thin woman with wild dark hair holding the door open. In her black capri pants and hot-pink metallic T-shirt, she looked eerily like Meghan. Alienation, take two, Isobel thought.

"That's a wonderful bookcase," the woman called out. "It's hand-painted, yeah?"

Isobel nodded. "Did it myself," she said, and set it down gently in the doorway.

The woman smiled. "It's your baby. I'll let you deal with it, then."

Nick came up the stairs behind Isobel, carrying several hangers' worth of clothes. "So this is your new roommate," he said.

"Oops," the dark-haired woman said. "Guess we should do the introductions, huh? I'm Elika Muraski."

She held out her hand, and Isobel took it; her touch was solid and warm. "Isobel Sivulka," she said. "And this is my stepdad, Nick Lewis."

Elika shook his hand as well. "My friend, you look like you could use a beer," she said.

Nick smiled, shy yet appreciative. "That obvious?" he said, wiping the sweat from his forehead.

Isobel pulled the bookcase inside to make way for him. The apartment was small and spartan, with an old-fashioned fan in the window, a black futon, and a television on a blond wood stand. Elika went into the tiny kitchen, which was empty save for an ancient microwave on a metal table. She knelt and rummaged through a huge cooler on the floor. "You want one, Isobel?" she yelled.

"Sure," Isobel said. "Why not."

Nick took his can of beer and headed back down the stairs. "I'll start on the boxes of books, okay?" he said.

"Good luck," Isobel said. She turned to Elika. "Books comprise pretty much everything I own. Sorry I couldn't bring more in the way of furniture to share."

"Don't worry about it," Elika said. "I'm a clotheshorse and a pack rat by nature, so we're covered." She popped the top on her beer can. "Your dad is a real sweetie."

"I know." Isobel didn't bother trying to correct her; Nick felt like her father by that point. "He's been such a help."

"My parents begged to move me in," Elika said, "but I wanted nothing to do with it. Let this be my own from the beginning, I said. I rounded up a few friends to carry the heavy stuff, bribed them with free pizza, and—"

"You're from around here?" Isobel said.

"God, no. Midwest by way of Far East." She took a long swallow of beer, then belched. "Whoa, excuse me. As you can tell, I also failed charm school."

Isobel laughed.

"But I did save the bigger bedroom for you," Elika said. "I figured you'd be here more than I would. I'm going to be living in an editing booth for the next few years."

"You are?"

"Yep. I'm a masochist—I mean, film and video student."

Elika leaned over and gave her a tight squeeze. "Hope I didn't scare you," she said afterward. "I'm big on hugs."

"Thank—thank you," Isobel said, surprised yet pleased. The affection that flowed from her new roommate felt genuine, not like Meghan's shrill, forced camaraderie, but she still didn't know how to respond.

"Rest assured," Elika said, her hand gliding lovingly over the top shelf of Isobel's bookcase. "I don't bite without permission. I promise."

⁘

Isobel watched with awe and envy as Elika took everything seemingly in stride. Elika knew that it would take her, in her words, "several centuries" to finish her MFA, and that slow pace suited her fine. She had a string of admirers, both male and female, but felt no piercing need or desire for any relationship the other side of platonic. Elika emanated cheerful, lucid stability, and it was fabulous yet maddening.

Meanwhile, Isobel grew more anxious as the time came to craft her dissertation. The summer before her work began in earnest, her mother suggested she take two weeks to relax at her grandparents' summer house in South Carolina. "Relaxing? What's that?" Isobel replied, but she accepted the offer anyway.

At first, her days in the Little River cottage fell into a blissful routine. She slept until eleven each morning, scrubbed dishes while listening to shag music, painted her toenails the color of blood oranges; she read on the front steps among the giant sunflowers, then would throw on a raggedy dress and head over to the yacht basin for dinner and to Marker 350, a little place overlooking the water, for chocolate cake. She'd bring it home and eat it on the porch while making notes, raising the fork to her mouth every few pages, one leg slung over the arm of an old tweed chair, the light spare and soft from the dim bulb above her head, the room swollen with the chirping of locusts and the mournful string arrangements of Russian composers on public radio.

Eventually, though, the heat made her queasy, and the sensuality of the place strangled her. It was her mother's lush world, not hers.

Chapter Eleven

Reykjavík

At Ragna's, Isobel fell easily and delightedly into the routines of family life. She walked Valdimar to his acting lessons so Ragna could get work done at the studio. They did the week's grocery shopping together at Nóatún, dancing in the meat aisle to American rap songs that played over the loudspeaker, unedited, while Valdi looked on, mortified at the behavior of two ancient, undignified women. Isobel's days grew so occupied that she had little time to contemplate her situation, which helped but also left her prone to sudden, delirious pangs of longing.

When Isobel returned briefly to Magga's flat for clothes, she found a message on the machine from Kjartan. Isobel returned his call on Ragna's mobile phone later that day, as they walked to a museum where Ragna's friend Bragi, the one who owed her

mountain climbing, had a few pieces displayed. The phone conversation simmered with static as Isobel crossed the street.

"Baby," he said. "I thought I would never hear from you."

"Are you sobered up yet?"

He sighed. "Isobel the inquisitor. When can I see you next?"

"I'm staying with a friend for now, until I get a better handle on
things."

Ragna motioned to her that they were approaching the museum.

"I have to go," Isobel said. "I'll let you know when I'm ready,
okay?"

"Soon, Isobel *mín,* please," he said. "I miss having you around
in the evenings."

"I . . . I've missed you, too," Isobel said, and handed the phone
back to Ragna.

"Was that bad?" Isobel asked her. "Was that horrible?"

"No," Ragna said, and held the door open for her. "Be kind to
yourself, my dear."

⤳

Ragna and Isobel were making dinner in the kitchen one night
when the doorbell rang. "I'll get it," Ragna said. "You keep an eye
on this young man and the couscous."

Isobel grabbed a wooden spoon and dished some on a plate.
"Hey Valdi," she said, "what do you think?"

He looked up from the portable electronic game he was engrossed in, and gave the meal a quick, appraising glance. "It looks
fucking gross," he said.

Isobel still hadn't adjusted to hearing an eleven-year-old with
such an unabashed mouth, but she laughed. "At least you're honest."

Ragna came back, her face tight with concern. "Isobel," she said,
"it's for you."

They stepped into the hall. Isobel spoke first. "Who—"

"It's a man. He says he needs to speak with you, that it's terribly important."

"Okay," Isobel said. "I'll only be a minute."

"If it's, you know, the one you told me about—"

"I'll be careful. I promise."

Isobel stepped outside to find Kjartan there, in his work clothes, his hair rumpled. He took both her hands. His forehead bore deep lines of desperation.

"Isobel," he said. "I couldn't wait any longer."

Isobel yanked out of his grip.

"How did you find me?" she said.

"It's a small city, baby. Not hard to do."

"Well, this isn't my house," Isobel said, "so you really shouldn't come around here."

"Meet me after work, then? At my place?"

"I'll meet you, but only in public. The restaurant, maybe."

"No. Somewhere else."

"Okay. Pick a venue."

"How about Kaffi List? Eleven o'clock?"

"Fine." Isobel backed up, her hand on the knob of the open door. "I have to go, dinner's ready."

He grabbed her arm. "One kiss before I leave."

Kjartan shoved his face closer to hers. She brushed her lips quickly against his, hoping to pacify him, but his grip on her tightened, and he pushed his tongue deep into her mouth. He tasted smoky, awful but wonderfully familiar. Isobel drew away.

"Eleven o'clock," she said.

༄

Ragna and Valdimar had already carried their plates into the dining room and were almost finished with the meal. Isobel sat down to a portion of couscous.

"Oh, that's not nearly hot enough for you," Ragna said. "Get her some off the stove, Valdi."

He rolled his eyes in languid protest but did as he was told. Ragna leaned toward Isobel. "Perhaps it's a bit nosy of me," she said, "but . . . was that him?"

Isobel nodded.

"He reminds me so much of Ólafur," Ragna said. Isobel said nothing in response. The idealist in her bristled with denial at the mention of Ragna's ex-husband.

"Don't let my musings influence you," Ragna said, almost as if she had intercepted Isobel's thoughts. "You're a big girl. You can make your own choices."

"I'm meeting him later tonight."

"Alone? Where?"

"At a bar."

"I'll give you my mobile phone and a spare key to the flat, in case you come in late."

"Ragna, you're fabulous."

"I wouldn't go that far," she said. "But thanks. And be cautious, all right? Call me at any hour."

Valdi came back in with a heaping plate of couscous.

"*Takk,*" Isobel said. "You're quite the gentleman."

He blushed, and Isobel wondered, How do you get to squalid disregard from such boisterous innocence?

༄

Kaffi List was a crowded tapas-serving pub festooned with red neon lights. Isobel found Kjartan slouched on a bar stool with his chin in one hand—a vaguely studious look, or more likely a premeditated pose of despair.

He rubbed his forehead. "Tonight is not a night for fifty-cent words, my brilliant girl."

She put her hand over his. "What is it this time?"

"There's an Icelandic word for my state," he said, voice cracked and dull. "*Mórall*. Like waking up with a hangover, only deeper, much worse. A more elemental regret."

Isobel didn't know whether to feel moved or impatient. Tenderness and cynicism swelled, two parallel seas, inside her.

"I want to be good to you, Isobel," he said. The magic sentence. She squeezed his hand.

༄

They walked up the front steps of his building, both of them sober and silent. He unlocked the entrance to his flat and gently put his hand on her elbow as Isobel stepped inside. He turned on the lamp beside the couch.

"My God," Isobel said, "it's so neat."

"I cleaned up," he said. He beamed like an unruly child who'd finally received a gold star for doing his chores.

They stood in the middle of the room for a moment, not touching, hands empty, uncertain. Then Isobel did the only thing she knew to do. She sat on the bed.

"We need some candles," he said. "Would you like that, Isobel *mín*?"

Isobel nodded and watched him move from table to table, bending lovingly to strike each match. The room sizzled, dense with smoke. Kjartan knelt before her and cupped her face in his broad hands. Isobel looked at him and saw Valdi, and the boys who played soccer on her sidewalk, and the kids at the corner who hawked newspapers from bright orange bags. Every image of vivacious, wide-eyed youth Isobel could find she grafted onto him, until she relaxed, heady with the elixir of sympathy.

Isobel drew him into her arms. Slid her hands beneath his shirt, kissed his ear and his shoulder. "*Elskan,*" he moaned, that longed-for foreign love-word, soft and raw. The candles flickered in hypnotic, soothing rhythm as she guided his mouth and his fingers. Images flew past her in a delusional flip-book of futile scenarios: she and him and Ingibjörg and Guðjón in Akureyri, visits from him in New York. "Isobel," he gasped. "Tell me what will make you feel good. Tell me what will make you happy."

Too shy to answer, Isobel simply tasted the salt on his skin. They came together, her breath rough, her fingertips pressed flat against his chest. They lay in bed, her head in the crook of his arm, and he traced the outline of her lips. "You are the most exquisite combination of body and mind," he said.

❧

Isobel returned to Ragna's at eleven the next morning. Ragna was in the kitchen, feet on a chair, stubbing her cigarette into an ashtray while she talked on the phone in rapid, animated Icelandic. She waved to Isobel with her free hand and motioned her into a chair.

"*Já, já,*" she said. "Okay. *Takk fyrir að hringja. Bless bless.*"

She hung up and lit another cigarette. "So," Ragna said, "how was your night?"

"Beautiful. The best I've ever spent with him."

"Beware Norsemen bearing drunken gifts."

Isobel laughed. "Did you worry about me?"

"Of course, Isobel. But I'm not your mum."

"No, you're much more fun."

Ragna smiled. "Want some *kleinur*?"

"Sure. I'm starving."

She tossed Isobel the full plastic bag. "I need to go out dancing tonight," she said, the same way you'd announce that you needed to pick up a carton of milk at the store. "Want to leave Valdi at my mother's and join me?"

"Seriously?"

"*Já.* I haven't been in so long."

"Umm . . . yeah, if you want to."

"Don't look so nervous. No drinking necessary, and we can protect each other from the assholes."

"That sounds great. Girls' night out."

"Better rest up," Ragna said. "I can be a bit of a wild one."

"Oh, I don't doubt that."

Ragna stood and plucked her keys from the table. "Off to escort my angelic son to his drama class." She gave Isobel a quick peck on the cheek. *"Sjáumst."*

⌇

That night, the purple-mouthed newscaster had already wished them *"Góða nótt"* before Ragna decided it was time for them to prepare. They crowded at the sink in her bathroom, primping like teenagers. "Let me do your hair," Ragna said, and stood behind Isobel to run her hands through it. "God, it's beautiful. Masses and masses of red."

"Trust me, you can have it."

"Here, I'll put it up with this." She grabbed a tortoiseshell clip from the counter and pulled Isobel's hair into it, then raked her own dark locks into a crazily dramatic topknot. "Off to my closet."

Ragna's bedroom was tiny, with an almost empty white particleboard armoire. She peeled out of her clothes without a shred of embarrassment and put on a plain black dress with spaghetti straps. Isobel thought to ask if she would get cold, but then remembered Ragna's resilience.

"How about this for you, Isobel?" she said, without a hint of Elika's playful but pushy insistence. She held up a tight orange halter top with a plunging neckline, and a long, swishy skirt in brown rayon.

"Those two? Together?"

"Why not? It'll be brilliant. Very striking."

"Sure. Why the hell not."

Isobel changed in the bathroom and came out with her head lowered.

"Isobel, you look smashing," Ragna said, pulling on a black down jacket. "Let's go."

Isobel felt less inhibited in the crisp, damp night air. They walked past the pond and toward Ingólfstorg. "What's that pub there?" Isobel said.

Ragna snorted. "Oh, that's Kaffi Reykavík," she said. "Good food, but it's a secondhand shop."

"What do you mean?"

"We'll step in for a minute, and you'll see."

They entered the white wooden building and found most of the middle-aged crowd clustered around the bar. A few brave souls gyrated on the small, dimly lit dance floor to a cover band's poor renditions of seventies American ballads.

Isobel gave it a discreet thumbs-down. Ragna laughed. "Told you," she said as they walked out. "Let's go to Astró."

"Where's that?"

"I'm sure you've seen it, on Austurstræti. An elegant little techno haven for the cocaine-addicted sons and daughters of wealthy businessmen."

"Ragna," Isobel said as they approached the club, "this is where I went my first night out."

"You've got excellent taste," she yelled over the din of the music. "Let's see if we can get in."

They opened the door to find a bouncer, female this time. She leaned down and spoke to Ragna in polite Icelandic, and Ragna took Isobel's arm and steered her outside.

"What did she say?" Isobel asked.

"It's a private party," she said. "Don't worry, I know where I can take you."

Isobel followed her down near the harbor, to Gaukur á Stöng, a pub that, Ragna explained, was Reykjavík's first proper venue for youth-oriented music. "It's a bit like a high school dance," she said, as they passed through its small foyer, "but I think you'll find it amusing."

The dance floor was tiny and packed, with a few tables around its fringes. On stage, under the spotlight, a band played everything from Britpop to hip-hop, while their audience thrashed in tight cliques or simply jumped up and down, dizzy with euphoria, as they sang along with the English lyrics, their accents near perfect save for occasional endearing glitches. Isobel hung back and watched their antics while Ragna went to the bar for a drink. She had been right; it was like a high school dance, complete with young men dressed in black, sitting on the sidelines. The way they eyed Isobel over their beers, coupled with the disapproving glances of one or two women, made her wonder if the orange halter had been a good idea, but she had little time to ponder before a stocky, pleasant-faced girl in a miniskirt and a denim jacket pulled Isobel into her circle. She yelled something Isobel couldn't understand as Isobel began to sway awkwardly to the music.

"I'm sorry," Isobel shouted back. "I couldn't hear you."

"Oh," the girl said, apparently nonplussed by the fact that Isobel was American. "I'm Dóra. What's your name?"

"Isobel," she said, and that was the extent of their conversation. They danced together to a song they both knew, singing along off-key, Dóra with better knowledge of the lyrics than Isobel. When the next tune began, Dóra noticed a friend of hers, a husky guy with glasses and a blond crew cut, and ran to throw her arms around him with a happy scream.

Abandoned, Isobel did the perfunctory step from side to side that those on the edge of the action do to convince themselves that they're part of the scene. A raucous, punk-flavored song began, and several people motioned for her to climb on top of a table with them. Isobel shocked herself by hopping onto a chair and taking the hand a statuesque woman in a white sleeveless dress offered to hoist her up. Isobel could barely move, and the tabletop's stability was precarious at best. The room smelled like ale and sweat. A man dove into the table, and Isobel had to grab the shoulder of the person next to her to keep from crashing to the floor. She couldn't see Ragna anywhere.

After the punk song, the rest of the dancers jumped down, surprisingly agile, and Isobel could breathe again. The next music genre of choice was reggae, and the lead singer sufficed as a decent Nordic Bob Marley. Alone on the table, Isobel began to unfold. Her body moved in sinuous, buttery ways, her hips smooth and open. Strands of her hair came loose from their tight clip, and she lifted them off her neck. A sly, absorbed smile sprung from her lips, and Isobel could tell she was garnering attention by the way Dóra's male friend stared up at her, mouth open wide, teeth gleaming with ferocity and lust. Her dance was not about seduction or flirtation, although she thrilled at the knowledge that she would turn all those eighteen-year-olds on and then walk away. No, her dance was a loose, unlocked tribute to the corporeal, a means of making love to the hurt fragments of herself that stubbornly refused the beautiful incarceration of living in a body.

The band took a break, and Isobel sat down on top of the table. A young man with messy brown hair, one of the more casual patrons in jeans and a sweatshirt, came over and mumbled what Isobel gathered from his tone was a come-on. She vaguely recognized him from Dóra's circle.

"*Fyrirgefdu mig,*" Isobel said. "*Ég er ekki Íslendinga.*"

Her plea of tourist ignorance, which Ragna had taught her, did not deter him. In fact, it intrigued him even more.

"You are the hottest table dancer here," he said, his accent so thick it was almost like a parody.

"Thanks," Isobel said, "but I'm not interested."

He leaned forward and put his hand, hard, around the back of her neck. Isobel stiffened, flattered yet panicked. Then she felt a cool, thin hand lift his moist one from her skin, and an unmistakably raspy voice shouting behind her.

The man backed away, his gaze still on Isobel. "You are new to Iceland," he said. "We all make mistakes."

"Góða nótt," Isobel murmured, but he had already made his way toward the bar. She turned to find Ragna, a grin on her face.

"Just call me the avenger," she said. "They'll try anything at one in the morning."

"What did you yell at him?"

"To get the fuck away from my friend, or else I'd ensure that he limped home."

"Thanks. He seemed pretty harmless, but you never know."

"He was, but when I saw him clamp on to you like that, my sisterly instincts went into overdrive."

"I'm glad. Did you get a chance to do any dancing?"

"Not really. It's sad, but it's hard to do your own thing without getting propositioned in these clubs. And I'm not particularly in the mood for cradle-robbing." She helped Isobel to the floor. "I saw you, though. You looked lovely, very in touch with yourself. Which I'm sure threatens the hell out of them, seeing as they think it's one big display for their erotic benefit." She made a face. "Want to get something to drink?"

Isobel nodded. Thankfully, her nemesis had already departed when they got to the bar. "What do you want?" Ragna asked. "I'll get it for you."

"Could I try a shot of *brennivín*?" Isobel was curious about the country's national drink.

"You can, but I don't know why you'd want to. I can't stand the stuff." The bartender came near them. *"Einn einfalden brennivín, takk!"*

A moment later, Ragna handed her a small shot glass. Isobel peered into it nervously, then tipped her head back and swallowed its contents in one foolish gulp of bravura. The liquid tasted like eighty-proof licorice on fire. Isobel grimaced.

"You're a madwoman," Ragna said.

"I feel fine," Isobel told her as they walked out.

"You say that now," she said, "but give it a few minutes."

As usual, Ragna was right. By the time they reached the pond again, Isobel had a searing headache. Her limbs felt spongy. Her senses swirled.

"Ragna," Isobel said, "I know this may sound silly, but I love you."

Ragna put her arm around her. *"Vína mín,* you're drunk."

"No. I mean, yes, I am, but that's not why I'm saying it. I do."

"That's very sweet of you." They turned onto Skálholtsstígur. "Let's get you off to bed."

Once inside her apartment, Isobel didn't bother with brushing her teeth or washing her face. She simply took off the skirt and the hair clip and crawled under the duvet, still wearing the orange halter top.

Ragna came into her room for a moment and stood over Isobel in her red satin robe. Her features reminded Isobel of the face on a Viking doll she'd seen in a souvenir shop: weathered yet graceful. "Do you need anything before I go to sleep?" Ragna said.

Hold me, Isobel thought. Tell me every piece in me isn't falling apart.

But she merely shook her head and thanked her for asking.

Letting the Body Lead

ॐ

That week, Ragna's friend Bragi finally got around to arranging the mountain-climbing trip, and she begged Isobel to come with them. "It'll be brilliant," she said. "You know the feeling you had dancing by yourself? Climbing is like that, only better."

Initially, Isobel balked. She told Ragna that she had never done something so physically strenuous and was apprehensive, which was true, but Isobel knew the real reason was far less honorable: she didn't want to leave Kjartan.

"Oh, don't worry about it," Ragna said in answer to Isobel's complaints that she didn't have hiking boots, and that she would slow the rest of the more experienced group down. "If you need to stop, you tell us, and we'll stop. There's no shame in that."

Isobel was cornered. She called Kjartan and told him she would be gone to Mount Esja all day Saturday.

"My beautiful, delicate girl," he said. "You're not built like us, you'll be marred by those sharp rocks."

For one piercing, poignant moment, Isobel thought of Sylvia's torn lip, and of her lie: *Oh, that. I slipped.*

"Stop being ridiculous," Isobel said. "We'll talk when I get back."

The afternoon they departed was stunning, the sky so blue Isobel had to squint and wonder whether it was a painted backdrop for some pastoral film. "You're a meteorological good-luck charm, Isobel," Ragna said as they got in her squat white car, she and Isobel in the front, Valdi in warm-up jacket and sunglasses—the epitome of preadolescent cool—in the backseat. "The weather's never this good normally, is it, Valdi?"

Walkman headphones firmly in place, he pretended not to hear her. They drove over to pick up Bragi and his girlfriend, Gréta, at their flat on Barónsstígur, a charming walk-up full of light and paintings and antiques. Gréta answered the door in full outdoors gear—down overalls, parka, high-tech socks. She and Bragi were so pink-cheeked and robust, so fresh off a well-to-do catalogue page, that Isobel felt drab and inept in her threadbare sweater and clunky boots borrowed from Ragna, yet somehow purified in their presence. They greeted her with affectionate handshakes and the inescapable "So how do you like Iceland?," and then it was time to cram back into Ragna's car for the drive to Esja. Gréta had to sit on Bragi's lap, and Isobel was stuck holding their bulging backpack.

"Isobel and I had a night out this week," Ragna said.

"*Já*, and they left me at Amma's," Valdimar said with only half-joking sourness.

"I hear you're a doctoral student," Gréta said to Isobel. "What were you doing at the discos?"

"Field study," Isobel said. They howled with laughter.

"Turn here, Ragna," Bragi shouted. She swerved across the road and into a parking area near the base of the mountain.

"Mama isn't known for her precise driving," Valdi said.

"I get you where you need to be, don't I?" As they piled out of the car, Ragna smiled at Isobel. "Ready for an adventure?"

The first portion of the climb was deceptively easy, but as it grew steeper, Isobel fell behind. Bragi and Gréta, the experts, remained in the lead, with Valdimar tagging along so as not to be outdone. Ragna stayed next to Isobel—"To pace myself," she said sweetly, which was her kind way of announcing she had volunteered to keep the slowpoke company. Several times Isobel had to clutch Ragna's arm to keep from tripping.

Every time she grew frustrated, however, all Isobel had to do was turn to view the rock she had traversed, and the countryside as it opened like the fingers of a verdant hand below her. Halfway to the top, they stopped on the side of the mountain to rest and rehydrate. Like a preschool teacher at snack time, Gréta doled out small cardboard boxes of orange juice, and even though Isobel felt like a three-year-old, she slurped the drink gladly, her taxed body rejoicing at its sticky citrus sweetness.

Isobel leaned back in the grass and closed her eyes. The breeze stroked her hair. If she reached out, she could touch Ragna or Valdi beside her. Nestled in a high embrace, Isobel dozed, then woke to laughter. Her blurred eyes fixed on the horizon, its washes of green and blue, and, terrified yet transfixed, she thought: I want to be the skyline, I think I am the skyline.

"*Jæja,*" Bragi said, stretching his arms. "Time to get going."

"Somebody wake Valdi," Isobel said, and pointed to him, fast asleep with his headphones still on.

Ragna shook her son's shoulder. "*Elskan,*" she said, "back on the trail."

He grumbled and yawned but then darted ahead of them. Isobel pulled off her sweater and tied it around her waist, stripping down to a tank top. Sweat began to dot her arms.

"How are you doing, Isobel?" Bragi asked. "Ready to quit yet?"

"Hell, no," she said. "I'm going the whole way up!"

As they reached the top, the path grew slippery and convoluted. Isobel flailed out at loose rocks, and a rough edge nicked her palm. Blood and dirt mingled together. She showed it to Gréta, who called, "Bragi, have you got a plaster?"

He nodded, and she unzipped his pack and dug through it for a Band-Aid. She bandaged Isobel's hand. "All better," she said. "Are you nervous? Here, take my arm."

Isobel held on to her for the last half hour of the trek. Her feet hurt, and her breath came deep and hard, but she accomplished her goal. Ragna ran over and gave Isobel a wild hug.

"You did it!" she said. "Sign the book."

She led Isobel over to a tall metal stand where a guest book lay. Ragna signed her name and handed the pen to Isobel. Isobel wrote carefully beneath her, and smiled at their pair of autographs:

RAGNA BJÖRK ARNARDÓTTIR, REYKJAVÍK, ÍSLAND
ISOBEL KATHRYN SIVULKA, NEW YORK CITY, U.S.A.

"Look," Ragna said, and gestured down below. "There's the valley where I grew up." She pronounced the *v* like a *w*.

"Really?" Isobel said. "You lived in the country?"

"Oh, yes, my dear, I'm a rural girl at heart. Halldór Laxness—you know, the author—grew up there, too." She waved. "Hello, my beloved valley! And see, over there is the harbor."

"Come on!" Valdi yelled. "We're going to eat!"

They grinned and joined the others to sit cross-legged in a circle, as if they were at summer camp. Gréta passed them small bottles of water, and Bragi got out flatbread, slices of lamb, and butter. "Here, Isobel," Valdimar said, rummaging in the backpack and tossing her a package of cookies. "Try the Pólo biscuits, they're good."

Isobel broke open the plastic and tried one. It was a delectable chocolate wafer with a faint coconut flavor, and by the time everyone else had been served the meat and bread, she had helped herself to half the cookies.

"Hey!" Valdi said. "Save some for me!"

"Don't listen to him," Gréta said. "We've got another package."

When they finished eating, Bragi brushed himself off and said, *"Jæja."* They all groaned and stumbled to their feet.

The first ten minutes of the climb down were horrific. Bragi and Gréta each grabbed one of Isobel's arms as she slammed, ass first, onto the slick ground. Her shirt billowed, and a huge rock slid inside it toward her chest. They hoisted her forward just as a man who they recognized came up the trail with a walking stick. Bragi and Gréta chatted with the man for a few minutes, then sent him on with a cheery *"Bless bless!"*

"Who was that?" Isobel asked.

"The Minister of the Environment," Bragi said.

"Shit," Isobel whispered to Gréta. "Leave it to me to meet political luminaries with sediment down my bra."

Gréta tipped her head back and laughed. She and Bragi guided Isobel until the route grew more stable. Their steps were light, and the air was cool. They jumped from stone to stone in a gurgling stream of brutal sapphire clarity, and refilled their bottles with its clear, icy water. Two hours later, they reached Ragna's car, achy and exhausted but content.

They drove back to Bragi and Gréta's, where the hosts cooked a full lamb dinner and offered Isobel, the resident foreigner, an introduction to Christmas brew, an odd combination of malt and orange soda that tasted fine on the first sip but soured in her stomach before she emptied the glass. By the time they sat at the table to eat, it was almost eleven in the evening, and through the curtained window the sky glistened, still pale and bright. They passed around bowls of corn and peas (or "green beans," as Gréta called them) and platters of baked potatoes, and when they were ready for dessert, Bragi said, "We're going on a longer trip next weekend. Would you like to join us, Isobel?"

"Beware," Valdi said. "When they say a longer trip, they mean it. Six-hour hikes."

"That would kill me," Isobel said.

"No, it wouldn't," Gréta said. "You're an excellent hiker, considering it was your first time."

"Especially given the awful shoes you had on," Bragi said.

Ragna threw a napkin at him. "Those are my shoes, thank you very much."

"In all seriousness, we'd love to have you," Bragi said. "It would be no problem making arrangements with the touring club."

Isobel rubbed her sore palm. Thought again of Sylvia.

"I'll do it," she said.

꿍

Buoyed by her foray into nature, Isobel spent most of the following week in a leisurely state of tranquil puttering. She sang in the shower, beat Valdi at video games, and, curled up on Ragna's red velvet couch, even managed to undertake a cursory, non-threatening reappraisal of her dissertation notes without spasms of anxiety.

Isobel did not call Kjartan. She knew she had broken a promise and realized she faced boundless theatrics, but she craved comfortable space, a clean bed, an existence free of *mórall*. That Thursday, Isobel received a postcard with her last name misspelled above Ragna's address. The picture on the reverse side advertised a nightspot called Wunderbar, and his barely legible message read:

Isobel mín (the amnesiac),

Have you forgotten how the telephone works in the midst of your frolics on mountaintops? Or are you merely ashamed to be seen with a boring, decrepit thing like me?

Hearts, flowers, etc. etc.

(or whatever brings my fickle girl in her wicked turquoise back round again)

Isobel couldn't decide whether to savor his pining wit or to rip up his letter. She tucked the postcard into her purse and told herself to forget it.

Letting the Body Lead

That night, after dinner, Ragna and Valdi went to visit her sister Áslaug, and Isobel told them she would stay behind and straighten up the kitchen. She washed the dishes, fed Siggi, read the children's page of the paper. At ten o'clock, she couldn't stand it anymore. Isobel wrote Ragna a note—*Gone out, will call later, no need to worry, love, I.*—and tucked it beneath a magnet on the refrigerator. She threw on her coat, put the spare key in her pocket, and headed straight for Kjartan's restaurant.

Isobel caught him at the end of his shift. He sat across from her at a table, shoulders slumped.

"We've got a good merlot," he said. "You want some?"

"Sure."

"Well then, you'll have to order it yourself, because I'm broke."

"Listen," Isobel said. "I'm sorry."

"You look positively aglow," he said. "So healthy and smooth and renewed from your little pilgrimage high above the city."

"If you're trying to induce guilt," Isobel said, "it's not working."

"I'm beyond guilt," he said, with a rueful, jagged laugh. His breath smelled fetid, like alcohol. He took her hand, caressed her wrist.

"What will you do in August, Isobel?" he said, so suddenly it stopped her. "When you go back to the States, what will you have learned? That we are all a bunch of superficial, insular creatures no matter what the travelogues say? That the sound of every textbook you have read slamming closed with a snap can never rival the song of your shaky, shivering breath as you come?"

She swallowed. *You may dance like them,* Isobel told herself, *but you're not one of the girls from your mentoring group back in Brooklyn. You're a grown woman. Stand.*

Isobel stood.

"Shut up," she said. She tossed her coat over her arm and ran for the door, bumping into a waitress as she passed. "*Afsakið,*"

Isobel said sharply, "excuse me." She took the steps two at a time so no one would see the tears that burned on her face. She bolted the whole way back to Ragna's and let herself in. Valdi stood in the hallway in his bare feet, gazing at her with a look of confused alarm.

"Mama!" he bellowed. "Isobel's crying!"

Ragna rushed in from the kitchen, her mobile phone tucked under her chin. She led Isobel into the living room, still talking to her friend. She handed Isobel a box of tissues, ended her call, and sat down beside her.

"Did you have a good time at Áslaug's?" Isobel said, sniffling.

"*Já,*" she said. "Valdi tore about the yard with her dog. But what's happened to you?"

Isobel told her the whole story. "There's no reason to make a fuss over me," she said, blowing her nose. "I brought it completely upon myself."

"Maybe you did, maybe you didn't, but it still hurts to be treated like shit."

Valdi, who had been lurking tentatively in the doorway, came and sat on the other side of Isobel. "Hey, don't cry, Isobel," he said. "I'll let you eat the whole packet of Pólo biscuits this weekend."

Isobel laughed. "It's hard to be melancholy around you guys for too long."

"I'll take that as a compliment," Ragna said. "And if you'd like, tomorrow we can go to Kringlan and find you a pair of proper hiking boots."

"*Já!* Kringlan!" Valdi shouted.

"I didn't know you had such an interest in shopping," Isobel said.

"You don't understand," he said, enunciating in the charming style of a child who'd learned English from imported television. "It's not just shopping—there is *games!*"

"Speaking of which," Isobel said, "I bet you a hundred krónur that I can beat you in that racing one we tried the other night."

"Okay," he said, and yanked her up from the couch. "But I'm gonna win!"

His prediction came true, because every time Isobel tried to concentrate on steering her car, her mind wandered toward the feel of her ex-lover's fingers on her wrist.

๛

The next day, Isobel busied herself on a shopping trip with Ragna. She bought the sought-after pair of boots and a handknit sweater for baby Laura, which Valdimar gave his infamous critique of "fucking gross."

"My son the crusader against provincialism," Ragna said, rolling her eyes as the salesgirls in the shop whispered to each other in disapproval of his manners. "Don't listen to a word he says, my dear."

They spent the rest of the afternoon packing for their trip to Þórsmörk. Isobel was warring with the zipper on her pack when Ragna came into the guest room and handed her a folded, stapled piece of paper. "This came in the mail," she said.

Isobel opened it and attempted to decipher Kjartan's handwriting amid the coffee stains:

Fervent apologies for bad behavior. Anything I can do to alienate you further, baby?

Sarcasm, stream of consciousness, all veiled, pedantic (I know you like that) attempts to say . . . ÉG SAKNA ÞÍN!

P.S. There is only one more week till August . . . !

Isobel showed it to Ragna. She shook her head. "He knows how to appeal to you, doesn't he?" she said. "But don't think about him right now. Just concentrate on what a brilliant, invigorating trip we're going to have."

"What does the Icelandic he wrote mean?" Isobel asked.

Ragna sighed.

"It's 'I miss you,'" she said.

∾

After an early dinner, they met Bragi and Gréta at the long-distance bus terminal on the outskirts of town. Loaded down with backpacks and rolled sleeping bags, they clambered onto a pale green bus for the several-hour trip. Isobel chose a seat near the front, by herself. The tour guide stood beside the driver and narrated in Icelandic, Valdi nodded in time with the music on his Walkman, and Isobel pulled out the slip of paper from Kjartan and read it over and over.

It was almost ten o'clock when they crossed the river that signified the entrance to the campsite. Water sloshed against the sides of the bus. Wheels ground over stones in a hard-edged lullaby. Everywhere Isobel looked, the grass lay dotted with small purple wildflowers that made her twitch with quiet hope. She looked over at Ragna, who was reading an English-language paperback of *She's Come Undone*, which had topped the best-seller lists for months back home. She noticed Isobel and smiled.

Once off the bus, Bragi led them up a hill to the wooden hut that would serve as their home for the next two nights. It consisted of one open common room, with shelves for their shoes; a closet-sized kitchen with a sink, camp stove, and cupboards full of tin plates; and two sleeping areas off the main foyer. They chose the barracks to their left, with bunks on three of its walls and a long table in the middle. The quarters were crammed but immaculate, and a friendly, eager air prevailed as they padded around in their woolen socks, setting up their makeshift beds.

Bragi and Gréta chose the top bunk on the far wall, and Ragna and Valdi took the top one above Isobel's, graciously allowing her the full bottom bunk. No sooner had Isobel unwound the neon-orange sleeping bag she had borrowed from Ragna, when Bragi, who had unpacked and organized in a matter of seconds, asked them, "So, who's up for a short walk?"

"Short," Valdi said. "That means we might be back in time for breakfast."

"No, it doesn't," Gréta said. "We don't want to wear out poor Isobel on her first night."

"Poor Isobel," Valdi said, "can kick our asses if we give her a chance."

They all laughed.

ᴖᶥ

They took a brief stroll up the hill in the twilight, and Ragna took photos of Valdi, slim and athletic, hopping about on a sturdy cliff. On their way back down toward the camp, they passed a village of tents.

"They don't stay out here for the rustic pleasure of it," Gréta whispered to Isobel. "They sleep in the tents so they can drink and be loud."

As usual, Isobel fell to the back of the line and encountered a little girl, no older than Ásta, who sat on her bottom at the base of the hill. Tears rolled down her face. Her nose dripped onto her adorable red sweater, which matched the ribbons that held up her corn-colored pigtails. She wore a child's knapsack, but it was far too heavily loaded for her, and in her lap she held a six-pack of Egils that she had obviously been assigned to carry.

Isobel knelt beside her and touched the small, hunched shoulder. She mustered every shred of Icelandic she could to ask, *"Ta-larðu ensku?"*

The little girl didn't answer, only sobbed harder. Isobel calmed her with soothing murmurs, those linguistic universals, enough that the girl would allow Isobel to help her take off the pack while waving furiously for Ragna.

Ragna and Gréta ran up from the hut. Ragna reached them first and guided the child to her feet. *"Ekki gráta,"* she said. *"Allt í lagi, elskan."*

She must have also asked what was wrong, because the little girl stammered a few words about *"pabbi minn."* My father.

Gréta slung the girl's knapsack over her shoulder, then picked up the beer with one hand and gently took the little girl's arm with the other.

"What happened?" Isobel asked Ragna as they watched Gréta and the little girl ascend toward the tents.

Ragna shook her head. "Her father gave her all that shit to carry," she said, "and when she fell, he just left her at the bottom of the hill."

"Jesus," Isobel said. "And making her deliver the booze, too."

"I know, but Gréta will take charge of it," Ragna said. "Look."

She pointed at a tall man in a plaid shirt and baggy jeans, clearly the child's father. They watched Gréta speak sharply but politely to him, and giggled as his daughter did a wiggly dance of happy reunion around him in her leggings and boots and flannel skirt. He ignored her until Gréta finished her lecture, and then they heard him scold the little girl: *"Ingibjörg!"*

Isobel turned away and shuddered.

"It's very strange," Ragna said, sensing Isobel's discomfort but immune to its source. "Children are usually treated so much better here."

They said nothing more about it as they got their toothbrushes from the hut and walked to another building, near the buses, which consisted of two restrooms with a set of water fountains in between. The ceiling in the women's room echoed with the sounds of chatter and laughter. Isobel had to wait ten minutes for a spot at the sink, and hurriedly brushed her teeth and splashed delightfully frigid water on her face.

Ragna was already waiting for her by the fountain when she emerged.

"How are you doing?" she said. "You look tired."

"This is definitely a departure for me," Isobel said, "but I feel good."

"I'm glad."

They linked arms, like sisters, and walked back to the bunk room. Isobel crawled into her sleeping bag and wrestled out of her jeans, too shy to undress before twenty strangers. Ragna climbed the ladder to join Valdi.

"Now, Isobel," he called down over the ever present hum of his rap music, "if she snores, just bang the wall and wake her up."

"Oh, hush, Tupac Shakur," Ragna said. *"Góða nótt."*

Isobel listened to Bragi and Gréta murmur to each other across the room, and pretended not to hear the delicate smack of their good-night kiss.

✺

Isobel slept so soundly that both Ragna and Valdi had jumped to the floor and made their breakfasts before she even wriggled from her sleeping bag.

"Góðan dag," Ragna said. "I've set out yogurt for you if you'd like some."

"Takk," Isobel said, and sat at the table in her rumpled T-shirt and jeans, the same outfit she had worn the day before and would wear the entire weekend. "Where are Bragi and Gréta?"

"Planning ways to torture us," Valdi said, mouth full.

"Valdimar, please." Ragna passed Isobel the container of milk. "They're outside consulting the map. The tour guide is asking *them* for advice."

"Did you hear the party last night?" Valdi asked Isobel.

"No, but I did hear you snoring."

"Bullshit!"

"Children, children," Ragna said in mock admonishment.

"Honestly," Isobel said, "I didn't hear a thing. I was out cold."

"Well, I wasn't," Valdi said. "Not with the people smashing bottles for fun at three in the morning."

"Ah, *Ísland*," Ragna said. "Come on, my darling squabblers. We don't want to keep the expeditioners waiting."

⌒⥾

The events of that day became fixed in Isobel's mind as a montage of radiant, earthen moments: running down a hill into a meadow from which it seemed she could see the whole world; clutching Bragi's arm while a sweet woman with salt-and-pepper hair clutched hers as they climbed across a huge chasm; eating Póló biscuits huddled in their anoraks under one umbrella during a surprise rain.

"This girl deserves a medal!" the tour guide shouted, pointing to Isobel as she slogged valiantly through the last half hour of the all-day hike. Isobel grinned weakly and staggered into Ragna.

"Here, you brilliant trooper," Ragna said, hoisting Isobel's pack onto her own shoulders. "Let me take the weight for a while."

When they reached the hut, Isobel's body was in such pain that Valdi had to help her out of her boots. She collapsed inside her sleeping bag, still in her damp jeans, and dozed. When she woke, the rain had slowed to a drizzle, and a jolly group had congregated in the common room. Someone had brought a guitar, and the crowd was singing Beatles songs.

Isobel hobbled into the kitchen to find Gréta and Ragna washing vegetables in the sink.

"Did you have a good nap, my dear?" Ragna said.

"Super. Can I help?"

"No, no," Gréta said. "Just sit yourself down and rest."

Isobel edged onto a chair next to a small table and watched their strong hands swirl in the water. She crossed one leg and pulled down her sock to reveal a huge, oozing blister on her ankle.

"Ugh," Isobel said. "I hope I'm not gangrenous."

Gréta peered over to examine. "Oh, my," she said. "That must hurt, but it will heal. We'll get Bragi to bandage it when he comes in."

"Where did he and Valdi go?" Isobel asked.

"Bragi is grilling the lamb," Ragna said, "and Valdi is either assisting or annoying, I'm not sure which."

Isobel grinned and, limping, helped them carry plates and silverware in to the table. Bragi returned with the lamb, and Valdi followed with the requisite platter of potatoes. "The drunks are all jealous of our fine dinner!" he said.

"What a tactful creature I've raised," Ragna said. "Set that plate down before you drop it."

Isobel's new friend with the salt-and-pepper hair came in, and they invited her to join them. She bound Isobel's foot with an ingenious sort of plaster, and they drank Peruvian wine from paper cups and played cards until midnight. Isobel beat Valdi but lay awake while he slept, listening to the shouts and shenanigans of the tent city as penance.

ॐ

The next day, the others went on one of Bragi's "short" walks, but, due to her blisters, Isobel abstained. She sat outside the hut on top of a wooden picnic table, and attempted to read Ragna's paperback. After almost two months in Iceland, however, the blunt, unadorned English words looked lifeless. Isobel took Kjartan's letter out of her pocket and traced its lines until they smudged.

Ragna was the first to return. She swung on top of the table and handed Isobel a sprig of the purple flowers she liked so much. "Bouquet for the invalid," she said.

"The invalid thanks you! How was the walk?"

"One of Bragi's more moderate routes. Brisk and lovely." She jumped down again. "Here they come. Let's pack it up, *vina mín.*"

They loaded their bags onto the bus, and as it pulled away, Isobel strained to look out the window, as if for something or someone (little tear-stained Ingibjörg?). Halfway through the trip, the bus stopped at a service station for a break. Isobel gave Gréta enough money to get her a bottle of lemonade at the snack counter, and waited in line at the restroom, unable to forget the image of Sylvia, her fingers stained with chocolate, in a similar shop with a man who had hit her. Isobel tore Kjartan's letter into tiny pieces and flushed it down the toilet.

☙

When they returned to the bus terminal, Bragi kissed Isobel goodbye on the cheek. She thought of how he had knelt on the floor to bandage her foot that morning, his face full of concern and genuine tenderness, as if Isobel were a grown-up daughter he was still proud to take care of. Isobel dabbed the corner of one eye with her windbreaker sleeve after she got into Ragna's car.

They had barely dragged their luggage into her flat when Valdi yelled, "Show her the drawing you did, Mama!"

"That can wait, Valdimar," she said, but came into Isobel's room a few minutes later while she was unpacking.

"This is what Valdi wanted me to show you," she said, and un-rolled a sheet of thick, high-quality paper.

It was a sketch, torn from a journal, of Isobel nestled on top of her sleeping bag after the long hike. Hands placed under her cheek, hair shrouding her face and misted with droplets of rain, Isobel slept, her features imbued with a serenity and luminous power she never knew she had. In the corner were Ragna's initials and the words *Resting Isobel at Þórsmörk*, with the date.

"I drew it at the table while you were asleep," Ragna said. "I hope you don't mind. You just looked so peaceful, and I wanted to capture that."

"*Mind?*" Isobel said. "Ragna, I love it. But it can't be me."

"Oh, yes, it is," she said, and pressed the page into Isobel's hands. "Here, keep it as a reminder of what you have—"

"*Mama, komdu hérna!*" Valdi called from his room.

Ragna shook her head. "Let me go attend to the master of the house. I'll be right back."

After she left, Isobel tucked the drawing in the corner of the bureau mirror, beside the wildflowers she had hung upside down to dry as a memento of the trip. Their deep-hued mouths cried out in a parched hunger, one that Isobel wanted to deny but was forced to recognize as her own.

Chapter Twelve

New York City

After her final mentoring session in Brooklyn, Isobel didn't leave her apartment for two weeks. Sleep became a shallow pool that she dove into and resurfaced from at ragged intervals, disoriented by dreams of the girls she could not help, the girls whose bodies she could not make feel right and whole again.

Usually she woke at about four in the afternoon, around the time the cartoons started on television, and she would lie there wrapped in her blankets and watch, and cry during the commercials, those perky ads awash in the bright studio light that shone on the gaily colored ponies whose pink-and-purple tails you could brush, the gaunt dolls with their vacant, painted-on blue eyes fixed in a permanent state of dazed euphoria at all the combinations of shimmering nylon and garish-colored fur they could

wear. Isobel wept at the child actresses, their excited proclama-
tions eerie with staged joy, their stubby six-year-old fingers moving the blank-faced toys across a stark tabletop landscape, their
innocence so sweet it was sinister.

Every day at five-thirty, when the news began, Elika came in
and sat on the edge of her bed and had dinner with her to make
sure she was still eating. She brought carry-out, mostly, Chinese
and pizza, which Isobel could barely bring herself to taste. She sat
huddled underneath the covers, and every so often she'd set down
her chopsticks or her napkin, grab Elika's arm, and say, "I can't go
back to school. I can't do it." Her panic scared her. She felt disconnected from her words and her own fear, and that frightened
her even more.

"You don't have to go back now," Elika said.

"But I have to go back eventually. I can't leave like this, not so
close to the end. I mean, look at how I—"

Elika turned Isobel's chin to face her.

"Listen to me," she said. "You don't have to go back now. You
will not fall apart if you don't graduate on time. I promise."

"Even if I quit with one month to go?"

Elika leaned down and kissed the top of Isobel's head. "Poor
thing," she said. "God forbid you should cut yourself some slack."

They would sit there like that, listening to the television as it
droned, Isobel with her eyes closed, cheek against Elika's shoulder, momentarily reassured. Soon, though, Elika would become
too much a creature of the outside world where people laughed
and talked and made love and hailed taxis, and Isobel would send
her out of the room and curl up once more, numb and hot and
shaky, waiting for the refrains to quiet in her head while the answering machine clicked on and the drawn blinds fluttered and
she fitfully dozed again.

❦

"My mother told me that she and my stepfather would send me abroad as a graduation present," Isobel said softly to Elika one night, slumped over on pillows with the remnants of a deli sandwich in her lap.

"That's nice of them," Elika said.

"Yeah. Who knows when or if I'll graduate, but I've been thinking about the trip anyway."

"Do you know where you'd like to go?"

"I want to go to Iceland."

"Seriously? How come?"

"It's a long story."

"I've got no curfew."

Isobel told her the story of Ms. J.'s trip there.

"Is she why you want to go?" Elika asked.

Isobel sighed. "It's childish, it's chasing mythology, I know."

"I don't think so. If you want to go, and you have the means to do it, you should. Debunk the myths later."

"Do you know how lucky I am to have you living with me?" Isobel said. "Do you know how much you keep me from jumping out the window?"

Elika looked away. "Isobel," she said, "I can't keep you from doing that. All I can do is remind you how many times I've crouched on the ledge myself."

❦

The next night Elika brought her dinner and a surprise wrapped in purple floral paper. "It'll make you feel better, I promise," she said. Isobel warily slid up from under the covers and scraped the Scotch tape from one end of the box with a bitten-down fingernail. She peeled off the wrapping and found what appeared to be a blank cassette tape.

"Elika," she said, "what—"

"Icelandic music," Elika said, "that I dug out of my collection. It's from a friend of my dad's who lives on the naval base at Keflavík. Mostly eighties stuff, but I thought you'd like it."

Isobel squeezed Elika's hand. "Yes. Thank you. Yes."

They ate their Chinese food there on the bed, the tape still in Isobel's lap. Isobel only picked at the chow mein, but this time her lack of appetite came out of a nervous excitement, a sense of opening inside her instead of the slammed-shut feral anxiety that had sent her crawling beneath dirty sheets. Every so often she would pick up the tape and run her thumb over the pristine white label, blank with promise.

When Elika left to go to a video screening on campus, Isobel curled up beneath the blankets again, hugging herself. She reached for the tape on the pillowcase; its spools, she knew, held some hissing clue. She breathed in deep, as if with each breath she might reform herself and rise from the dank, murky contours of where she lay, her spongy trembling self replaced finger by finger, toe by toe, hardened into the bones and angles of an invincible woman.

After a few minutes, she swung over the side of the bed and shakily pulled on her robe. She ran her fingers through her hair in an attempt to remedy its tangled shagginess, to prepare for what she perceived to be an important ritual. She gripped the bedpost and pulled herself up, swaying on her feet. She felt hot, dizzy. Her mouth tasted sour. She hobbled around the bed, shoulders hunched, the tape tight in her fist. The floorboards creaked beneath her feet; the rooms loomed before her, terrifying in their white openness. She skimmed her hands across the walls to guide herself, her fingers crackling with the pain of rekindled energy, her legs' stiffness shooting through her with every jerky step. I have to close the curtains, she thought as she approached the living room. I can't look out onto the street. It was the first time she'd walked the whole way across the apartment in fifteen days.

She knelt before the stereo, knees rubbery now, and put the tape in the deck. Her furry brain's fog parted enough for her to remember which button to hit.

The first song took her by surprise: jangly country-western, slightly ridiculous but strangely sweet in its earnestness. She laughed, and the sound of her own voice—tremorous, metallic—surprised her even more. She turned the volume down a little. Her head hurt; she didn't know if she could stand again. She crawled across the floor to the kitchen, struck by the eerie sadness of the yellow linoleum tiles. She hoisted herself up, her hands gripping the counter. She shuffled through her kitchen with a dreamlike sense of fear and wonder; it was like walking around in the house of a dead woman, that aura of stopped life, dusty interruption. She opened cabinets gently, then the refrigerator. Peanut-butter jars. A bottle of cheap wine left over from Gavin's birthday. Silverware in the sink. The calendar on the wall still on April, its photograph of an English thatched cottage awash in glistening color. It was May now, wasn't it? She flipped one month forward, was about to tack it solidly up when she saw her defense appointment penned in glaring red on the eighth. She let the months fly back to April's bland bucolic scene and pulled her robe tighter.

The country-western song ended, and she tottered back toward the living room and leaned against the doorjamb to listen to the next one. Its opening notes undulated through her, spare and slightly jazzy, melancholy piano giving way to a deep, throaty male voice, hoarse and husky with ragged seduction; behind him came spare, soft washes of bare percussion and smoky guitar, like the brush of lips across a rapidly turning neck, a whisper heard in half-sleep. She pressed a hand to her mouth. She felt warm and open and completely splintered. She staggered across the carpet, moving toward the windows, arms wide. The singer's blissful rasp poured into Isobel's ears, her fear poured out of her, and as she gazed down onto the dusky street, she thought: I'm leaving.

♫

After that moment of jazz and revelation, Isobel expected some sort of wild change in her life, a miraculous shift that would spill energy through her and grant her the power to put on presentable clothes and enter the game of real life again.

But it didn't happen. The street sounds outside her window loomed with just as much loud danger as before, and a ringing phone sent her curling tighter under the covers. It was only in that spare evening hour of badly dubbed tape that calm came, enough to at least pace about the apartment, pick at the remains of her dinner with Elika, and listen to two weeks' worth of answering-machine ramblings.

"Isobel, please call your adviser. This is the third message I've left and I'm worried. I understand you're under a lot of stress, but you do realize that you have the defense in a week, don't you?"

Click.

"Hey, Isobel, it's me. Your godchild has started to kick, and I was so excited I just had to share. Hope your thesis is going super. Love ya. Call whenever."

Click.

"Isobel, sweetheart, it's Mom. Are you okay? We haven't heard from you in a while. Give us a call. We miss you."

Click.

"Isobel. Please call me. I've talked with Elika, I've been calling

you for days, and I just . . . I just want to see you, that's all. I'll try
again later. I love you."

Click.

She turned the stereo up louder. So loud she couldn't hear him
at all.

༄

One night after Elika left to go to a bar with some friends, Isobel put on the tape, took out her carton of the evening's leftovers,
and sat cross-legged on the living room rug. Shafts of burnished
shadow and stripes of fading sunlight fell across the floor and her
face. She shook a little, still quavery with the newness of being up,
but strangely satisfied as she nibbled at vegetable pakoras and
hummed along to the now familiar music.

At the end of the country-western song, she heard what she
thought was a knock at the door. She tensed. Swirled a samosa in
chutney. It's nothing, she told herself. Her jazz song came on, and
she cranked the volume. Lately she'd started to dance to it, in an
idiosyncratic, swaying stagger, an attempt to bring fluidity back to
her cramped, tight body. She shoved herself up from the floor and
waltzed across the room, slow and sinuous, the container of Indian food in one hand as if it were a dancing partner. She heard
the knock again, more insistent this time. She set the food down
on the carpet. Ignore it, she thought, and went back to her sultry
whirl. She tipped her head back. The entire room was suffused in
a deep peach glow.

"Isobel!" she heard. "Isobel!"

A desperate pounding.

She turned and glided away from the window toward the door.
If the music doesn't stop, she thought, maybe I can do this. Trembling, she undid the latch.

Letting the Body Lead

Gavin stood there in his faded khaki coat.

"Isobel, honey," he said, and opened his arms.

Even though she knew it was more for his benefit than hers, she let him hold her. He stroked her hair. "I haven't washed it in days," she said quietly.

"It's okay," he said, and, as if to prove his point, kissed the top of her head.

The song ended. She began to shiver.

"Oh, here, here," he said, and took off his jacket. "You're so cold. Put this on."

She shrugged it on over her thin sleeveless nightgown, feeling like an obedient child. They sat on the living room floor. She returned to her dinner, toying with the dumplings and yogurt sauce. "Do you want some?" she asked.

He shook his head. "Why haven't you called me?"

"I . . . I don't know. I don't have the energy anymore."

"For me?"

"For anything."

"Isobel, for Christ's sake. I was worried about you."

He pulled the collar of his jacket away and down, and kissed the back of her neck, her shoulder blade. Warmth rushed through her. She curled tighter in on herself, thinking, No, yes, don't do this, I care about you, I don't want to care for you, just hold me, go home. She leaned back against the futon and motioned him into her arms. He rested his head on her shoulder.

With his cheek against her bare skin, she closed her eyes and let her mind drift to thoughts of plane tickets, passport stamps, ascent. They sat there until the sunset turned the color of a fresh bruise, and then she asked him, meekly, if she could be alone again. "Yes," he said, "but you have to promise that you won't disappear on me for weeks."

"Fair enough," she said. She sat with her arms hooked limply around her drawn knees, her head tilted toward the window. Elika's tape had long since clicked off.

He got to his feet, then bent down, pressed his lips to her forehead. His mouth was moist, his kiss both forceful and tentative.

"I want to go to Iceland," she said.

"You what?" he said, laughing a little.

"You heard me."

"When? This summer?"

"No. Now. In May."

"What about your defense?"

"I can't do it."

"It's in a week."

"I don't care."

"You want to go to some random country instead of finishing your doctorate?" He cupped her face in his palm. "Come on. You're just upset, you're not making sense."

She dropped her chin. "Let me, then. Please, please, please let Isobel not make sense, just this once, okay?"

He drew his hand away. "All right. But you'll call me?"

She nodded and closed her eyes.

❧

"You're doing a lot better," Elika said the next night as they sat on the futon. Isobel had taken a shower and put on old jeans.

"Thanks," she said. "I figured that if I'm going to escape academic hell by fleeing the country, I might as well get dressed first."

Elika laughed. "You're still planning to forgo the defense?"

"Yeah. For better or for worse."

"Have you told your adviser?"

Isobel picked at a loose thread on her T-shirt. "No. She's left me a ton of messages, though."

"You should call her back."

She frowned. "I know, but she'll give me a whole litany of reasons why I shouldn't back out."

"Tell her thanks for the input, but no thanks, babe," Elika said, tucking a stray strand of Isobel's damp hair behind her ear. "You can decide what you want, but at least you owe the big bad bureaucracy a response."

"You're right."

"Okay, then, do it now."

"Elika, no, I can't—"

"Sure you can."

"I don't want to call her at home during dinner."

"Leave a message at her office. Here." Elika jumped up and handed her the phone with a smile. "Go on. It's all yours."

"Not now. Please. I can't tell her like this."

"At the very least, make an appointment to talk before your defense date. What are you going to do, skip it and go crying to her afterward?"

"Of course not. But what do I tell her, that I've been an absolute sloth for the last two weeks?"

"Say you were sick. It's not a total lie."

Isobel dialed, listened to Natalie's brief but cheerful voice mail, and mumbled a quick, breathless apology for taking so long to return her call, along with a request to meet before the eighth. She tossed the phone back to Elika. "Happy now?"

"You needed to do that, and you know it," Elika said. "Don't you feel relieved?"

"No."

"Well, you will once you hear my good news." She sat back down, one satin-clad leg thrust over the arm of the couch. "I talked to my dad last night, and I told him about your trip to Iceland. He said that he can check with those friends of his on the base about finding you a place to stay."

"Really? That would be wonderful." Isobel sighed. "Here you are, serving as my ad hoc therapist and travel agent, and I haven't even asked you how you're doing."

"Enough with the tertiary masochism, girlfriend; I'm not offended."

"You're never offended, but still . . . how's the documentary going?"

"The editing is taking fucking forever. I'll be lucky to finish by the end of the summer."

"I could still be away then," Isobel said softly.

༒

Gavin took the following afternoon off to be with Isobel. She answered the door wearing a pair of fresh pajamas in his honor, and was not prepared for the haggard look on his face or his red-rimmed eyes. It occurred to her that the past two weeks had done him as much damage as it had her. Tenderness pushed purpose into her idle body. "Come here," she said.

She led him into her bedroom, pulled back the covers, and guided him under them. They undressed languidly, their clothes a precisely discordant pile at the bottom of the quilt: her pale aqua top, his tie printed with sunflowers. He ran his fingers across her hipbone. It jutted out, like a secret that can no longer stay hidden. She moved his fingers down farther.

He settled above her. "Isobel, are you sure?"

The ambiguity of the question—*Are you sure you want this? Are you sure you'll leave?*—snagged in her head. She pressed her palm into the hollow of his neck.

"Go slowly," she said, "okay?"

Letting the Body Lead

❧

Afterward, they lay there, his back to her, and she ran her hands over his shoulders. He sighed. "You aren't really serious about Iceland, are you?"

"Ah, so I see what this is about," she said, smiling in spite of her irritation. "A lovely midafternoon nap as a vehicle of interrogation. It's brilliant, I have to hand it to you."

"Please. I just want to know why you've suddenly got the urge to go on some weird pilgrimage."

His words sent her fantasies of blissful escape tumbling into ruins. She sat up and yanked the blankets around herself, as if to protect her fragile dreams from his mockery. "Some weird pilgrimage?" she said.

"Well, it is, honey. You've never been off the East Coast before, much less out of the country, and face it, you're vulnerable."

"Just because I've had a rough time lately?"

"I'm not trying to be harsh. I only wish you'd think about the logistics, about your own safety. The last thing I want is to get a call from you in the middle of the North Atlantic telling me how lonely you are."

"Don't flatter yourself," she said.

"What was that about?"

"Come on," she said, "you know the main reason my plans are bugging you is because you can't bear the thought of us being apart."

He swung his legs over the side of the bed. "Listen, Isobel, I've got needs, too. And maybe if you snapped out of your self-absorption for all of two seconds, you'd see that my need to be near you is just as strong and valid as your desire to run an ocean away."

He pulled on his clothes before she could even respond, and

headed for the kitchen. She grabbed her robe and followed him. He turned in the doorway to face her.

"You're absolutely right," she said. "And the time I've spent with you has been light, and gorgeous, and more fun than I've ever had in my life."

He frowned. "I just thought that you, of all people, would see it as meaningful. Something more."

"I do. But can't you understand . . . don't you see that that's the point, that I've been searching for meaning so long that I need to learn how to just be, I need to stop analyzing, I—"

"You need some ephemeral *fun.*"

"Would you stop oversimplifying me?"

With an angry scrape, he pulled out a chair and straddled it. "I'll stop oversimplifying you when you stop trying to evade reality by flying to a foreign country."

"This isn't about fucking Iceland," she said. "It's about where I want to go with my life."

"Okay, then. Tell me."

She braced her arms to steady herself as she leaned against the kitchen counter. How do I say it? she thought, her throat clogged with wordless pleas for empathy. She paused.

"I want to take time off from school," she said finally. "I want no obligations."

"And what does that mean for us?"

"Look," she said, "we had an understanding. We were going to be reasonable, we were going to be open and honest and enjoy each other's company but not get snared in a web of romanticism. Remember?"

"Yes, but—"

"But what?"

"I love you."

She sighed, and crossed the room and rested her cheek against his hair, her arms draped loosely around his neck. "I love you, too," she said, "but love isn't a license to delude each other."

"You're such a cynic."

"No, I'm not."

"Don't you trust me?"

"Of course I trust you. You're one of the steadiest people I've ever met. I just feel like . . . lately you've been wanting more from me than I've got."

"I want things to be serious. That's all."

Stroking his face, she thought: You are dear and luminous and persuasively cute, but you are too much right now.

"Serious," she said. "Oh, sweetheart."

He pressed his palm to her cheek. She had the overwhelming urge to pry his fingers away and graze her mouth against his broad knuckles all at the same time.

"I'm not sure how to explain this to you," she said, "but I have been a serious student and a serious lover, and I have worn this serious little face for so damn long that, well, sometimes I want to tear it off. That's me. And I can't do serious right now. I just can't."

She felt his shoulders sag. "That doesn't mean that I don't care about what happens to us," she said. "But can't we just live from day to day?"

He looked up at her, his eyes wide with boyish mourning. "I wish I could say yes."

"Please don't do this to me. We aren't Colette and Brian."

"No."

"And we won't be."

"Isobel—"

"I'm sorry, but we won't."

She untangled herself from him and sat across the table, her head resting on her arms. She gazed up at him.

"I'll still be here when you get back," he said.

༌

The following Tuesday, Isobel went to see Natalie in her office. It was the first time she had left the apartment in three weeks, and she stumbled up the stairs still stricken with the sensory overload of a walk through the Village in bright sunlight. Both Gavin and Elika had offered to come with her, but she had insisted on going by herself.

Natalie met her at the door. "Isobel," she said, "are you all right?"

"I'm . . . better than I was," Isobel said.

"Sit down. Please."

Isobel took a seat, arranging the loose folds of her sundress. She'd put on a little lipstick for the illusion of normalcy, but she knew she looked wan.

"I don't want to pry," Natalie said, "but something tells me it was more than just illness that kept you away."

"I'm not doing the defense this week."

Natalie paused for a moment, then plucked Isobel's file from a stack on her desk.

"I won't say I'm not disappointed," she said, "because I am, very deeply. But you know what you can handle, and I'm not about to argue with that."

Isobel stared at her hands. "Thank you."

"You have read the policies in the graduate catalogue, I assume? You do realize the fees and administrative heartache that await you in the fall?"

Isobel nodded, stunned at Natalie's nonchalance. She probably sees this all the time, Isobel thought, but why doesn't she berate me for it, the way I do myself?

"Okay, then." Natalie smiled. "I almost hate to ask, but what are you doing this summer? I mean, other than decompressing?"

"I think I might go to Iceland."

Natalie raised one eyebrow. "Really? Fascinating country, from what I've heard. Pack warm clothes, and send me a postcard."

"I'll do that."

"And, Isobel, do yourself a favor while you're at it."

"Yes?"

"If you feel yourself slipping again, get some help. Don't think you have to save all of womankind by the ripe old age of twenty-five."

Isobel laughed. "Believe me, I don't."

"I hate to cut this short," Natalie said, checking her watch, "but I have a department meeting at four."

⌒♉

Isobel broke up with Gavin later that night. She sat on the floor in the living room, huddled in an afghan, listening to her Icelandic tape. Gavin lay with his head in her lap.

She stroked his hair and thought, My bright boy, fresh out of business school, clean-cut as a J. Crew ad, the first man I made love to, so well adjusted I was shocked you wanted me. Her mind stuttered with fragmented endearments: *oh, lovely, lovely, sweet.*

"You look so peaceful," was all she said.

He smiled drowsily. "Of course," he said, his voice no more than a murmur. "I'm in your arms, aren't I?"

She swallowed. "Gavin," she said, "this isn't working."

He eased himself up on his elbows. "Isobel, no," he said. "Don't say that just yet. You're under so much stress, and it's been rough for us lately, but give things—give them another chance."

She shook her head. "It's not the last few weeks," she said. "It's me."

"You don't know that," he said, sitting up all the way, taking her hands. "Give yourself the summer. Go on your trip, take some time to think. I won't give you a hard time about it, I promise."

"There's no 'we' about this," she said. "I want to float back into myself. I need to be weightless. I'm sorry."

He let go of her, dropped his face in his palms, and began to cry. She put her arms around him, caressing his back, and rested her chin on his shoulder. She watched the green numbers on the tape deck's counter climb higher, higher.

"Could you turn that off, please?" he said, sniffling.

"Sure," she said, and reached over in silent concession to eject the tape. It was the least she could do.

She held him for a few more minutes, listening to the moist, shuddery sounds of his breathing as it quieted. She felt dead inside.

"I guess I'll go now," he said.

"You don't have to," she said.

"Yes," he said sharply. "I should."

He stood and pulled on his jacket. His face shimmered in the sunset, fire-ripened, round and pleading, a delicate peach.

"You'll let me know how your trip goes?" he said.

She slid her arms around her knees and down to the floor, as if to draw a circle around herself, bend her frame into some yoga pose of autonomy.

"Of course," she said.

༉

The next day, Elika dragged Isobel to the film lab with her. "You need to get out," she said. "No maudlin dwelling on what you just did."

Isobel frowned as Elika unlocked an editing room, but she obediently took a seat, crossing her arms over her chest in what, she realized, must look like an adolescent pose of defiance.

"Welcome to the monster known as the Avid editor," Elika said, gesturing around the booth. She fed in her MiniDV tape, fiddled with some dials, and turned on the monitor. "Here we go. Ready to see yourself as a star?"

A blur of images rolled past with a screech. With one masterful, slender finger, Elika paused the footage at just the right spot. On the screen, Isobel saw her face rise to the surface, brows furrowed, hair a bright shock. Her features were molded in a wrinkled cry of fright or agony or passion, as if someone had just hurt her, as if she were coming.

"Turn it off," she said.

Chapter Thirteen

Reykjavík

*O*ne evening after the Þorsmörk trip, Valdi was showing Isobel a new computer game he'd gotten when Ragna came into his room, somber-faced.

"Isobel," she said. "You have a gentleman caller."

Isobel answered the phone in the kitchen.

"Baby, you've got to help me," Kjartan said. His voice was jittery, panicked.

"Why in the hell do you have this number?"

"I'm sorry, my girl, but you've got—you've got to—"

"What?"

"I lost the job, Isobel. They fired me tonight, and—"

"How much have you had to drink?"

"I don't—don't know . . ."

"Stay with me, damn it," Isobel said. "What did you have?"

"Can't remember."

"Not a good sign," Isobel said. "Listen, I'm going to hang up, and I'll be right over, okay? Do *not* fall asleep on me. Don't you dare."

"I'll try, baby."

Isobel went to Valdi's door. "I'll be back in a few hours," she said to Ragna.

Ragna looked up from the computer screen. "Everything fine?"

"I just need to make sure Kjartan doesn't have alcohol poisoning."

"Oh, God," Ragna said. "You're far more noble than I would be."

"Can't you stay to watch the last round of this game?" Valdi asked her.

"Afraid not, kiddo. We'll play tomorrow. Promise."

Isobel walked outside with her hands stuffed in her coat pockets, vacillating between the desire to rush to Kjartan's aid and fury at her fuzzy boundaries.

She found him thrashing in bed, vomit crusted in his hair. Empty bottles lay, overturned, at her feet.

Isobel cleared a path to sit on the dusty floor beside him. He clawed at her sleeves, grabbing her arms. "Isobel the savior," he rasped.

"You need to get medical attention," Isobel said. "I'll take you."

"*Nei, nei,*" he said, and shook his head. "I'll live, baby."

"Then why did you call me over here?"

"There's no one I'd rather see in my . . . in my . . . *Hvað er þetta á ensku?*"

"Don't expect me to read your mind," Isobel said, getting up. "I came because I thought you were on your deathbed, that's all."

Kjartan clutched her. Tears welled in his eyes. "Please don't leave," he said. "You're the only thing I have left, it's all been taken from me—my children, my job . . ."

"And whose fault is that?" Isobel said. "Look, you're sick and you're scared, and you shouldn't be alone right now. But if you think I'm going to crawl into bed with you for a sympathy fuck, you couldn't be more wrong."

"You drive a hard bargain, Isobel *mín*," he said. "Can you find it in your stony little heart to sit with me until I fall asleep?"

Isobel nodded, and he rolled onto his back, still holding her hand. He closed his eyes, and she listened to his moist, shallow breaths. When the clock on his nightstand read eleven, Isobel extricated herself from his grip and moved onto the couch to dial Ragna.

Ragna answered after the third ring, sounding drowsy.

"I'm sorry," Isobel said. "Did I wake you?"

"*Já,*" she said, "but don't feel bad. I just nodded off in front of the television. Hold on." She covered the mouthpiece with her hand and said something to Valdi. "*Afsakið.* How are your nurse-maid duties going?"

"Fair enough. He'll have a hellish hangover tomorrow."

"Isobel," she said, "can I give you a bit of unsolicited advice?"

"By all means."

"You say he's in no immediate danger, and you don't want to baby-sit him for hours on end, am I right?"

"Yes."

"Then do yourself a favor and come home."

Isobel glanced over at Kjartan. Her heart quivered. "Ragna," she said, "I don't know if I can—"

"*Elskan,* you must," Ragna said. "I'm not telling you this because I'd rather have you here with me and Valdi. I tell you this because I know where you've been. I'm sure he looks so soft and dear, like a naughty little boy you're convinced you can reform, but trust me, *vina mín,* morning will come, and it will not be pretty."

Her words held a grim certainty that rendered them almost prophetic.

"Okay," Isobel said softly. "I'll leave now. Will you wait up for me?"

"Of course."

Isobel set the phone down and walked across the room. The walls glistened like wet golden skin. She took Kjartan's face in her hands, smoothed back a strand of his tangled dark-blond hair, and kissed his sweaty forehead. He breathed deeper but did not stir.

In the same book Isobel had left him her number at Magga's, she wrote a small note now:

Hope you feel better by the time you read this, and that things work out for you.

Bless bless,
Isobel

It was, Isobel realized, the bland sort of farewell you'd write to a foreign pen pal.

When she got home, Isobel encountered Valdi asleep on the couch amid a pile of pillows and blankets. Ragna sat at the kitchen table, smoking her prebed cigarette. She looked up at Isobel, surprised, as if she had expected tears, histrionics, avalanches of regret.

Vile pain throbbed in Isobel's face. She didn't know how to explain to Ragna that she had no emotions left.

༚

The next afternoon, Isobel went into the old city center to pick up a few things. She was terrified at the prospect of meeting Kjartan there. The driver of a car that looked like his yelled out the window as he passed her, and Isobel ducked down Skólavör-ðurstígur and into a jewelry shop to escape. While there, she discovered handmade glass-and-metal pendants in a variety of colors, and she bought one each for Colette, her mother, and Elika (who, upon receiving it, would later shriek, "Oh, thank you, it's just what I wanted—a sperm talisman!").

Her paranoia subdued, Isobel went back onto the main street, shopping bags in hand, and searched for a quiet place with a secluded table where she could write and get a cup of coffee. She discovered it on Þingholtsstræti, in a dark, near-empty Mediterranean restaurant full of wrought iron. Isobel chose a spot by the window, ordered a cappuccino, took out her unfinished postcards, and began to write.

Dear Natalie,

Here, as promised, is your postcard—I actually climbed this mountain! My time in Iceland has taught me much, and I hope to come back more sane if not fully rejuvenated.

I've decided to continue with the dissertation, but I won't let it drag me under again. It's not the whole of me, I've learned—and for pushing me toward that knowledge, for stubbornly refusing to pacify me, for making me find the answers myself, I thank you.

Hope your summer is going well, and we'll talk in the fall.

Isobel

Dear Shireen,

Góðan dag *from Iceland! I am sending this postcard to Mrs. Sullivan in the hopes that she will pass it on to you. (I climbed the mountain in the picture on the other side—cool, huh?)*

I hope you are having a good summer, and wish you the best of luck in high school. I'm sorry I couldn't help you more this past year, and I hope the new one finds you happy and strong and feeling better.

Hugs,
Isobel

Dear Sylvia,

Well here I am! Does the landscape look familiar? You really ought to come back and stand at the top of this mountain—beautiful and invigorating!

Thank you so much for your letter. Don't worry, we all tango with the inappropriate—I certainly have while here, and what a dance it's been! You did it with gentleness and good intentions, though, and that I will always remember.

I'll call when I get home so we can catch up.

Much love,
Isobel

Isobel wiped the corners of her moist eyes with her sleeve. The waitress came back with Isobel's second cappuccino. Her face was bright, her hair dark and perfect above the unwrinkled collar of her silk blouse.

"Gertu svo vel," she said. "Here you are."

꿎

When Isobel returned home that afternoon, she found a message from Kristín on Ragna's answering machine, asking Isobel to call her. She phoned her back right away.

"I hate to impose on you like this," Kristín began, "but . . . I need someone to watch Ásta for me, and I would have asked my mother, but Ásta requested you."

"Well, how can I refuse?" Isobel said. "I'd love to. Will you be out long?"

"I could," she said shyly. "I've got a date."

Isobel arrived at Kristín's small flat across from the lake at a few minutes before eight. Kristín met her at the door in stockings and a red dress.

"I'm running late," she said, and kissed Isobel on the cheek. "I'm a bit nervous. Because of Ásta it's been a long time."

"You look wonderful," Isobel said, getting the words out just before Ásta raced into the room, skidding on the hardwood floors in her footed pajamas, and lunged to hug Isobel's knees.

"She's prepared a whole film festival for you," Kristín said, and gestured toward a blond wood television cabinet where a stack of American children's videos lay.

"We're going to watch them *all,*" Ásta said firmly.

"As long as she's in bed by ten," Kristín said. "I'll be back out in a second."

She disappeared into the bedroom she and Ásta shared, and Ásta took Isobel by the hand and led her to a low bookcase, where she proceeded to pull out a pile of picture books. "Let's read these now," she said.

"Oh, honey," Isobel said, "I don't think I know enough Icelandic."

"Don't worry," Ásta said as they settled on the burgundy leather couch. "I'll read them to you."

The doorbell rang, and Kristín, now in high heels, ran to answer it while putting on her earrings. She said a quick hello to her date, Pétur, a striking fellow with a shaved head, and gave a kiss to Ásta. "I'll call later," she said, "to see how she's doing."

"We'll be fine," Isobel said. "Good luck."

She watched as Kristín and her date walked out the door and onto the second-floor landing. Isobel saw Pétur take Kristín's arm, and remembered the sensation of fingertips on skin, the potent emotional cocktail of longing laced with fear.

We were never taught what we needed to know, she thought angrily. Years and years of school, but nothing to show for it. They never told us how to be both passionate and safe, or even that we could.

Ásta tugged Isobel's arm. "Can I read to you now?" she asked. The breeze from the white lace curtains blew her fine blond hair. In her small face, Isobel saw a child who knew how to move in her body, who might not have to hurt herself before she could feel good.

"Of course," Isobel said.

✧

That night, Isobel dreamt of the thirteen-year-old girl. She huddled on her knees in the corner of Isobel's room. Her eyes were wet with tears, her hair a messy tangle. Isobel crossed the room and knelt before her, lifted her chin gently with her hand. A bruise glistened by the girl's lip; a fresh scratch scrawled, red and raw, across her cheek. There was a hole in her sweater. She gazed at Isobel, wary yet hopeful. "Will you stay with me?" she said.

Isobel nodded. Hesitated for one fumbling moment, then took her in her arms.

ɼ

Her last evening in the city, Isobel went to a sushi bar with Ragna and Kristín. The Japanese restaurant was empty, save for a drunken Greenlander who was arguing with the lone hostess. Noticing Ragna and grateful for a diversion, the hostess left her slurring, irate patron to seat the three women. They slid into a booth, ordered sake to start, and watched the waitress hash out the bill with the man through the ornate screen that partitioned them. Their conversation was in English—the Asian woman's accentless, the Greenlandic man's thick and slurred—so Isobel caught a few words. Finally they agreed, or at least agreed to disagree, and the waitress said, deadpan, "We hope to see you again soon."

"This is my only trip to Iceland," he said. "I'll never be back."

"All because of the sushi?" Isobel whispered. Ragna put her hand over her mouth to stifle a laugh.

"Well . . . enjoy the rest of your stay," the waitress said, faltering.

Wallet in hand, the man stumbled away. When he reached the door, he called over his shoulder, almost as an afterthought, "Have a nice life!"

The trio laughed even harder. By the time their beleaguered server returned to take their order, they were all a little tipsy from the sweet, numbing sting of the sake, but it was a good, friendly buzz, the kind that reassured them they could be safe and silly together, with no regrets the following morning.

Their first plate of sushi arrived, and, hands tingling, Isobel fumbled with the chopsticks, dropping them the first few times, unable to cram each piece of fish into her mouth whole the way the other two women could.

"Poor Isobel," Ragna said. "These Icelandic-sized portions are giving her trouble."

"Here," Kristín said, demonstrating with her chopsticks. "Maybe if you try like this . . ."

"That's right, my dear," Ragna said, "like that. Pinch them. They like to be pinched."

They burst into giggles yet again at the makeshift tutorial, and ordered a second platter and another pot of wine. Ragna got a pack of cigarettes. Kristín gazed at it longingly.

"Having some nostalgia, Stína *mín?*" Ragna said after an especially long drag.

Kristín nodded. "I quit smoking a few months ago," she said to Isobel. "My daughter got asthma, so I thought it would be best."

"Such a devoted mum," Ragna said. "Valdi would have to be near death for me to give it up."

The waitress came back with their bill. They paid it without dissent and left her a large tip for her trouble, but couldn't resist chorusing, "Have a nice life!" as they filed out.

"Shameless, we are shameless," Isobel said.

"How about a stop at Kaffi List?" Ragna said. "I promised someone I'd meet him there."

"Who is it?" Kristín asked.

Ragna told her, and whoever he was, he elicited a nod of approval. Isobel winced internally. His first name was Kjartan.

"Is that okay with you, Isobel?" Kristín asked.

Isobel shrugged. Remembering her last journey to the Spanish pub left her a little achy, but she told herself that she'd be fine with everyone else in tow.

The place was crowded when they got there, but thanks to Ragna's good graces, they snagged a table that allowed them a prime view of the comings and goings at the bar. The girls ordered Isobel a ten-dollar glass of red wine as a parting gift. She touched it only out of gratitude.

Isobel was on the lookout for Ragna's friend—"He'll have spiky hair and tortoiseshell glasses," Ragna said—when she froze. It was her Kjartan, making his way from the entrance to the bar. He looked surprisingly good, to one who didn't know the details of what he'd done to himself in the past week. Isobel knew the details, however, and she could spot them: the ragged bits of stubble on his chin; the tiny stain on his shirt, barely discernible, a daub of alcohol right where his heart should be. She slid her fingers over the cool rim of her goblet, wanting to corner him, coil around him to comfort, plant brazen kisses. Then she pictured Sylvia with her fractured lip, and Ragna's back slammed against the wall. *No,* Isobel thought, and averted her eyes.

"What is it?" Ragna said.

Isobel looked slowly from her to him and back again. Mouthed his name and added, "Not the one we want to see."

Kristín leaned over to Ragna, asked for an explanation. Ragna whispered one in her ear in Icelandic. When she was finished, Kristín nodded, and her normally placid face went tight and angry.

"Is it a problem," Ragna said, "if we stay?"

Kristín put her hand over Isobel's. Isobel took a sip of her wine. Tasted bitter.

At first Isobel couldn't respond. It would take years for her to fully come to terms with the summer she had spent in Iceland, but right then, it was summed up entirely by her friends' wishes for better for each other, their attempts at justice, no matter how ludicrous, no matter how small—all those things shone under the festive red neon, giving way to the possibility for a new kind of desire, one much richer, much more fully defined.

"Not at all," Isobel said. "Not at all."

꿍

A half hour later, Ragna's Kjartan arrived, and after the perfunctory round of introductions, Isobel excused herself. Much as
she loved their company, Isobel needed the rest of the evening to
be hers alone, to say a private goodbye to the city. "I hope you'll
understand," she told them.

Ragna waved a hand at her. "Don't apologize," she said. "It's a
smashing idea."

Isobel went around the table and hugged them each in turn.
Kristín squeezed her tightly and produced a piece of paper from
her purse. "Here," she said. "Ásta drew this, and she wanted you
to have it."

The sheet of heavy butcher-block paper revealed a crayon
sketch of Ásta, Kristín, and Isobel feeding the ducks at Tjörnin.
Ásta had made Isobel's hair a wild, garish scribble of red, and
the sky an endearingly accurate ribbon of blue. Isobel's eyes
welled up.

"Tell her I think it's beautiful," Isobel said, "and that I'll be
sure to save it. Give my best to your mother, okay?"

Ragna was next. She gave Isobel one of her crazy, one-armed
hugs, and said, "Breakfast tomorrow, *kanski?*"

Isobel nodded. They would go to Café París the next day, for a
late brunch, and when the waiter was slow in bringing Isobel's
meal, Ragna would pull him aside and, in a whisper, explain that
"We have a very famous intellectual from America here who will
not think too kindly upon our country unless you deliver her some
jam and pancakes soon." Afterward, still laughing at her audacity,
they would part ways for real outside of Hótel Borg. Looking like a
lovely amalgam of Sylvia's empathy, Natalie's blunt earthiness,
and Elika's coy flamboyance, Ragna would stuff her hands in her
pockets, suddenly reserved, and say breezily, "Love to your mum

and everyone," even though she had never met Isobel's mother. Like Isobel, her nonchalance would only mask her sadness. Isobel would later sit in the Keflavík airport outside the duty-free shop, eating fistfuls of Ópal licorice drops and sniffling softly until her flight was called.

Now Isobel mumbled a quick "Nice to meet you" to Ragna's male friend with the unfortunate name and made them all promise to stay with her if they were ever in New York. Then Isobel edged cautiously past the bar, where she sneaked a quick glance at her former lover. He was talking with a woman in a pale pink silk tunic, his face intent on hers, listening—or at least pretending to listen—to her every word. Isobel slipped out with her head lowered, relieved and yet disappointed that he had not looked up to greet her.

On the walk home, Isobel's mood brightened as her thoughts shifted away from him and to the town she must bid farewell. She was filled with urgent affection for the scruffy yet cosmopolitan city, and it occurred to her that there were too many things she hadn't had time to discover, too many places she hadn't explored, both in that landscape and the one slowly being charted inside her. Isobel wanted to spin like a child in the twilight hour, dervish through back alleyways in the evening air. On Vesturgata, the world was a carnival beneath a peach sunset. An ambulance swerved around the corner. A pack of sixteen-year-olds in platform sneakers and nylon jackets crossed the street. Isobel heard the cry of gulls, smelled the sharpness of salt. Within her came a voice, like warm breath from a kind mouth, murmuring, Nothing wrong with wanting, *allt í lagi*, it's all right.